# INVISIBLE
## KAZAKHSTAN

## OTHER TITLES IN THE SAS OPERATION SERIES

*Behind Iraqi Lines*
*Mission to Argentina*
*Sniper Fire in Belfast*
*Desert Raiders*
*Samarkand Hijack*
*Embassy Siege*
*Guerrillas in the Jungle*
*Secret War in Arabia*
*Colombian Cocaine War*
*Heroes of the South Atlantic*
*Counter-insurgency in Aden*
*Gambian Bluff*
*Bosnian Inferno*
*Night Fighters in France*
*Death on Gibraltar*
*Into Vietnam*
*For King and Country*
*Kashmir Rescue*
*Guatemala – Journey into Evil*
*Headhunters of Borneo*
*Kidnap the Emperor!*
*War on the Streets*
*Bandit Country*
*Days of the Dead*

# SAS
# OPERATION

*Invisible Enemy in Kazakhstan*

PETER CAVE

HARPER

*Harper*
An imprint of HarperCollins*Publishers*
1 London Bridge Street,
London SE1 9GF
www.harpercollins.co.uk

This paperback edition 2016
1

First published by 22 Books/Bloomsbury Publishing plc 1994

A catalogue record for this book
is available from the British Library

ISBN: 978 0 00 815515 5

Set in Sabon by Born Group using Atomik ePublisher from Easypress

Printed and bound in Great Britain

**MIX**
Paper from
responsible sources
**FSC** **FSC˚ C007454**
www.fsc.org

# 1

*Moscow – March 1945*

General Sergei Oropov sucked deeply on a thin, knobbly cheroot of black Balkan tobacco, inhaling the acrid smoke and attempting to savour it. Failing, he sprayed it out from between his clenched teeth, sending it jetting on its way with a convulsive, chesty cough. The faintly blue smoke rose towards the high ceiling of the large, overheated and airless office, blending into a murky pall made thicker by the steam escaping from a leaking radiator. The heating system, along with the ventilation fans, had been faulty for over three months now, and it was still impossible to find labour sufficiently skilled to fix it.

'Thank God this damned war will soon be over,' Oropov muttered testily, knowing that it could be merely a matter of weeks before Germany was finally forced to capitulate. Russian troops had almost reached the Oder, the Western Allies had established a firm bridgehead east of the Rhine and troopers of Britain's already legendary 1 and 2 Squadron SAS ranged throughout Europe, organizing and arming local resistance fighters and carrying out long-range reconnaissance and sabotage attacks as far north as Hamburg and Lübeck.

The remark was not really intended as dialogue, more as a private thought expressed aloud. Nevertheless, Oropov's companion took it up, seizing on the opportunity for a mild rebuke to be administered, a propaganda point to be gained.

Tovan Leveski's thin lips parted slightly in a mirthless smile. 'One does not thank God any more – one thanks Stalin. It was the strength of the Russian bear which crushed the German jackal to death. But of course, comrade, I agree with your sentiments, at least. It will be good to have our brave young men back from the German front – to finish our necessary business in Poland.'

It was Oropov's turn to smile, but with faintly malicious humour.

'That too, of course. Although, personally, I was more looking forward to buying some decent Cuban cigars.'

Oropov's grey eyes twinkled briefly as Leveski twitched, reacting uncomfortably to the obvious jibe. It felt good to score a point over the man, whom Oropov both disliked and distrusted. It was not just the fact that he was, basically, a civilian; it went a lot deeper than that, with potentially more sinister implications.

Leveski represented a new and unknown quantity. The exact nature of his sudden new post was ill-defined, as if deliberately vague. There were mutterings and rumours in the corridors of the Kremlin. No longer obsessed with matters of war, Stalin was stirring politically again. There was talk of new purges to come, of heads rolling and personnel once again disappearing at short notice and in suspicious circumstances. Stalin's feared secret police, previously concerned with purely internal matters, were now extending their awesome powers. Now the newly formed KGB, with people like Leveski at its head, were moving in to take an active interest in military, European and overseas matters. It impinged directly on Oropov's authority as head of wartime intelligence, and it was extremely disquieting. It was definitely a time for staying on top, and being clearly seen to be on top. A time to know exactly what was happening all around oneself – and, even more important, who was making it happen and why.

With these thoughts in mind, Oropov decided it was politic to adopt a more conciliatory attitude towards his companion.

'Speaking of Poland, Tovan Leveski, what news from Warsaw?'

Leveski shrugged, a gesture of vague irritation. 'Mixed, as ever. Confused and conflicting reports, rumours, snatches of Allied propaganda. The usual wartime rubbish. The very thing my new department was set up to rationalize.' He broke off to nod deferentially towards Oropov. 'With your cooperation, of course, comrade.'

'Of course,' Oropov said, nodding, his face suddenly more serious. 'I was merely a soldier, doing a soldier's job in a time of war. Now we must all work together in the cause of peace, and for the good of the Motherland.'

The brief speech presumed a response. Predictably, Leveski obliged.

'A toast, comrade?' he suggested.

'A toast indeed.'

Oropov slid open a drawer in his desk and drew out a quarter-full bottle of Stolichnaya and two conical, stemless glasses. He handed one to Leveski, filled it, then splashed a generous measure into his own.

'*Rodina*,' Oropov grunted, waving the glass briefly in the air before placing it to his lips and draining the fiery vodka at a single gulp.

'*Rodina*' Leveski responded with suitable fervour in his voice. The word translated simply as The Motherland', but it carried the patriotic zeal of an entire national anthem to anyone with a drop of Russian blood in their veins. In a society which had largely turned its back on the Church, it was the litany of a new and potent religion.

The time for pleasantries was over, Oropov decided. It was obvious that Leveski had not entered his office on a purely social visit. He returned the bottle of vodka to his desk, smiling up at the man politely. 'Well, Tovan Leveski, what can I do for you?'

The little man cleared his throat, managing to make the apparently innocent gesture a censure of Oropov's smoking habit.

'We are a little concerned about the lack of information currently on file regarding Allied armaments projects.'

Oropov ignored yet another implied rebuke. He raised one shaggy eyebrow the faintest fraction of an inch. '*We*, comrade?'

'I', Leveski corrected himself hastily, uncomfortably aware that he had just let something slip, without fully understanding its relevance. Just like General Oropov, he had yet to adjust fully to the scope of his position and powers. 'I find myself slightly worried about the gaps in our intelligence. I was briefed to acquaint myself fully with current military research, but I find some of your dossiers and files rather sparse, to say the least.'

Oropov made a steeple of his fingers, pressing them gently against his lips. He eyed Leveski stonily. 'Specifically?'

'Specifically, this "Manhattan Project". As a military man, you must surely appreciate the momentous implications of a nuclear fission bomb. Yet we appear to have no idea at all just how advanced the Americans are in its development. Cause for worry, would you not agree, General?'

'Indeed,' Oropov agreed. 'And, equally, a matter for the tightest and most efficient security screen we have ever encountered. The potential power of atomic weaponry is not lost on the Americans, either. Our files represent our finest efforts and the deaths of two top agents. I assume you have followed up on the cross-reference file relating to the German research facility at Telemark?'

Leveski nodded. 'Of course. Again, a woefully thin report and a disgusting fiasco. The damned Norwegians and the Allies made fools of us. It should have been Russian troops who stormed that laboratory. Then the secret of heavy-water production would be in Soviet hands, not at the bottom of some damned fiord.'

'Our troops were otherwise engaged at the time,' Oropov pointed out rather icily. 'But a tragic loss to Soviet science, I agree. However, I understand our own atomic research facility is now well established.'

Leveski's lips curled into a sneer. 'Oh yes, two or three years behind the blasted Allies, at a conservative estimate.'

He hunched his shoulders, as if to subdue a shiver of rage, finally releasing only a faint shrug. 'However, that is past news. What matters now is the future. Do we have any active personnel inside the Manhattan Project?'

Oropov shook his head. 'No one with scientific knowledge, I'm afraid. There is a woman – a minor clerical worker – who is able to send us copies of purchasing invoices, interdepartmental memos, that sort of thing. We are able to glean a little theoretical knowledge, but not much else.'

Leveski digested all this information for a while, assimilating it into the dossier in his brain.

'Have we made any attempts to get to the man Oppenheimer direct?' he asked finally. 'Our records suggest that in his postgraduate days, at least, he had certain . . . sympathies?'

Oropov spread his hands in a gesture of resignation. 'A fact also realized by the Americans. Oppenheimer is a very important man, and a deeply mistrusted one. His every move is closely monitored. It is impossible to get an agent within shouting distance of him.'

'So we have nothing? No one? No chance of further information. Is that what you are telling me?'

Oropov was beginning to wilt under the mounting attack. 'It's not as bad as that,' he countered, somewhat lamely.

'No? Then please tell me how bad it actually is, comrade.'

Leveski knew that he had his man on the run now. There was little point in any further pretence at friendliness.

'There *is* one man – in England. Klaus Fuchs. We have him as a sleeper. He is not attached to the Manhattan Project, but his work involves him in a closely related field. In a year or two, perhaps, he may be of great use to us.'

'A year or two?' Leveski said dismissively. He rose from his high-backed chair, his mouth twitching angrily with barely repressed frustration. 'In a year or two, comrade Oropov, Russian science will be left behind like a sick, abandoned animal. Out in the cold, waiting to die.'

There was a slight tremor in Oropov's voice when he finally spoke again. He was acutely aware that Leveski had only just started to show his claws, and the Kremlin rumours were beginning to assume a chilling reality.

'What is expected of me, comrade Leveski?'

'You don't know? Then I had better spell it out for you,' Leveski sneered. 'The demands of this war, and sheer Nazi fervour, have resulted in one of the greatest explosions of science and technology this world has ever known. Those scientific breakthroughs are the key to the future – the richest and most precious spoils of war. At this very minute the Allies are picking their way across Europe like scavengers, snatching up the juiciest morsels. Physicists, rocket experts, engineers, designers, the finest brains of Germany – all falling into capitalist hands. Any day now the Western powers may have the secret of the atomic bomb. In a matter of a few years, the power to deliver it across oceans and continents. In a decade, world domination in their pockets. And if that happens, comrade, we might as well sell our bodies and souls back to the Tsars, because we will have lost everything this great nation has struggled and bled for. Something the Russian people would never forgive, General. And perhaps more important to you, personally, something that *I* would never forgive.'

The gauntlet was down. Oropov struggled to control a nervous shiver, and failed. His voice was little more than a croak.

'What do you want me to do, comrade Leveski?'

The man was now regarding him with undisguised contempt. 'I'm glad that you finally realize how high the stakes are, General. And, no doubt, the penalties for failure. I want a short-term plan. A definite and positive strategy to ensure that Russia snatches some worthwhile prize from this war. Give me a phoenix from the ashes, General – that is all.'

Leveski turned on his heel and moved towards the door. He delivered his parting shot over his shoulder, without turning round. 'You have forty-eight hours, General. I expect to see a detailed report on my desk by Thursday.'

He closed the door quietly, almost gently behind him. Strangely, this seemed to reinforce the aura of menace he left behind him rather than lessen it.

Alone now, Oropov gave up the uneven struggle to stop his hands from shaking. He delved into his desk, pulled out the vodka bottle and uncorked it with his teeth. Holding the bottle directly to his lips, he gulped down the harsh spirit. It did little to thaw out the icy chill he felt in the pit of his belly.

He stared blankly across his office at the closed door through which Leveski had exited, racking his brain for a single optimistic thought. There was nothing. One realization swamped everything else. War, or at least *his* kind of war, was coming to an end, and a completely new kind of war was about to begin. With a terrible sense of resignation, he knew that he had little if any part to play in the waging of it.[1]

---

[1] In August 1945, three days after the second atomic bomb fell on Nagasaki, General Sergei Oropov was arrested by the KGB, found guilty of treasonous activities against the State, and executed by firing squad. All files relating to his last assignment, which he had code-named Project Phoenix and put into operation some two months previously, were removed from Military Intelligence and taken to KGB headquarters.

# 2

*Berlin – June 1945*

The two jeeps zigzagged through the rubble-strewn streets on the outskirts of what had once been the thriving city of Berlin. Another brilliant innovation from David Stirling, who had created the concept of the SAS in 1941, the small, nippy and versatile American vehicles were ideal for the war-torn terrain. Gutted, smashed and burned-out buildings formed an almost surrealist landscape which could have come straight from the tortured imagination of Hieronymus Bosch.

Corporal Arnold Baker, known affectionately to his comrades as 'Pig-sticker', or usually just 'Piggy', in tribute to his prowess with a knife, surveyed the dead city from the passenger seat of the leading jeep.

'Jesus, this was some savage fucking war,' he said gravely, shaking his head as though he still could not quite believe the evidence of his own eyes.

His driver, Trooper Andy Wellerby, sniffed dismissively. 'Save your bleeding pity, Corp. When was the last time you saw London? Or Coventry, for that matter.'

'Yeah.' Piggy took the point, tearing his eyes away from the desolation and concentrating once more on the road in front of him. 'What's that up ahead?'

Wellerby waved his arm over the side of the battered Willys jeep, signalling for the vehicle behind him to slow down. He tapped lightly on the brake and squinted into the distance. Just over a quarter of a mile further up the long, straight road towards Brandenburg, a line of military vehicles sealed it off. Wellerby could make out a line of about a dozen uniformed figures standing guard beside the vehicles. He groaned aloud.

'Not another bleeding roadblock? Bloody Yanks again, I'll bet. It's about time somebody told those bastards that it was us Brits who invented red tape.'

Piggy was also concentrating on the grey-uniformed soldiers. He shook his head slowly. 'No, they're not GIs, that's for sure. Uniform looks all wrong.'

Wellerby let out a slightly nervous giggle. 'Maybe it's a bunch of fucking jerries who don't know the war's over yet.'

It was meant to be a joke, but one hand was already off the steering wheel and unclipping the soft holster of his Webley .38 dangling from his webbing. At the same time Piggy was checking the drums on the twin Vickers K aircraft machine-guns welded to the top of the jeep's bonnet. In the utter chaos of postwar Germany, just about anything was possible. All sorts of armed groups were out on the streets, both official and unofficial, from half a dozen nations which had been caught up in the conflict. Quite apart from regular soldiers and covert operations groups, there were resistance fighters with old scores to settle and ordinary citizens with murder in their hearts. Even a shambling line of what appeared to be civilian refugees or released concentration camp prisoners might conceal one or two still dedicated and still fanatical Waffen SS officers who would kill rather than surrender.

'Damn me. They're bloody Russkies,' Piggy blurted out,

as he finally recognized the uniforms. He sounded indignant rather than surprised.

'What the hell are the Russians doing setting up roadblocks?' Wellerby wanted to know.

Piggy shrugged. 'Christ knows. Everyone's getting in on the act. And I thought we had enough problems with the Yanks, the Anzacs and our own bloody mob.'

It was the light-hearted complaint of a fighting soldier increasingly bogged down in the problems of peace. The war might be over, but Berlin was still a battleground of bureaucracy, with checkpoints and roadblocks everywhere and dozens of garrisons of different military groups still waiting for Supreme Allied Command to work out a concerted policy of occupation. For the time being, it was still largely a policy of 'grab something and hold on to it'. Or just follow the orders one had, and muddle through.

But even so, it did not pay to take chances. The intensive training, both physical and mental, which any potential SAS trooper had to undergo did more than just produce a soldier whose reflexes and abilities were honed to near-perfection. It developed a sixth sense, an instinct for trouble. And Piggy Baker had that instinct now. There was something not quite right about the situation – he could feel it in his bones.

'Pull up,' he muttered to Wellerby out of the corner of his mouth. As the jeep stopped, he turned to the second vehicle as it, too, came to a halt some six yards behind.

Behind the wheel, Trooper Mike 'Mad Dog' Mardon looked up with a thoughtful smile on his face. 'Trouble, boss?'

Piggy shrugged uneasily. 'I don't know,' he admitted. 'But something smells.'

Mad Dog grinned. 'Probably just our passenger. The little bastard's been shitting himself ever since we picked him up.'

Piggy glanced at the small, bespectacled civilian sitting stiffly and uncomfortably in the rear of the vehicle. Stripped of its usual spare jerrycans and other equipment, the jeep was just about capable of carrying two passengers on its fold-down dicky seat. Just as he had throughout the journey, the German looked blankly straight ahead, ignoring Trooper Pat O'Neill, who guarded him with his drawn Webley held across his lap.

'Pat, I need you up at the front,' Piggy said. He nodded at the jeep's own pair of Vickers guns. 'On the bacon slicer, just in case.'

O'Neill glanced sideways at his prisoner. 'And what about Florence Nightingale here? Little bastard might decide to do a runner.'

'Improvise,' Piggy told him.

'Right.' O'Neill cast his eyes quickly around the jeep, finding a length of cord used to lash down fuel cans and fashioning it into a makeshift slip-noose. Dropping it over the German's neck, he pulled it tight and secured the loose end to the mounting of the spare wheel. Satisfied with his work, he crawled into the passenger seat and primed both the Vickers for action.

Piggy felt a little easier now, but there was just one last little precaution to take. He reached to the floor of the jeep and hefted up his heavy M1 Thompson sub-machine-gun. Slamming a fresh magazine into place, he slipped off the safety-catch and leaned out over the side of the jeep, jamming the weapon into a makeshift holster formed by the elasticated webbing round the spare water cans. The weapon was now concealed on the blind side of the Russian troops, and ready for action if it became necessary.

There was not much more he could do, Piggy thought. He glanced sideways at Wellerby. 'Right, take us in – nice and slow.'

The two jeeps approached the Russian roadblock at a crawl. Despite Winston Churchill's eventual conviction that Stalin was one of the good guys after all, there was still a deep-seated mistrust between the two armies.

As Wellerby brought the leading vehicle to a halt, Baker studied the line of twelve Russian soldiers some ten yards in front of him. They stood, stonily, each cradling a PPS-41 sub-machine-gun equipped with an old Thompson-like circular drum magazine. If it had not been for the uniforms, they would have looked exactly like a bunch of desperadoes from a Hollywood gangster film.

There was something about their stance which made Baker feel even more uneasy. In the heady aftermath of victory, most Allied soldiers had tended to let discipline relax, and embrace a general feeling of camaraderie. These Russians looked as though they were fresh out of intensive training and ready to ship out to the front line.

He stood up in the jeep, scanning the line for any sign of an officer. There was none. 'Who is in charge here? Does anyone speak English?' he asked in a calm, authoritative tone.

There was no response. The Russian soldiers continued to stare straight through him, virtually unblinking. Several seconds passed in strained silence.

Inside the cab of one of the covered Russian personnel carriers, Tovan Leveski examined the occupants of the two jeeps thoughtfully. He too had been a little confused about their uniforms from a distance, having been briefed to expect a standard British Army patrol. Now, at close hand, he could see that these were no ordinary British soldiers. Clad in dispatch rider's breeches, motorcycle boots and camouflaged 'Denison' smocks, they could have been anything. But it was their headgear which finally gave the clue. The beige berets, sporting the unique winged-dagger badge, clearly identified them as members of that small, élite force which had already started to become almost legendary. Clearly, even four SAS men were not to be taken lightly.

Quietly, Leveski murmured his orders to the eight more armed soldiers concealed in the truck behind him. Satisfied, he opened the passenger door and dropped down to the ground.

Piggy regarded him cautiously. Although the man ostensibly sported the uniform and badging of a full major in the Red Army, he seemed to lack a military bearing. However, the 7.62mm Tokarev TT-33 self-loading pistol in his hand certainly looked official enough.

'I am in charge of this detachment, Corporal,' Leveski said in flawless English.

It was a sticky stand-off situation, Piggy thought to himself. Even with the incredibly destructive firepower of the Vickers to hand, he and his men were hopelessly outnumbered – and there was no way of knowing how many other armed troops were inside the vehicles which made up the roadblock. Besides, military bearing or not, the officer still outranked him. For the moment there was nothing to do except play it by ear. They were no longer in a war situation, after all. Apart from the Germans and Italians, everyone was supposed to be on the same side now.

'Do you mind telling me the purpose of this roadblock?' Piggy demanded.

Leveski smiled thinly. 'Certainly. My orders are to monitor all military movement on this road, Corporal. Perhaps you in turn would be so good as to tell me the exact nature and purpose of your convoy.'

Piggy considered the matter for a few seconds, unsure of what to do. His orders had been specific, but were not, as far as he was aware, secret. He could think of no valid reason to withhold information, yet something rankled.

'With respect, Major, I fail to see what business that is of the Russian Army.'

Leveski shrugged faintly. 'Your failure to understand is of absolutely no concern to me, Corporal. What does concern me, however, is your apparent lack of respect for a superior officer and your refusal to cooperate.'

Piggy conceded the point, grudgingly and despite the dubious circumstances. 'All right, Major. I am leading a four-man patrol to escort a German prisoner of war to the railway marshalling yards at Brandenburg. And, since I have a strict schedule to adhere to, I would appreciate it if you would order your men to clear the road so that we can continue.'

'I'm afraid I can't do that,' the Russian said in a flat, emotionless tone. 'You and your men are in breach of the Geneva Convention, and I cannot allow you to continue.'

Piggy stared at the Russian in disbelief, starting to lose his temper.

'Since when has it been against the rules of the Convention to transport prisoners of war?'

'Military prisoners are one thing, Corporal. Civilians are another matter,' Leveski informed him calmly. 'You do have a civilian in your custody, do you not? One Klaus Mencken – Dr Mencken?'

'Doctor?' Piggy spat out the word, in a mixture of loathing and ridicule. 'My men and I have come directly from Buchenwald concentration camp, Major. This "doctor" was in charge of horrific, inhuman experiments on Jewish internees there. His speciality, I understand, was removing five-month foetuses from the womb for dissection. The man is a war criminal, Major, and is on his way to an international trial to answer for those crimes against humanity. So don't quote the Geneva Convention to me.'

The impassioned speech seemed to have had no effect on the Russian, who continued to speak in a calm, emotionless voice. 'I must insist that you hand Dr Mencken over to me.'

'By what damned authority?' snapped Piggy, openly angry now, having had more than a bellyful of the Russians.

'By the authority of superior strength.'

The new voice came from a few yards away.

Baker's eyes strayed to his right, where a Russian captain had just jumped down from the back of one of the personnel carriers. The man walked unhurriedly towards the leading jeep, being very careful to stay out of the line of fire of the Vickers.

'I am Captain Zhann,' he announced. 'You and your men are in the direct line of fire of no less than eighteen automatic weapons. Now please, Corporal, I must ask you to move back from that machine-gun and order your men to step calmly out and away from your vehicles. If you do not comply, my men have orders to open fire. You would be cut to ribbons, I can assure you.'

It was a threat that Piggy found easy to believe. Assuming that the remainder of the concealed troops also carried the thirty-five-round PPSh-41 sub-machine-guns which were on display, the Russian captain had the cards fully stacked in his favour. Each individual weapon had an automatic firing rate of 105 rounds a minute, and in a full burst, a cyclic firing rate approaching 900 rounds a minute. And the 7.62mm slugs were real body-rippers. At that range, they would all be dead in the first five seconds. Still, there remained time for at least a token show of defiance.

'And if I refuse?' Piggy asked.

Zhann shrugged. 'Then you and your men will be slaughtered needlessly. A pointless gesture, wouldn't you say?'

Piggy could only stare at the Russian in disbelief. The whole thing was crazy. It was peacetime, for Chrissake. They had all just fought the most bitter and savage war in human history. It was unthinkable that anyone would want to carry on the killing.

'You're bluffing,' he blurted out at last, suddenly convinced that it was the only explanation. 'Apart from which, you'd never get away with it.'

Leveski stepped forward again. 'I can assure you that Captain Zhann is conducting himself according to my specific orders,' he muttered chillingly. 'And what would there be to "get away with", as you put it? A simple mistake, in the confusion of a postwar city. A tragic accident. The authorities would have no choice but to accept that verdict.'

Piggy's fingers tightened around the firing mechanism of the Vickers. He moved the twin barrels a fraction of an inch from side to side – mainly to show Leveski that he had control.

'Aren't you and your captain forgetting something, Major?' he pointed out. 'If it comes to a shoot-out, it'll be far from one-sided. I can virtually cut your vehicles in half with one of these babies.'

The Russian gave one of his chilling smiles. 'What I believe the Americans call a Mexican stand-off,' he observed. 'However, we would still appear to have the advantage. As you see, I have four covered lorries. Only one of them contains armed troops. Your problem, Corporal, would be in knowing which one to fire on first. You must surely appreciate that you wouldn't get time for a second guess.'

It was becoming like a game of poker, Piggy thought. But what made the stakes so high? It made no sense at all. Unless, of course, the Russian *was* bluffing. No stranger to a deck of cards, Piggy decided to call Leveski's hand.

'You must understand that my men and I cannot be expected to surrender our weapons,' he said in a flat, businesslike tone. 'And I cannot believe that you would push this insanity to its logical conclusion.'

As if understanding his corporal's reticence to surrender without a fight, Trooper Wellerby spoke up.

'We ain't got a choice, have we, Corp? What's a piece of rubbish like Mencken to us, anyway? If the Russkies want him that bad, you can bet your sweet fucking life they ain't planning to take him to no birthday party.'

Piggy could not repress a thin smile. In attempting to make light of the situation, Wellerby had hit the nail on the head. He was right: what were the lives of three brave troopers measured against the Butcher of Buchenwald? If only a tenth of the stories about him were true, he deserved not an ounce of human consideration. Whether Mencken died from a British noose or a Russian bullet, it made no difference at all. On the other hand, Piggy knew that he had no moral right to condemn his men to almost certain death. He returned his attention to Leveski.

'All right, Major,' he said, 'in the interests of avoiding conflict, I will allow you to take the prisoner. But I must point out that I regard this as an act of hijacking and I will be reporting it to higher authorities as soon as we reach Brandenburg.'

Leveski allowed the faintest trace of satisfaction to cross his face. 'Your objections are noted, Corporal.' He began to walk towards the second jeep. Releasing the hastily made noose, he gestured for Mencken to alight and led the German towards the waiting Russian convoy.

Even now, the Nazi was arrogant. He still felt justified. He had just been obeying orders, he had done no wrong.

He glared at Leveski defiantly. 'I suppose you Russian dogs intend to shoot me. Then do it, and get it over with. I would not expect the luxury of a trial from Bolshevik lackeys.'

Leveski ignored the insults, switching on his chilling smile. 'Shoot you, Herr Doktor?' he murmured in a low voice. 'Oh no. On the contrary, we are going to treat you like a VIP. You are going to Russia to join some of your colleagues. You will soon be working for us, Doctor – doing what you appear to enjoy doing most.'

He took Mencken by the arm, escorting him towards the nearest truck and bundling him up into the cab. Jumping in behind him, Leveski barked instructions to the driver, who fired the vehicle up into life and prepared to move off with a crunch of gears.

As the truck started to move, Leveski stuck his head out of the open window, nodding towards Captain Zhann. 'You have your orders, Captain,' he said in a low voice. 'We cannot afford any survivors to tell the tale.'

Zhann nodded curtly in acknowledgement, but his face was as grim as his heart was heavy. He was a good soldier, a professional soldier. And the job of the soldier was to kill the enemy, not murder what amounted to an ally. But an order was an order, and much as he detested the increasing power and influence of the KGB in military matters, to defy a command was to place his own life on the line.

He glanced at Piggy. It was a mistake which was to cost him his life. For in that fleeting look, Piggy saw something beyond the expression of respect for a fellow soldier. He saw regret, and he saw pity. Even as Zhann's hand twitched at his side in a prearranged signal, Piggy's highly tuned senses were already primed. That very special instinct was alerted, and his body tensed to respond.

Ninety-nine soldiers out of 100 would have missed the faint, muted click of a dozen PPSh sub-machine-guns being cocked simultaneously. Piggy did not. More importantly, he pinpointed the exact source of the sound immediately: third lorry, fifteen degrees to his right.

'Shake out,' he screamed at the top of his voice. Even as he yelled, the Vickers in his hands was pumping out its devastating 500 rounds a minute – a lethal cocktail of tracer, armour-piercing shells, incendiary and ball. Beside him, Wellerby had already dived over the side of the jeep, retrieved the Thompson and rolled back under the vehicle, from where he began raking the legs of the Russian soldiers who had been standing in line.

Piggy swung the spitting machine-gun along the side of the third lorry from the cab to the tailgate, concentrating his fire at the level where the side panel met the canvas cover. The fabric of the canopy shredded away like mist evaporating in the sunshine, whole sections of it bursting into flame and drifting into the air on its own convection currents. The side panel disintegrated into splinters of wood and metal, finally revealing the inside of the truck like the stage of some monstrous puppet theatre on which life-sized marionettes jerked and twitched in an obscene dance of death.

Caught on the hop, the rest of the Russian troops had reacted with commendable speed. Leaving their unfortunate colleagues who had caught Wellerby's raking ground-level burst from under the jeep writhing on the ground with shattered legs and kneecaps, those who could still move threw themselves down and rolled for what cover they could find.

The second set of Vickers never had a chance to open up. Pat O'Neill took a chest full of rib-splintering 7.62mm slugs which lifted him out of the jeep and threw him several feet behind it. He was dead before he hit the ground. Seconds later, Mad Dog caught it in the gut and slid lifelessly down in his seat, his head bowed forward like a man in prayer. Beyond the arc of the sub-machine-guns, two surviving Russian soldiers had rolled into a position from which they had a clear line of fire to the underside of the lead jeep. Andy Wellerby did not stand a chance as a deadly cone of fire from the two guns converged on his trapped and prone form.

Piggy had only the satisfaction of seeing Colonel Zhann's upper torso dissolve into a massive bloody stump before the Russian fire came up over the side of the jeep and caught him in the thighs and groin. He fell sideways, landing half in and half out of the jeep as the clatter of gunfire finally ceased.

Pain swamped his senses, but his eyes were still open and his brain could still register what they saw. Just before the blackness came down, Piggy saw the lorry containing Leveski and Mencken dwindling into the distance.

'We owe you one, you bastards,' he grunted from between clenched teeth just before he collapsed into unconsciousness.

Miraculously, Piggy survived. But he was to hobble for the rest of his life on a pair of crutches and one tin leg. Just one year after leaving the military hospital, he joined the Operations Planning and Intelligence Unit at Stirling Lines – ironically enough, nicknamed 'The Kremlin' – and had a distinguished career until his retirement in 1986. Throughout his service years, his colleagues would come to know him for one particular conviction, which became almost a catch-phrase.

'Never trust a fucking Russian,' Piggy would say. 'Never trust a fucking Russian.'

# 3

*Puerto Gaiba, Bolivia – May 1951*

The man who called himself Conrad Weiss watched the two strangers walking along the shabby riverside and knew that the day he had feared and dreaded for six years had finally arrived.

They were coming for him; of that Weiss had absolutely no doubt. The two men were smartly dressed and obviously Europeans – both extreme rarities in a little Bolivian backwater town on the River Paraguay. He assumed that they had been to his house and extracted directions to the boat from his wife. He hoped that they had not tortured or hurt her. Although he had originally taken Conceptua in bigamous marriage purely for reasons of political expediency, Weiss had grown genuinely fond of her and the two olive-skinned sons she had borne him.

The two men strolled unhurriedly towards the luxury motor cruiser, which stood out like a sore thumb among the jumble of dilapidated river fishing craft. Weiss thought, momentarily, of the loaded Luger he kept in his cabin locker, quickly dismissing it. If the men were coming for him they would be trained agents, armed and alert. Besides, even if he did manage to kill them both, others would follow. They knew where he was now.

It seemed best to play innocent, attempt to bluff it out. There was at least a reasonable chance of getting away with it, Weiss reasoned. His false Swiss identity papers were the flawless work of a master forger, and his assumed identity was rock solid. And, even if that failed to impress his investigators, he had distributed vast sums in bribes to corrupt Bolivian officials in high places. That should protect him against any official attempts at extradition. Of course, they might have plans to smuggle him out of South America forcibly. Or simply to kill him where he was. In which case, his six-year run of good luck would have finally run out.

Weiss had developed a philosophical attitude to what had basically been a second life for him. He had been incredibly lucky, and more than a little cunning. When the Allies had liberated Auschwitz, he had managed to slip through the net disguised as one of the Jewish prisoners. Undetected even after six weeks in a temporary transit camp, he had finally managed to buy his ticket to freedom from an American sergeant for a handful of gold nuggets. Whether that sergeant had ever known that those nuggets came from the dental fillings of murdered Jews, Weiss had never known, or cared. He had evaded everybody – even the British SAS units on special duty to round up and arrest known and suspected war criminals. At the time, that was all that had mattered.

For the gold itself, Weiss had cared even less, for it had represented but a small fraction of the fortune in stolen jewelry and valuables he had amassed during his four years in the death camp. It was that fortune which had bought him the identity of Conrad Weiss, a retired Swiss watchmaker, and his passage to Bolivia.

But luck was at best a temporary phenomenon. The two men now mounting the gangplank of his boat both testified to that.

Bluff it out, then. Play the cards you held and hope for the best, Weiss decided. Propping himself up against the stern rail, he tried to look innocently surprised.

The first man aboard had a smile on his face, but his eyes were cold.

'Herr Weiss?'

The reply was non-committal. 'Who wants to know?'

'Ah, you are worried, cautious. As of course you should be,' Tovan Leveski murmured in good German. His hand dropped slowly and gently towards the front of his well-cut jacket, slipping open the buttons. He studied Weiss's eyes, following every move.

'Let me assure you, Herr Weiss, that we mean you no harm. We are not what you probably think we are. For a start, both of us are completely unarmed.' Leveski pulled his jacket aside carefully, to show that he was not wearing a waist or shoulder holster. He half-turned to his companion, motioning for him to do the same.

Weiss's surprise was genuine now. 'Who are you? What is it you want with me?'

'Just to talk. We have a little proposition to put to you. One that I think you will find extremely fascinating, my dear Doctor.'

The German's sharply honed survival instinct cut in automatically, despite Leveski's disarming manner.

'Doctor? Why do you call me doctor? I was a simple watchmaker in Switzerland until my retirement.'

The cold smile dropped from Leveski's face. 'Please do me the courtesy of crediting me with intelligence, Doctor. I have not come all this way to be insulted. You are Dr Franz Steiner.

You were in charge of the medical research facility at Auschwitz from 1941 to 1945. Your highly specialized work concerned the grafting and transplantation of amputated limbs in human subjects. You were several years ahead of your time in recognizing the problems of spontaneous rejection – a problem which, I might add, has since been much more widely studied.'

Something told Steiner that, armed or not, Leveski was not a man to antagonize. His bluff had been called, yet no threats had been offered – only a tantalizing reference to his work. Steiner found himself increasingly fascinated.

'You have overcome the rejection problem? Isolated the antibodies which cause it?'

Leveski shook his head. 'Not yet, Doctor. But we will – or rather, you will. With our help, of course.'

Steiner suddenly realized that his first question remained unanswered. He repeated it. 'Who are you? What do you want with me?'

Leveski dipped his hand carefully into the inside pocket of his jacket and drew out his identity card, which he flashed under Steiner's nose. 'My name is Tovan Leveski. My companion is Viktor Yaleta. As you see, we are both official representatives of the government of the USSR.'

Leveski saw the look of uncertainty which flickered across the German's ice-blue eyes. 'You are surprised, Doctor. You should not be. The fact that we may have been enemies in the past has no relevance to our business here today. It is something which transcends accidents of birth, mere geographical boundaries. We are talking about science, Doctor – pure science. Medical reasearch – the very future of the human race. Does that not interest you?'

Steiner shrugged off the pointless question. 'Of course. Who could fail to be interested?'

Leveski nodded towards the hatch which led down to the boat's cabin. 'Then perhaps we can discuss this in greater comfort?'

Nodding thoughtfully, Steiner turned, leading the two Russians to the short companionway.

'So, how did you find me?' Steiner asked, more relaxed now that the danger seemed to have passed, and mellowed by a large glass of local brandy.

Leveski smiled. 'Find you, Doctor?' He inclined one shaggy eyebrow. 'We never lost you. We have known your exact whereabouts since 1946. We simply had no use for your particular talents until now. Your work was well ahead of its time, as you probably realize.'

Steiner sipped at his brandy. 'And what exactly are you offering me?'

Leveski spread his hands in an expansive gesture. 'Virtually anything, my dear Doctor. The resources of the finest and most comprehensive research facility in the world. Unlimited funds, an inexhaustible supply of human subjects for experimentation. And, probably most important to you, Doctor, total freedom to conduct biological experiments without any ethical or moral restraints. The chance to play God, in fact.'

Even if Steiner had not already been hooked, this last phrase would have clinched it. His eyes had a dreamy, faraway glaze to them. 'This research establishment you spoke of. What is its actual purpose?'

'To push the boundaries of medicine, surgery and biochemistry to their ultimate limits – and then beyond,' Leveski said grandly. 'To dream impossible dreams, and then to make those dreams come true. To travel on unknown roads – and to make new maps for others to follow in the future.'

Steiner's heart surged. It seemed that he had heard such dreams outlined before, not so long ago. But those dreams had gone sour, decried and finally smashed to dust by a world which did not understand. Now, suddenly, it was as if he were being given a second chance.

'And my colleagues? Who would I be working with?' he wanted to know.

'Others like yourself. Scientists who have dared to work in areas avoided by the squeamish and faint-hearted. We scoured Europe for them – the concentration camps, the germ-warfare establishments, the genetic study centres set up by your late Führer in his dream of a pure master race. All supplemented with the cream of our own scientists, of course.'

'The human subjects? You would use your own people for such experiments?'

Leveski shrugged carelessly. 'Some. Dissidents, activists, criminals, lunatics – the scum of our society. Polish Jews, prisoners of war, Mongolian peasants – the world is seething with displaced and expendable people, Doctor. As I told you, our supply of subjects is virtually inexhaustible.'

There was only one, comparatively minor question left to ask.

'What about my wife and sons?' Steiner wanted to know.

Leveski shook his head firmly. 'I am afraid that our offer is for you alone, Dr Steiner. You must simply disappear without trace. They would be well provided for, of course. Your own needs would also be well catered for. There will be no shortage of available women where you are going.'

Steiner considered the matter unemotionally. There was just one last point to be cleared up.

'Suppose I turn down this proposition?' he asked.

'Ah.' Leveski looked apologetic. 'Unfortunately, you now know too much to be left alive. Perhaps you are aware that at this moment several Israeli assassination teams are highly active throughout South America. We would simply pass on our information about your whereabouts to one of them. It would then be just a matter of time.'

The Russian broke off, to turn to his compatriot. 'Viktor, why don't you tell the good doctor how the Israelis' victims die?'

The other man spoke for the first time, in a deep, guttural voice. His thick lips cracked open in a bestial, malicious grin. 'Choked to death on their own genitals,' he grunted, with obvious relish. 'Hacked off and stuffed down their throats.'

Leveski stared Steiner coldly in the eyes, letting the image sink in. 'Mind you, they might have something a bit more special for someone who used to perform surgical amputations without anaesthetic,' he volunteered.

Steiner held the Russian's gaze, the ghost of a smile playing over his lips. 'When do we leave?' he asked.

# 4

*London – January 1993*

Lieutenant-Colonel Barney Davies glanced around the Foreign Office conference room with a slight sense of surprise. He had not been expecting such a high-powered meeting. Nothing in the message he had received had given any indication that this was to be any more than a briefing session. Now, noting the sheer number of personnel already assembled, and the prominence of some of them, Davies could tell that this was to be no mere briefing. It looked more like a full-blown security conference.

He reviewed the cluster of faces hovering around the large, oval-shaped table. Nobody seemed prepared to sit down yet; they were all still waiting for the guest of honour to arrive. It had to be pretty high brass, Davies figured to himself, for he recognized at least two Foreign Office ministers, either of whom could quite comfortably head up any meeting up to and perhaps including Cabinet level. He teased his brain, trying to put names to the faces.

He identified Clive Murchison almost immediately. He had had some dealings with the man during the Gulf War, the successful conclusion of which probably had something to do with Murchison's obvious and rapid climb up the bureaucratic ladder. Tending towards the curt, but irritatingly efficient, Murchison was of the old school, the 'send a gunboat' brigade. His presence alone reinforced Davies's feeling that this meeting was serious stuff.

Naming Murchison's colleague proved a little trickier. Windley? Windsor? Neither name seemed quite right. It fell into place, eventually. A double-barrelled name. Wynne-Tilsley, that was it. Michael Wynne-Tilsley. Still technically a junior minister but well connected, tipped for higher things. Word was that he had the PM's ear, or maybe knew a few things he should not. In political circles, Davies reflected, that was the equivalent of a ticket to the front of the queue.

There were half a dozen other people who meant nothing whatsoever to Davies. Whether they were civil servants or civilian advisers, he had no idea, although there was probably the odd man from MI6 or the 'green slime' in there somewhere.

There was, however, one more face that he definitely did recognize. Davies's face broke into a friendly grin as he strolled across to the slightly hunched figure in the electric wheelchair. Reaching down, he gave the man's shoulder an affectionate squeeze.

'Well, you old bastard, what are you doing here? Thought you'd retired.'

Piggy Baker looked up, grinning back. 'I had . . . have. They dug me up again to bring me in as a special adviser on this one.' The man extended his hand. 'Barney, good to see you.'

The two men shook hands warmly. Finally, Davies drew back slightly, appraising his old comrade. He noted that Piggy no longer bothered to wear his artificial leg.

'So what happened to the pogo stick? Thought they would have rebuilt you as the six billion dollar man by now. All this new technology, prosthetics and stuff.'

Piggy shrugged carelessly. 'They did offer, a couple of years back. But what the hell? I'm too old to go around all tarted up like Robocop.' He broke off, nodding down at the wheelchair. 'These days, I'm happy enough to ponce around in this most of the time.'

Davies nodded, his face suddenly becoming serious. 'So, what's all this about? Looks like high-powered stuff.'

Baker's face was apologetic. 'Sorry, Barney, but I can't tell you a thing until the briefing. OSA and all that, you know.'

'Yes, of course.' Davies had not really expected much else. He knew all about the Official Secrets Act, and official protocol. He had come up against it himself enough times.

There was a sudden stir of movement in the room. The babble of voices hushed abruptly. Glancing towards the large double doors, Davies was not really surprised to see the Foreign Secretary enter the room. He had not been expecting anyone less.

The Foreign Secretary headed straight for one end of the oval table and sat down. 'Well, gentlemen, shall we get down to business?' he said crisply. He glanced across at Wynne-Tilsley as everyone took their chairs. 'Perhaps you would be so good as to introduce everybody before we begin the briefing.'

Wynne-Tilsley went round the table in an anticlockwise direction. Just as Davies had supposed, most of the personnel were civilian advisers or from the green slime, the Intelligence Corps.

The introductions over, the Foreign Secretary took over once more. 'Gentlemen, we have a problem,' he announced flatly. 'The purpose of this meeting is to determine what we do about it. Let me say at this juncture that it is not so much a question of should we get involved as *can* we get involved. Which is why I have invited Lieutenant-Colonel Davies, of

33

22 SAS, here today.' He paused briefly to nod towards Davies in acknowledgement, before turning to Murchison. 'Perhaps you would outline the situation for us.'

Murchison rose to his feet, riffling through the sheaf of papers and notes in front of him. He spoke in a clear, confident tone – the voice of a man well used to public speaking and being listened to.

'Essentially, we've been asked by the Chinese to infiltrate former Soviet territory,' he announced, pausing for a few moments to let the shock sink in. He waited until the brief buzz of startled exclamations and hastily exchanged words were over. 'Which, as you might gather, gentlemen, makes this a very sticky problem indeed.' Murchison then turned to face Davies directly. 'The general feeling was that this is an operation which could only be tackled by the SAS if it could be tackled at all – although the complexities and nature of the specific problem could prove even beyond their capabilities.'

It seemed like a challenge which demanded a response. Davies rose to his feet slowly, addressing the Foreign Secretary directly.

'You used the word "infiltrate",' he said thoughtfully. 'An ambiguous word at the best of times. Some clarification would be appreciated.'

The Foreign Secretary nodded. 'I appreciate your concern, Lieutenant-Colonel, and I understand your reserve. Just let me assure you that we are not talking about an invasion force here, nor would we go in with any hostile intent. However, it is possible that your men would encounter hostile forces.'

Not much wiser, Davies sank back into his chair. 'Perhaps I'd better hear the rest of the briefing,' he muttered.

Murchison rose to his feet again. 'I think the background to the problem will be best explained by Captain Baker,' he said. 'I know Lieutenant-Colonel Davies is well aware of his colleague's position, but for the rest of you I had better explain that Captain Baker was for many years with SAS Operations Planning and Intelligence. He has been called here today because he has been close to this particular story for a long time.'

With a curt nod in Piggy's direction, he yielded the table and sat down again.

'You'll excuse me if I don't stand, gentlemen,' Piggy began, a wry grin on his face. He paused for a while, marshalling his thoughts. Finally, he took a deep breath and launched into his rehearsed brief.

'Just after the Second World War, it became apparent that the Russians were gathering together scientists, doctors and medical staff from all over Europe for some sort of secret project,' he announced. Turning towards Davies, he added a piece of more personal and intimate information. 'As it happens, I had a personal encounter at the time, and there are three plaques mounted outside the Regimental Chapel at Stirling Lines because of it. So you might say that I have always had a deep and personal interest in the ongoing story.'

So, Davies thought, it was personal – to them both. Family business. An old score that needed settling. But why now? Why the Chinese involvement? He listened intently as his old friend went on, now with a deeper sense of commitment.

'Suffice it to say that when I moved to OPI I initiated a monitoring operation on this project, which has been kept up to the present day,' Piggy continued. 'And although there has been no official liaison with our own Intelligence Corps, I believe that they too have been keeping an eye open, as, indeed, have our American counterparts.'

Davies broke off briefly to cast a questioning glance towards Grieves, the officer from the green slime. The man nodded his head wordlessly, confirming Piggy's suspicions.

'We know that the original project was code-named Phoenix by the Russians,' Piggy went on. 'Everything suggests that it was never officially embraced by the Soviet government, but placed largely under the control of the KGB, and kept under tight security wraps. For that reason, our intelligence is patchy, to say the least, and we have had to surmise quite a lot of what we were unable to know for fact. What we *do* know, however, is that in 1947 a secret research facility was set up in a fairly remote and mountainous region of Kazakhstan, fairly close to the Mongolian border. While we still do not know the exact purpose of this original facility, we have always assumed it to be a biological research project of some kind. It is also logical to assume that the underlying concept of this research facility was in military application, although there may have been some spin-offs into mainstream science. It is more than possible, for instance, that the dominance of Soviet and Eastern Bloc athletes during the fifties and sixties was directly due to steroids and other performance-enhancing drugs which were developed in the Kazakhstan facility.'

The Foreign Secretary had been busy making notes. He looked up now, tapping his pen on the table to draw Piggy's attention.

'So what you are saying, in effect, is that this project has never actually offered any direct, or perceived, threat to the Western powers, or us in particular? At worst, in fact, it might have cost us a few gold medals in the Olympics?'

Piggy nodded, conceding the point. 'Up to now, yes. But recent developments have given us cause to think again.'

The Foreign Secretary chewed his bottom lip thoughtfully. 'And what are these new developments?'

'With respect, sir, I believe I can best answer that,' Grieves said, rising to his feet and waving a buff-coloured dossier in one hand. Satisfied that he had the floor, he cleared his throat with a slight cough and carried on. 'About three months ago, GCHQ monitored what appeared to be some kind of distress signal sent out from the Kazakhstan facility to the old KGB HQ in Moscow. From this, we must deduce two things – A, that some sort of accident or emergency situation had occurred within the complex, and B, the personnel inside are seemingly unaware that the KGB has been virtually broken up and disbanded over the past year or so. This further suggests that they might be completely out of touch with what has been going on inside the Soviet Union and the world at large.'

'But how can that be?' the Foreign Secretary wanted to know. 'Surely they must have regular contact with the outside world – supplies, that sort of thing.'

Grieves shook his head. 'Not necessarily, sir. Our intelligence has always suggested that the facility was designed to be virtually self-sustaining. As long ago as 1969 an American spy satellite carrying out routine surveillance of the Soviet nuclear weapons testing facility at Semipalatinsk happened to overfly the base and monitor an internal nuclear power source. This suggests that it has its own closed power source, and it is probable that they also have their own hydroponic food-production facility along with a pretty sophisticated recycling system. The very nature of the complex has always been secretive, even autonomous. It is more than likely that it even has its own security system – a private army, in effect.'

'Just what are we actually talking about here?' Lieutenant-Colonel Davies interrupted. 'A scientific research facility or a bloody garrison? Just how big is this damned place, anyway?'

If the Foreign Secretary found Davies's language at all offensive, he gave no sign. 'A good question,' he muttered, glancing questioningly at Grieves.

The Intelligence officer shrugged faintly. 'Again, inconclusive evidence,' he said. 'Satellite observation suggests that much of the complex is built underground, but we don't know how many subterranean levels there might be. Basically, we have no way of knowing the actual size and personnel strength of the establishment. It might house a few dozen scientists and support staff. Or it could be an autonomous, full-scale community, of several hundred people living in a miniature city. Don't forget that this place has been established for nearly fifty years now. There's no guessing how it has developed.'

Grieves fell silent for several seconds. When he spoke again, his face was grim and his tone sombre. 'Of course, personnel numbers could well be a purely academic point. They may, in fact, all be dead anyway. Which, incidentally, is where the Chinese come in. They're afraid that some sort of chemical or biological contamination may have escaped from within the complex, and may already have crossed the Mongolian border.' He paused again, longer this time, to allow the full significance of his words to register.

Finally, Davies attempted a brief recap. 'So what you're suggesting is that this place may have been engaged in chemical or bacteriological warfare research, and something nasty might have got loose?'

Grieves nodded. 'In essence, yes.'

'Have the Chinese any direct evidence for this?' Davies asked. 'Have there been any actual deaths?'

Grieves consulted his notes briefly. 'It's difficult to be absolutely sure,' he replied. 'You have to understand the unique background and make-up of Kazakhstan itself. It's vast – almost unbelievably so. You could fit Britain, France, Germany, Spain, Finland and Sweden into it quite comfortably. Yet it only has a total population of some seventeen million – an improbable mix of races and cultures including native Kazakhs, Tartars, Uzbeks and Uigurs along with emigrant Russians, Germans and others. In Stalin's heyday, Kazakhstan was Gulag territory. When the concentration camps were disbanded, many of the inmates settled in the area. Stalin also used the region as a dumping ground for vast numbers of people he considered "political undesirables" – Volga Germans, Meskhetian Turks, Crimean Tartars and Karachais to name but a few. So we're talking about millions of square miles still sparsely populated by people of widely differing religions, cultures and languages. And we are also dealing with a particularly remote region, in mountainous terrain not far from Mount Belushka. Because of the nature of this terrain, and the scattered, semi-nomadic distribution of the peasant population, there is no direct communications network. Any information which comes out of the area is essentially rumour, or word-of-mouth reports which might have been passed through several dozen very simple people before reaching the ears of the authorities. However, there are enough reports of dead and missing goatherds, peasant farmers and the like filtering through to give these Chinese fears some credibility.'

'So why can't they go in and sort it out for themselves?' Davies asked. 'After all, they're right there on the spot.'

Grieves did not attempt to answer. Instead, he glanced towards the Foreign Secretary.

'With respect, Lieutenant-Colonel,' said the latter, addressing Davies directly, 'you're looking at this through the eyes of a military man, without taking into account the highly complex and sensitive political issues involved here. This whole region is a territorial minefield. There have been border clashes between the Chinese and Russians for the last three decades, and stability balances on a knife-edge. The Chinese don't dare to make a serious incursion into Russian territory for fear of sparking off a major incident.'

'Then it's up to the Russians to sort it out for themselves, surely?' Davies suggested.

The Foreign Secretary smiled thinly. 'Perhaps you're forgetting that there is virtually no longer any centralized decision-making inside former Soviet territory,' he pointed out. 'Every region, every state is in turmoil – fragmented and politically unstable if not actively in the throes of civil war. The Kazakhstan region is no exception. There are perhaps up to half a dozen different guerrilla groups and political and religious factions already fighting for territory virtually on a village by village, valley by valley basis. You only have to look to Georgia, just across the Caspian, to get an idea of what's going on there.'

Davies nodded thoughtfully. Grieves coughed faintly again, drawing attention back to himself.

'Actually, to answer Lieutenant-Colonel Davies's last question, I ought to point out that we believe the Russians *did* manage to send in at least one military team to investigate,' he volunteered. 'Our intelligence suggests that they disappeared without trace, with absolutely no clues as to what happened to them. We have no way of knowing if they even managed to get anywhere near the research facility.'

'But I still fail to understand how the Chinese reckon to get us involved in all this,' Davies said, becoming increasingly bogged down in the political intricacy of the entire affair.

The Foreign Secretary treated him to another thin, almost cynical smile. 'Politics sometimes makes for strange bedfellows,' he said. 'The Chinese are desperate for Western acceptance after the Tiananmen Square massacre. They are equally desperate for access to European trade markets, and, rightly or wrongly, they seem to believe that Britain could be holding the top cards in the Euro-deck right now. And, as we are already involved in close association over the Hong Kong business, they feel they have an ace of their own to play.'

Davies started to understand at last. 'So it's a threat, basically?' he said. 'Unless we play ball with them, they'll make the Hong Kong negotiations more difficult?'

The Foreign Secretary smiled openly now. 'I see you're beginning to get a grasp of modern-day diplomacy,' he murmured, without obvious sarcasm. He paused to take a slow, deep breath. 'So, Lieutenant-Colonel Davies, that's it, in a nutshell. We appear to be stuck with the problem, and the SAS would appear to be our only hope.'

'To do what, exactly?' Davies demanded. He was still not quite sure what was actually being asked of him.

The Foreign Secretary stared him directly in the eye. 'To get in there, monitor the situation and neutralize it if possible. Of course, you understand that we are talking about some of the most difficult and inhospitable terrain in the world, under the most extreme climatic conditions. As I understand it, the difference between daytime and night-time temperatures can be as much as 20°C. Once you're up into the mountains, you can expect extremes as low as minus thirty – plus fierce and bitter northerly winds straight down from Siberia.'

Davies nodded thoughtfully. 'Not exactly the Brecon Beacons,' he muttered. The reference to the SAS testing and training grounds went over the top of the Foreign Secretary's head.

'You would, of course, be given the full support of the Intelligence Corps and access to all the relevant files,' the latter went on. 'You would be expected to liaise with Captain Baker about the finer points of the operation, including more detailed briefing about the geography of the region. All I require from you at this stage is a gut assessment as to the feasibility of the operation. In short, could your men get a small team of scientists into that complex with a reasonable hope of success?'

The last sentence was a sudden and totally unexpected sting in the tail. Davies jumped to his feet angrily, quite forgetting the company he was in as he banged his fist down on the table. 'No bloody way,' he shouted, vehemently.

The Foreign Secretary kept his cool admirably, merely raising one eyebrow quizzically.

'Come now, Lieutenant-Colonel. I would have thought this was right up your street.'

'No bloody civilians, no bloody way,' Davies repeated, virtually ignoring him. 'The SAS isn't a babysitting service for a bunch of boffins who probably couldn't even step over a puddle without getting their feet wet. If we go in at all, we go in alone. And if we need any specialist know-how, we'll take it in our heads.'

The Foreign Secretary seemed unperturbed. 'Yes, Captain Baker more or less warned me that that would be your reaction,' he observed philosophically. He thought for a few moments. 'Well, as I can't order you, we shall have to resort to Plan B. Your men will secure the area and neutralize any obvious threat to an Anglo-Chinese team of scientific experts who will be airlifted in behind you. Can you do that much?'

Davies simmered down. 'We can have a damned good try,' he said emphatically. 'What about insertion into the area?'

'That's one of the matters we're going to have to discuss,' Piggy put in. 'But basically you'd probably have to assemble somewhere neutral like Hong Kong. You'd go in as civilians, of course – either as tourists or visiting businessmen. From there you would be contacted by the Chinese and transferred to a military base on the mainland. We would expect the Chinese to put you over the border somewhere just inside Sinkiang Province, probably 100 miles north-east of Tacheng. You would then be facing a foot trek of around 350 miles. It's going to give you supply problems, but there's a possibility the Chinks would be willing to risk a brief air incursion into Soviet territory to drop you one advance cache. Certainly no more, since the official Kazakhstan government is extremely well armed with the latest high-tech kit. The republic has even managed to retain nearly fifteen per cent of the former Soviet total nuclear arsenal, much to the Kremlin's annoyance.'

'In that sort of mountainous terrain?' Davies shook his head. 'No, we'd probably never find it. And if we put it in with a homing beacon there's every chance someone else would get to it before we did. No, we'd have to go in on a self-sustaining basis. What's the local wildlife situation?'

Piggy shrugged. 'Sparse – particularly at this time of year. Probably a few rabbits or even wild deer in the foothills, but not much else. Your best bet would probably be airborne. Carrion crow, the odd golden eagle – probably not much different to turkey if you eat 'em with your eyes shut.'

'Sorry, but you two gentlemen seem to have lost me,' the Foreign Secretary put in. 'I thought we were discussing a military operation, not a gourmet's picnic'

The politician went up an immediate notch in Davies's estimation. The man had a sense of humour.

'It's a question of weight and distance ratio,' Davies hastened to explain. 'With a round trip of 700 miles, my men are going to be limited in the amount of food and supplies they can carry in their bergens. They're already going to have to be wearing heavy thermal protection gear and, from the sound of it, Noddy suits as well.'

43

'Noddy suits?' the Foreign Secretary queried.

The SAS man smiled. 'Sorry, sir. I mean nuclear, chemical and biological warfare protection. Cumbersome, uncomfortable, and all additional weight. Quite simply, it's going to be physically impossible to carry all the gear they will need for an operation of this size and complexity. So we cut non-essential supplies such as food. Troopers are trained to live off the land where necessary.'

'They could, of course, take in a couple of goats with them,' Piggy suggested. It was not intended to be a facetious remark, but Davies glared at him all the same.

'I'm concerned about keeping them alive – not their bloody sex lives,' he said dismissively. 'And in that respect, where do we get kitted up, if we're going in as civvies?'

'No problem,' Piggy assured him. 'We can arrange for anything you ask for to be ready and waiting for you when you arrive at your Chinese base.'

The Foreign Secretary was standing up and gathering his papers together. 'So I can leave you two to sort out the details?' he asked, beginning to feel slightly uncomfortable and superfluous. 'How soon do you think you might be able to come up with a reasonable plan of operations?'

Davies shrugged. 'Six, seven weeks maybe. There's a lot of groundwork to be done.'

'Ah.' The Foreign Secretary frowned. 'I'm afraid we don't have the luxury of that sort of timescale,' he said. 'There is another problem.'

'Which is?' Davies wanted to know.

Murchison answered for the Foreign Secretary. 'It's a question of climate and temperature,' he explained. 'If there *has* been a biological leak, our experts seem to think that the extreme cold might well keep any widespread contagion in check for a while at least. Come the spring, and warmer weather, it could be a different picture altogether. We had been thinking in terms of getting something off the ground in three weeks maximum.'

Davies sucked in a deep breath and blew it out slowly over his bottom lip. It was a tall order, even for the SAS. He looked at the Foreign Secretary with a faint shrug. 'I'll see what I can do,' he said quietly, unwilling to make any firmer promise at that stage.

The Foreign Secretary nodded understandingly. 'I'm sure you will do everything you can, Lieutenant-Colonel.' He glanced almost nervously around the table before directing his attention back to Davies. 'You understand, of course, that if anything goes wrong, this meeting never took place?'

Davies grinned. It was a story he had often heard before. 'Of course,' he muttered. 'They never do, do they?'

The two men exchanged a last brief, knowing glance which established that they were both fully aware of the rules of the game. Then the Foreign Secretary picked up his papers, nodded to his two ministers and led the way out of the conference room.

Left alone, Davies crossed over to Piggy and slapped him on the back. 'Well, I think you and I need to go and sink a few jars somewhere,' he suggested.

# 5

'So, what's your gut feeling on this one?' Davies asked Piggy after he had helped install his electric wheelchair in the lift down to the high-security underground car park.

Piggy let out a short, explosive sound halfway between a grunt and a cynical laugh. 'You know my views on anything to do with the fucking Russians,' he replied. 'And I'm not too sure about the bloody Chinks, either. Personally, I'm inclined to the view that every takeaway in London is part of a plot to poison us all with monosodium glutamate.'

Davies grinned. 'You're a bloody xenophobe.'

Piggy shook his head, a mock expression of indignation on his face. 'That's a vicious rumour put about by those jealous bastards at Stirling Lines. I take my sex straight.' He paused to flash Davies a rueful grin. 'At least, I do when Pam hasn't got a bloody headache these days.'

Davies smiled back. 'Christ, are you two still at it? You dirty old man.'

'*Lucky* old man,' Piggy corrected him. 'Actually, I think it's just the delayed effect of all those hormones I was taking for forty years.'

Davies's eyes strayed briefy to the wheelchair, and Piggy's

truncated torso. 'You never had any problems, then?' he asked, a little awkwardly.

Piggy grinned again. 'No, the old Spitfire still flies. They may have shot the undercarriage to hell, but there was nothing wrong with the fuselage. The hormone treatment did the rest.' His face suddenly became serious again, almost sad. 'No kids, of course – that's the only part that still hurts.'

Children were a sore point with Davies as well. 'Count yourself lucky,' he muttered. 'Mine hardly ever bother to even talk to me these days. Now they've got a new dad and a new baby-sister, I'm just a relic from the past.'

'You never bothered to remarry, then?'

Davies laughed ironically. 'Like the old cliché – I married the job,' he said. 'And the SAS can be a jealous bitch. Besides, there aren't that many understanding women like your Pam around these days.'

They had reached the car park level. Piggy looked up into Davies's eyes as the lift doors hissed open, a wry smile on his face. 'We're still doing it, aren't we?' he murmured.

'Doing what?' Davies didn't quite understand.

'The bullshit,' Piggy said, referring to the casual banter which virtually all SAS men exchanged before operations.

Davies gave no reply. He helped steer the wheelchair through the doors into the underground car park. Instinctively, he began to walk towards his own BMW, suddenly pausing in mid-stride and looking back at Piggy somewhat awkwardly.

'Look, I've only just realized that my car isn't equipped to take that chariot of yours,' he muttered in embarrassment.

Piggy smiled easily. 'No problem, I do have my own transport, you know.'

'Yes, of course.' Davies relaxed, feeling a bit better about his near-gaffe. 'So, where would you like to go for a drink?

I'm afraid I'm not really up on London pubs these days.'

Piggy looked at him with a faint look of surprise. 'Who said anything about a London pub? There's only one place for a pair of old troopers like us to have a drink – and we both know exactly where that is.'

It was Davies's turn to look a little bemused. 'The Paludrine Club?' he said, referring to the Regiment's exclusive little watering-hole back at Stirling Lines in Hereford.

'And why not?' Piggy prompted. 'We can do it in just over two hours, given a following wind. Besides, we're going to have to do some serious planning, and where better than the Kremlin?'

Davies glanced at his BMW again, the sense of embarrassment returning. 'Two hours flat out is some hard driving – even for me,' he pointed out awkwardly.

Piggy followed the direction of his gaze and then broke out into an open laugh. 'Christ Almighty, Barney, do you think I'm driving a fucking three-wheeler or something?' He fingered the controls on the arm of his electric wheelchair, steering it over towards a black and silver Mitsubishi Shogun. Pulling a small remote control panel from his pocket, he activated the door lock and automatic winching gear. As the lifting plate sighed down to ground level, Piggy rolled the wheelchair onto it, locked the wheels in position and set the controls again. Effortlessly, the powerful motor hoisted wheelchair and occupant up into the driving cab.

Davies looked up at him, impressed. 'Last one there buys the drinks,' he said, grinning. 'I assume you're planning to stay at my place for a couple of days?'

Piggy smiled down as the wheelchair started to slide into the driving position. 'You assume correctly, my old friend. Everything's already packed in the back.'

He pulled the door closed behind him. Seconds later the Shogun roared into life and lurched away towards the exit with a squeal of rubber on concrete.

Laughing like a schoolboy, Davies broke into a run towards his own car. They were off. But he could already feel the surge of adrenalin in his system which told him he was setting out on something far more challenging than a race up the M4. And something potentially far more dangerous, he reminded himself as he slipped in the ignition key and gunned the powerful BMW into life.

Davies walked away from the bar after paying for the drinks – a small brandy for himself and a double gin and tonic for Piggy. He had not deliberately let Piggy win, he told himself. Perhaps it was just that he was a little more cautious these days, with a little more respect for things like speed limits. Or perhaps it was simply that Piggy still had that extra something to prove to himself. Either way, he actually felt quite good about buying the drinks. Reaching the table, he set them down and sat eyeing Piggy over the rim of his balloon glass, waiting for him to open the conversation.

Piggy picked up his cue. 'First thoughts?' he queried.

Davies sipped at his brandy. 'Two four-man patrols, over the same route but spaced about two hours apart.'

His companion nodded thoughtfully. 'Sweep and clean. And back-up if necessary. Makes good sense. Any thoughts on personnel yet?'

'Mike Hailsham springs to mind.'

Again, Piggy seemed in general agreement. 'Yeah, Major Hailsham's a good CO. Any special reasons?'

'Two main ones. Firstly he has intensive experience of anti-bacteriological equipment and techniques from the Gulf War. He skippered the frontline undercover raids on the Scud bases when we still thought Saddam was going to start dumping anthrax on the Israelis.'

'And second?' Piggy wanted to know.

'And he has fluent Russian,' Davies said. 'Although how much use that's likely to be, I'm not too sure at this point.' He broke off to look questioningly at Piggy. 'You've studied the region. What's likely to be the most common language?'

'Russian's probably as good as anything,' Piggy said. 'The native Kazakhs do have their own tongue, basically derived from Turkish, but most of the younger ones have probably been taught Russian as a second language by now. You can forget the older generation. Before 1917 they didn't have a written language at all – no books, no schools, no permanent records of any kind. It was just a very simple nomadic culture, and basic storytelling or folk song were about the only ways of communicating information.' He tailed off, realizing that he was starting to ramble a bit. 'Anyone else in mind?'

'Andrew Winston would be a good bet, I think,' Davies said. 'Again for the basic reason that he was with Hailsham in Iraq and knows the score. 'And he's a tough bastard. If anyone can nip up a mountain with a full bergen on his back, that big black sonofabitch can. In fact, he'd probably beat everybody else just so he could have ten minutes on his own to sit on the top and write a couple of poems.'

Piggy listened to his friend's eulogy without really understanding it, not knowing the mild-mannered but combat-lethal Barbadian sergeant. Soldiers like Winston were the members of a new breed of SAS men – thinkers and idealists rather than the hardened death-or-glory boys of his own early years.

'And Cyclops, of course,' Davies was going on. 'If you're right and we're going to have shoot down bloody eagles to stay alive, then I want the best sniper in the Regiment.'

Again, Piggy was not personally familiar with the man, but his shooting prowess was legendary. Already five times Army sharpshooting champion, Corporal Billy Clements was the undisputed king of the L96A1, otherwise known as the Accuracy International PM. In his hands the 7.62mm calibre weapon was as accurate and as lethal at 800 yards as a stiletto is at six inches. It was a skill born of almost fanatical practice on the firing range, and one which had given Clements his odd nickname since he appeared to be almost constantly squinting down the eyepiece of a telescopic sight. However, stories that he was incapable of reading even the largest print at less than arm's length remained unproven, since no one had ever actually seen Cyclops trying to read anything.

'Well, that's three names to conjure with for a start,' Davies said as he turned his attention back to his brandy. 'I'll issue recalls this evening and we'll set up a prelim briefing in the Kremlin for 09.00 hours the day after tomorrow.'

He drained his glass after swilling the last few droplets around the bowl and inhaling the fumes with genuine appreciation. Placing it back on the table, he pushed it in Piggy's direction.

'Your round, I think. If we're going to get religiously pissed, we'd better get a move on.'

# 6

To an outsider, it would have been inconceivable that the apparently ill-assorted bunch of men assembled in the briefing room in the 'Kremlin' could function as the most cohesive and effective fighting unit in the world. But *they* knew, and that was what counted. They knew themselves as few men ever do; and they knew each other, and each other's capabilities.

Major Mike Hailsham glanced around the room at the small gathering with almost paternal affection. Not that any of them really needed fathering, he reflected. Used strictly as a term of endearment, the word 'bastards' fitted them all rather neatly as individuals. But collectively, that was a different matter entirely, and it was from this standpoint that Hailsham's sense of pride emanated.

Considering the short notice, he had done rather well, Hailsham told himself. Davies's brief had been nothing if not explicit. 'Imagine the shittiest, toughest assignment you can and get me two teams by the day after tomorrow.' The names of Sergeant Andrew Winston and Corporal Billy Clements had already been dropped into the hat. The rest were his own personal choice, only arrived at after a great deal of thought. Given a brief like that, a man picked his companions very carefully indeed.

Piggy sat directly beneath the large stuffed water-buffalo head which decorated one wall of the briefing room. A memento of the Regiment's days in Malaya, it was also a symbol of unity, of exclusivity – the totem of a closed and quasi-secret brotherhood. For the SAS was indeed a brotherhood, and Stirling Lines was their highly exclusive lodge.

Piggy also reviewed the assembled men, but from a slightly different perspective. Most were strangers to him, and yet he felt that he knew them all as intimately as he knew his own family. Personal acquaintance did not really enter the equation, and time meant nothing. There were blood ties. These unfamiliar faces were direct descendants, the inheritors of a strict line of succession which stretched unbroken from the summer of 1941 to the present day. A quietly spoken Scots Guards lieutenant named David Stirling had conceived a crazy idea, and the idea had spawned a legend.

Yes, they were all brothers under the skin, Piggy thought – and it helped to fill the void of knowing that his own direct family line would end with his death.

Davies respected them all, but he envied them too. They would go, and he would stay behind. Ahead of them, these men faced danger, incredible hardship and conditions that a man would not want to inflict on his worst enemy. But to them it was life, Davies knew. A life that they had chosen to live, sucking out every precious moment and savouring it until it ran dry of juice and the clock stopped ticking. With his own safe, desk-bound job and retirement looming up, Davies might be seen by others to be one of the lucky ones, a man who had survived the odds and finally beaten the clock. Yet he feared the day as it drew inexorably closer. The end of his service career might not be a death, Davies thought bitterly, but it would be an amputation. His eyes strayed briefly to

Piggy's mutilated body in the wheelchair, and he drew uncomfortable comparisons. With a conscious effort, he pushed away his thoughts and tried to concentrate on the job in hand.

Cyclops was bemoaning to Andrew Winston the fact that he had been recalled from leave.

'The trouble with this bloody job is that you never know where you are,' he complained bitterly. 'One minute I'm romping around in a king-sized waterbed with a pair of nympho sisters and the next I'm kipping down in the spider with a bunch of smelly bastards with tattooed arses.'

Andrew's black face broke open into a dismissive grin, revealing a double keyboard of gleaming white teeth. 'You'd never manage to fuck two sisters, you lying bastard,' he teased. 'Everyone in the Regiment knows you've got a prick like a rifle. Too long, too thin, and only one shot up the spout before you have to reload.'

Cyclops was not going to be put down so easily. 'Try a Franchi SPAS pump shotgun and you're a bit nearer the mark,' he countered. 'Fat, fast and ferocious, and enough charge to spray an entire room with one shot.'

'Dream on, man,' Andrew said, laughing. He turned away, moving across the room to talk to Troopers McVitie and Naughton, both only twenty-one but chosen by Major Hailsham on Andrew's personal recommendation. Neither seemed particularly grateful for this singular honour.

'Well, what have you got us into this time, you black bastard?' Jimmy McVitie demanded in his gruff Glasgow accent.

'Whatever it is, I hope we can knock it out in a couple of days,' Barry Naughton added optimistically. 'I'm due for leave in just over a week's time.'

Andrew grinned benignly. 'In answer to your two kind enquiries, A, we're going on a nice little trip to China, and

B, you could both have grey hairs on your goolies before we get home again.'

Barry chose to see the bright side. His eyes flashed with eager anticipation.

'Great, I've always wanted to screw a Chinese bird,' he said, enthusiastically.

Jimmy regarded him with a serious expression on his face. 'Ye ken a Chinese woman's cunt runs the other way, do ye not?' he said. 'Straight across, like a little yellow letterbox.'

His companion's face creased into a sceptical smile. 'That's bullshit,' he muttered, but there was just the faintest suggestion of doubt in his voice. He looked up at Andrew, seeking a second opinion. 'It's not true, is it, boss?'

The sergeant's face was grave. 'Oh, it's true enough,' he confirmed. 'That's why you never see Chinese women sliding down banisters.'

Barry looked at them both blankly, now totally confused. As if at some secret signal, Andrew and Jimmy both raised their forefingers to their mouths at the same time, rubbing them rapidly up and down over their lips. Blubba-dubba-dubba-dubba-dubba-dubba.

They both collapsed into silent laughter as Barry's face told them that he had been well and truly suckered. The young trooper glared at them both without malice. 'You pair of prats,' he spluttered, then fell silent as a faint flush of embarrassment began to spread over his face. He slunk away, looking for someone to take his revenge on.

Finding himself heading in the general direction of Corporal Max Epps, Barry paused for a moment. The tall, burly Mancunian was not known for his sense of humour, nor for his ability to engage in witty repartee. The man was essentially a loner – a trait which had given birth to his nickname, 'the

Thinker'. Under normal circumstances, he was quite happy with his own company, and those who knew him respected that as they respected the man himself. What counted was his contribution to the team when circumstances were not normal. For under fire, or when the going got tough, Epps's character was a mirror-image of his physical presence. Sturdy, dependable, rock-solid. With twenty-six years of intensive soldiering under his belt, he was a comforting man to have around.

But he was definitely not a man to wind up, Barry decided. He veered away across the briefing room, homing in on Tweedledum and Tweedledee, who were, as ever, looking like a pair of Siamese twins who had been separated against their will.

Terry Marks and Tony Tofield had got used to the smutty, but basically good-natured jokes about the closeness of their friendship. Both young, both Londoners and both only recently badged, they accepted the ribaldry of their fellow SAS men because they knew that no one seriously thought that there was anything unnatural about their liking for each other's company, or had any doubts about their sexual orientation. So Terry and Tony had become a natural pair, soon shortened to 'T One' and 'T Two' because it rolled off the tongue better, and finally Tweedledum and Tweedledee.

The pair exchanged a knowing glance as Barry sauntered towards them. Even to a couple of comparative newcomers, the young trooper's gullibility was well known. Baiting him was already a regimental sport.

Innocent as ever, Barry walked right into the trap. 'Hey, you guys. Have you heard? We're going to China,' he announced briskly. 'I suppose you've heard the story about Chinese women's fannies?' He paused expectantly, waiting for a feed-in line. None came. Instead, Tweedledee just nodded knowingly. 'What, about them being so small?' he asked.

Barry was thrown. 'How do you mean?' he asked uncertainly.

Tweedledee held his thumb and forefinger an inch or so apart. 'They're only about this big – about an inch long,' he said in a matter-of-fact way.

He was not going to get caught again, Barry decided. But it was already too late. The trap had been sprung.

'In fact, they're hardly what you'd call a crack at all,' Tweedledee continued, then glanced aside at his companion with a big grin on his face.

'No, more of a little chink, really,' Tweedledum finished for him. It was a pretty pathetic joke, but they both laughed uproariously.

'Bastards!' Barry exploded. More irritable than ever, he turned away and went to sulk in a corner.

It was time to cut the bullshit and get down to business, Davies decided. Picking up a wall pointer, he rapped it a couple of times on the table. 'Gentlemen, can I have your attention,' he demanded loudly.

All at once the buzz of conversation ceased and smiles faded from faces. The atmosphere of casual conviviality in the room was instantly replaced by an air of earnest anticipation.

'Thank you,' Davies said. He gestured over to Piggy, who had taken up position under the wall display and large-scale maps of the Kazakhstan region. 'For those of you who don't know, this is Captain Baker, ex-SAS and ex-OPI. He will give you an initial briefing on our theatre of operations and a rough idea of what you can expect. Afterwards, I shall hand over to Major Hailsham and we'll be holding a Chinese parliament, so you can all have your say.'

The 'Chinese parliament' represented the essence of SAS philosophy, in minimizing the importance of mere rank in favour of military experience. It was an informal discussion held by the CO of an operation at which each man, regardless of rank, was free to offer advice and criticism and suggest his own alternatives. Valuable in its own right, the system also reinforced the Regiment's classless and truly democratic outlook and the belief that every man had his own valued and important contribution to make.

There was a long silence after Piggy finished his briefing on the geography and climatic conditions of the target area. News that they might also be facing a threat from unknown chemical or bacteriological agents merely extended it.

It was inevitable that the silence would be broken with a joke. Both Davies and Major Hailsham had been fully expecting the typical response of men facing up to a life or death challenge. It was a mantra against the terrors of the unknown.

Surprisingly, it came from a totally unexpected source.

'Well, I'll be all right,' the Thinker intoned in a rich, deep baritone. 'My old dad kept his Mickey Mouse gas mask from the Second World War in the garage for years. I'll just nip home and get it.'

'You're not talking about one of those things with two flaps of rubber over the nose-piece and a flexible tube on the mouth, are you?' Cyclops jeered. 'That wasn't a gas mask, you plonker. Everybody knows those things were standard Army-issue condoms. The idea was to make sex so fucking boring that all the men couldn't wait to get back to barracks.'

'Yeah, only they didn't work too well,' Jimmy put in. 'That's probably why you were born, Thinker. We've often wondered.'

A loud chorus of cathartic laughter rippled around the briefing room. Major Hailsham let it die away naturally before addressing the men.

'On a more serious note, gentlemen, you will all, of course, have to report for a three-day refresher course in anti-chemical warfare protection. After that, we'll all be taking a nice week's holiday in the country.'

'A bit of mountain scenery, perhaps?' Jimmy asked, sensing what was coming.

Hailsham smiled. 'Good guess, Trooper. Yes, we'll all be tripping off to the Brecon Beacons for some climbing practice. Two or three runs up Pen-y-Fan with a bergen full of bricks on our backs should soon have us all leaping about like a bunch of mountain goats.'

This news was greeted by a loud chorus of groans, none of them louder than those from the younger troopers like Tweedledum and Tweedledee, for whom the harsh basic training in the Welsh mountains was still a comparatively recent ordeal. Yet they all realized its importance and value. Even the biting gale-force winds and icy blizzards of a Welsh winter would seem benign compared with the conditions they could expect on the mission.

'So, your suggestions, gentlemen,' Hailsham said, throwing the briefing open. 'And if anyone says, "Let's go to Majorca instead", I'll personally kick his arse round the Clock Tower.'

'What's the latest intelligence on guerrilla activity in the region, boss?' Andrew asked.

'Good question,' Davies commented, taking over. He consulted the notes which Major Grieves had handed him the previous evening. 'Basically, our latest information is that things are hotting up fast. The Uzbek Popular Front, the Birlik, appears to be gaining a lot of ground recently, and the principal Muslim brotherhoods are beginning to splinter into different Sunni and Shiite factions. Without putting too fine a point on it, Kazakhstan is rapidly shaping up as another Yugoslavia.

What's more important from our point of view is that any one of these guerrilla groups is likely to regard us as a strictly hostile presence. And you can forget any notions of a bunch of simple peasant farmers armed with pitchforks and the odd shotgun. Many of these groups are exceedingly well armed with Kalashnikovs, mortars and grenade-launchers. And what they might lack in training is compensated for by the fact that this is their home patch. As a result, they know how to use the terrain to their advantage. They know instinctively where to hide, where to launch an ambush and how to disappear after they've hit. It's a formidable technique, gentlemen, and one which the Russians found out to their cost in Afghanistan.'

'And what's our brief if we get bumped by one of these outfits?' Cyclops asked. 'Shoot 'em in the legs and let 'em limp away?'

Davies looked at them all gravely. 'I don't need to remind you that this is not our war,' he said simply. 'Obviously you will be expected to avoid direct confrontation if at all possible. If not, your lives, and the integrity of this mission, become your number one priorities. You'll have to make up your own minds if and when the occasion arises.' He paused, looking around the room. 'Now, are there any more questions?'

There was a long pause, broken by a few odd mutterings but nothing spoken publicly. Hailsham looked round one more time before finally nodding. 'Then go out and have a good time tonight, lads. As of tomorrow you'll all be confined to barracks until this mission is completed. We expect to go in two weeks.'

Davies walked over to Piggy as Hailsham followed his men out of the briefing room. 'Do you think they have any real idea what could be in store for them?' he asked.

Piggy shrugged. 'I doubt it,' he said, honestly.

# 7

High in the Sailyukem Mountains, in the southwestern fringes of the Western Sayan range, the building seemed to be nothing more than a low, flat expanse of grey concrete which seemed to melt into the rocky hills surrounding it. Snow-covered and desolate, it was merely a vaguely geometric shape which looked oddly out of keeping with the peaks and contours of the enclosing terrain. Other than the dozen or so frozen human bodies which had not yet been completely covered by the swirling snow, or the burnt-out shell of the Russian MIL Mi-6 'Hook' helicopter 100 yards away, there was nothing to suggest the Phoenix Project was anything but abandoned.

But deep inside there was life, even though here too, there was also much evidence of death. Silent and locked laboratories, sealed corridors and entire closed-off wings of the upper levels were littered with corpses, some human, some animal, some hideously indefinable. Hermetically sealed, and with all heating and power sources isolated, the building was a cryogenic mausoleum, preserving the bodies in much the same condition as when they had dropped, some four months previously.

On the fifth subterranean level, Tovan Leveski paced his small air-conditioned office and wondered if and when a second attack would come. He did not fully understand the first, any more than he could understand why his KGB paymasters had ceased all communication over a year earlier.

But then there was much that he could not comprehend any more. Although his body was over eighty in strict chronological age, he had the outward physique and appearance of a fit and healthy man of less that half that age – the direct result of one of the first of the project's long-term experiments into arresting the ageing process, an initial step towards the dream of human immortality. Like so many of those early, hopeful experiments, it had been long abandoned. Too late, the scientists had realized that the drugs worked well enough on the physical body but could not arrest the insidious decay of the brain which comes with ageing. In fact, they even accelerated it. So Leveski survived, but with the mind of a centenarian trapped inside a middle-aged body. A mind which even at the height of its powers had fringed on the psychotic.

There were still a few brief moments of clarity left to the Russian, although they were becoming increasingly infrequent. When the epidemic had first become apparent, he had still retained the mental power to order the lower levels to be sealed off, condemning the healthy and uninfected to die along with their sick companions. And when the Army assault helicopter had arrived, in response to an unauthorized distress signal, it had been Leveski who had masterminded its destruction and the slaughter of those few soldiers who managed to escape from the burning wreck.

Now he waited, wondering if they would try again, and failing to understand why the once-prestigious Phoenix

Project seemed to have been so abruptly and utterly abandoned by those who had so enthusiastically supported and nurtured it for so long.

But though slow and feeble, Leveski's mind was still capable of sporadic cunning. He had taken precautions. If they did come again, Phoenix was ready for them. He still had control over eighty to ninety per cent of his original security force. The outer perimeter of the complex had been electronically mined and the wrecked helicopter and several of the Russian corpses booby-trapped. Any new intruders would die as the first ones had. This thought afforded Leveski a degree of satisfaction, despite his prevailing depression and sense of abandonment. Outsiders were unwelcome, and must be killed. In his confused state, he was incapable of conceiving that the assault force had been on a mission of mercy and rescue. To Leveski, they had been simply invaders, coming to unveil the secrets of the Phoenix Project.

And many of those secrets were too dark, too guilty, to ever be revealed to the outside world. For nearly fifty years, Phoenix had been inviolate, a law unto itself. Funded by secretive agencies without reserve and staffed by experimental scientists without principles, Phoenix had carried out a range of experimentation which was without precedent and almost beyond the imagination of a normal mind. Using the unfortunate inmates of Soviet labour camps and asylums as basic stock, the Phoenix scientists simply bred their next subjects in much the same way as a battery farm would produce new chickens. By the mid-1950s they were able to incorporate new discoveries in the field of hormone research to force male and female children into sexual maturity at a much younger age, thus saving a few extra years on each new generation. A decade later a generation had been reduced to just ten years, and *in vitro* fertilization techniques and the use of fertility drugs to create multiple births were increasing both the breeding stock and the available gene pool.

But with the 1980s came the new climate of *détente* and *glasnost*. Official Kremlin interest in the Phoenix Project, which had never really been acknowledged in any case, began to wane. Soviet scientists in the mainstream of research became convinced that they had more than made good any technology gap with the West, in all branches of science. Phoenix, although it continued to be well funded by the KGB, became something of an embarrassment, and best forgotten.

Increasingly cut off from the outside world, the Kazakhstan complex rapidly became fanatically and fiercely independent – a secretive and self-sufficient community which closed ranks around itself and its short but terrible history.


Cyclops motioned the nearest air hostess over with a wave of his finger and ordered two more cans of beer, ignoring the faint look of disapproval on her face. Reaching down into the webbed pocket on the back of the seat in front of him, he retrieved the four previous mangled cans and placed them on her tray.

Jimmy McVitie accepted one of the offered beers with a wry grin. 'Well, I'm bloody glad I don't have any shares in British Airways,' he said. 'You'll have drunk 'em into bankruptcy before we reach Hong Kong.'

Cyclops opened his can expertly and held it to his lips, taking a deep draught before answering. 'Make the most of it while you can. You'll find it pretty difficult sinking a pint with a bloody respirator over your face.'

Jimmy shuddered just thinking about it. 'God I hate those bloody things,' he said with distaste. 'That's going to be the worst part of this little jaunt.'

Cyclops grinned. 'You could always take the new Irish version,' he suggested. 'You carry two rats in a little cage – like miners used to take live canaries down the pits. When they keel over, you know it's time to close your mouth and stop breathing. It's not only foolproof – it actually serves a dual purpose.'

Jimmy bought into the gag. 'Oh aye, and what's that?'

Cyclops eyed his companion over the rim of his can. 'When you get hungry, you can eat the fucking rats.'

The Glaswegian was not amused. 'Don't even joke about it,' he warned his mate. 'With the sort of scran we're likely to be getting our teeth into, rats might be a bloody delicacy.'

It was a sobering thought. 'Mind you,' Jimmy went on philosophically, 'I did a four-day survival course on Dartmoor once and the boss had us eating worms. You sort of stir-fry the wriggly little bastards into a goo. A bit like grey porridge, really.'

'Aw, Christ,' Cyclops groaned, wrinkling up his nose in disgust. 'What do they taste like, for God's sake?'

Jimmy shrugged. 'Not too bad, funnily enough. Fucking gritty, though. The trick is to suck it down without chewing too much.' Having imparted this nauseating piece of culinary information, he returned to his beer with no apparent damage to his appetite.

Food and drink were not high on Major Hailsham's list of priorities at that precise moment. With six hours still to go before their own Cathay Pacific flight to Hong Kong, and a fast car waiting to whisk them directly to Heathrow airport, he sat in the ops room at Stirling Lines with Sergeant Andrew Winston, running a final check on the list of arms and equipment they would need on the mission.

'So we're decided on bullpups, are we?' Hailsham asked, referring to the somewhat controversial Enfield L85A1 SA-80 assault rifles which had been made available to the Regiment just before the Gulf War. The weapon had suffered from several teething problems, including vital bits such as magazines falling off under combat conditions. These early design faults had now been largely corrected, but the gun retained a somewhat dubious reputation.

Andrew nodded. 'I think so. Weight has got to be one of our primary considerations, and the SA-80 offers an appreciable saving over a conventional SLR or an M16.'

It was not a point which Hailsham was prepared to argue with. The chunky 5.56mm weapon might not be popular, but it was ideally suited to the operation, being easy to wield and possessing high accuracy up to a range of 300 yards. The fact that its design incorporated a plastic stock and foregrip made it markedly lighter than any other assault rifle with similar fire-power, weighing less than 11lb when fully loaded with a thirty-round box magazine. In addition, each man would be wearing the back-up of a standard Browning High Power 9mm handgun on his hip – a valuable addition to his personal armoury.

Cyclops's L96A1 sniper rifle was another priority. Hailsham and Winston had considered the possibility of including a second and heavier 12.7mm Barret as back-up and rejected it. If Cyclops went down, any one of them could still handle the L96A1 creditably, if not with the same uncanny skill. And the weapon itself was by now proven reliable. Short of actual combat damage, it was rugged enough to survive most conditions.

A pair of general-purpose machine-guns, or GPMGs, were equally essential. The SAS had always made extensive use of this weapon, and it was rare for any four-man patrol to venture out without at least one. Although heavy, weighing in at nearly 24lb without ammunition, its belt-fed, devastating and accurate fire-power at ranges of up to 1500 yards had demonstrated it to be a life-saver in any situation where heavy cover was required. As was often the practice, the 200-round spare ammunition belts would be shared out and carried by all the other members of the team.

There is one minor blessing,' Andrew pointed out. 'At least up in the mountains we're unlikely to come up against anything really heavy. So we can safely do without any anti-armour capability.'

Hailsham thought this over for a few seconds, before finally nodding thoughtfully. 'Our main weakness is going to be attack from the air,' he then said. 'If we're anywhere near rebel activity, it's a sure bet that the official Kazakhstan Army is going to be monitoring the area with regular helicopter patrols. It would be nice to justify carting along a Stinger, but I think it's going to be out of the question. What do you think?'

Andrew shook his head slowly and doubtfully. 'I agree that it probably wouldn't be feasible to take it all the way,' he agreed. 'But you're right – being without any SAM cover at all leaves us extremely vulnerable. How about a compromise? We take a Stinger and say four missiles in with us as far as the lower foothills and then cache it at our first RV point for retrieval later? That way we would at least have some protection while we were still out in open country.'

It was a good suggestion, and Hailsham considered it carefully. The American Stinger system was a very effective hand-held surface-to-air missile, ideal for protecting small, isolated units from enemy air attack. It had certainly proved its worth in the Falklands, in similar terrain to the miles of steppe that they would have to cross before reaching the foothills of the

Western Sayan. The weapon's main drawback, from the point of view of this, or any other SAS patrol, was that the launcher alone carried a 33lb penalty and its individual missiles were each a similar weight. It was a lot of extra baggage for a threat which might not even materialize. Hailsham was in two minds about it.

'I'll volunteer to carry it, if it makes any difference to your decision,' Andrew put in, noting Hailsham's continued hesitation. 'And that's not sheer masochism – I'd feel happier.'

The major thought for a couple more seconds, then said: 'All right, you've got it. But we dump it as soon as we start any serious climbing. Hopefully the mountains themselves will give us reasonably adequate air cover.'

Andrew grinned with relief. 'Understood, boss. Now, what about mortars?'

This did not need as much thinking about. 'We've only got one choice, haven't we?' Hailsham asked. 'It'll have to be a couple of 51mm. Anything heavier is out of the question. I'll take one; the Thinker can carry the other. Ammo?'

'Mixed bag,' Andrew said without hesitation. 'Frags and smoke for daytime use; flares for night.'

Hailsham ticked off the last two items on the personal list he had scribbled out earlier. 'Add a Claymore for each team and six fragmentation and four stun grenades apiece and that should take care of the hardware. We won't be exactly travelling light, but it's a step up from water pistols and a big stick.'

It was intended as a joke, but it reinforced what they both knew – the two patrols were cutting armaments to a bare minimum, perhaps even below adequate protection levels.

'Mind you,' Hailsham added, trying to put things in a better perspective. 'We should keep in mind that we're not actually supposed to be fighting anybody.'

70

Andrew smiled thinly. 'Yeah, but has anyone told those bastards that?'

It was not a question that Hailsham wanted to answer. He scooped up his little pile of notes from the table. 'Well, we've done our shopping list. Let's just hope the delivery service is making house calls to China this week.'

'In plain brown envelopes, of course,' Andrew joked.

Hailsham laughed. 'More like a couple of wooden crates labelled "agricultural machinery". Or maybe "atomic warheads for Iraq" – that should guarantee priority service,' he added wryly.

Tweedledum and Tweedledee were already in Hong Kong, having flown in to Kai Tak airport on a charter flight the previous day. Not surprisingly, they had forgone a sightseeing trip of the city they called the 'New York of Asia' in favour of a round of its myriad bars and brothels. They sat now in the opulent, over-ornate vestibule of a particularly up-market whorehouse in downtown Kowloon, eyeing the dozen or so beautiful young Chinese girls who were parading coquettishly about in their colourful *cheong-sams*, giggling and winking as they competed for the two troopers' custom.

It was a difficult choice. Tweedledee's face was rapturous as he ran his eyes over the feast of ripe young bodies, assessing each one like a choice cut of meat in a butcher's window. A ten-hour diet of beer and wine had put him in an expansive mood.

'Not a bad life, this SAS lark,' he observed to his soul-mate. 'Lots of good healthy exercise, foreign travel and the chance to fuck exotic women.'

Tweedledum grinned drunkenly. He pulled one of his standard-issue condoms from his pocket, ripped open the foil and dangled the limp latex tube under Tweedledee's nose. 'And they look after us like a mother hen,' he said, giggling. 'We might get shot, blown to fuck, gassed, poisoned or fried, but at least we'll die with clean dicks.'

The irony of the statement eluded Tweedledee's drink-befuddled brain. He merely grinned vacantly and pointed to a pair of girls dressed in identical yellow *cheong-sams*. They looked like twins.

'How about those two?'

Tweedledum nodded enthusiastically. 'I'll ask the *mama-san* if she's got a double room,' he said, licking his lips in anticipation.

Tweedledee looked at his companion slightly dubiously, but said nothing. There were times, he felt, when doing things together could be taken a bit too far.

Across the city, Trooper Barry Naughton was just returning to the room in the Royal Pacific Hotel which he was sharing with Corporal Max Epps. He floated several inches above the floor, for it had been an unbelievably magical evening, and he was in seventh heaven.

Sung Lu, the girl had said her name was. And she was not a whore, Barry reminded himself – even though she had demanded money after they had made love in her sordid little hotel room. It was, as she had explained in her tiny sing-song voice, merely to convince her sick and elderly mother that she had been a good girl and stayed at her job in the bar on Wing Sing Street, where he had met her.

And she had told him that no man had ever made love to her so wonderfully before. She had even told him that she loved him. 'I love you, soldier-boy,' she had murmured frequently during their brief but frantic embrace. Somehow, it did not seem to matter that she could not actually remember his name, or that she dressed with almost indecent haste after it was all over.

Barry had made love to a beautiful young Chinese girl, and she had told him that she loved him. He was almost bursting with pride and happiness as he let himself into the hotel room. He had to tell someone, even if it was only the Thinker.

'I'm in love,' he announced dreamily as he walked in through the door.

His room-mate looked up from his bed, where he had spent the evening writing a long and thoughtful letter to his wife.

'Ya daft prat,' the Thinker muttered dismissively, bursting the bubble.

# 8

The rendezvous point on the Chinese mainland was the White Swan Hotel in Canton. Major Hailsham and Andrew had flown in direct, having changed planes without ever leaving the confines of Kai Tak airport. Tweedledum and Tweedledee had tagged themselves on to a party of British and German package tourists making a 'Chinese Highlights' sightseeing tour, and Cyclops, Jimmy and Barry had taken the train from Hong Kong. The Thinker, different as ever, had opted for a fairly leisurely boat trip up the Pearl River.

Now, all finally assembled in one of the hotel's small conference rooms, they waited for their promised Chinese contact. The atmosphere was unusually subdued, even slightly tense. The transition from Hong Kong to 'foreign' territory was subtle, but tangible. Although they were still dressed as civilians, there was no longer any doubt that they were really soldiers, or that the mission was for real. Even Tweedledum and Tweedledee, who might normally have been expected to regale the group with lurid and wildly exaggerated accounts of their night in a Hong Kong whorehouse, sat uncharacteristically apart, saying nothing.

They all sipped weak green tea from delicate porcelain cups, mostly under sufferance. Alcohol was banned now, for the duration of the mission. The next real drink to touch their lips would be consumed in the Paludrine Club either as a celebratory toast to all those who had made it back, or as a homage to the ones who had failed to beat the clock. Even in a regiment which made its own rules and ignored much of the more formal military discipline, there were still unspoken routines, and customs to be observed.

Hailsham consulted his watch. There were still two minutes to go before the appointed time, and their Chinese contact would be punctual to the second, he knew. As with many Eastern cultures, courtesy and politeness were highly important, even stylized, and it was considered as much of an insult to arrive early as to be late for an appointment.

At precisely three-fifteen, the conference room door opened and a bellboy ushered in the Chinese delegation. There were three of them: two men and, surprisingly, a woman carrying what appeared to be a medical bag. They were all dressed in civilian clothes.

Hailsham nodded politely to the obvious leader. He was tall for a Chinese, and with an unusually dark complexion which betrayed an ancestry stretching back to the days when the Mongol-Tartar hordes swept through central and eastern Asia. He reminded the major of pictures he had seen of North American Indians.

He acknowledged Hailsham's nod with a polite smile, although he made no attempt at a formal greeting. 'I am General Chang,' he announced in flawless English. This is Captain Leng Pui and Dr Su.' He glanced around the room. 'Are you all taking part in this mission?'

Hailsham nodded. 'What you see is what you get.'

'Good.'

General Chang motioned to the woman, who stepped forward, laid her bag on the desk and opened it. She withdrew a small membrane-sealed bottle containing a colourless liquid and several disposable syringes.

'Perhaps you and your men would be so good as to roll up your sleeves,' Chang suggested, looking at Hailsham again. 'Dr Su will administer a small injection to each of you.'

A slight frown clouded Hailsham's features. 'Injection?' he queried. 'We weren't briefed on this. What is it?'

Dr Su was carefully loading each syringe and laying them down in a neat row along the table. 'It is nothing,' she murmured soothingly. 'Just a little booster vaccine, that is all. We have no specific knowledge of what biological contaminants you might be exposed to. This will give you some measure of protection against some of the possible viral strains.'

Hailsham was still not sure. 'What about after-effects?' he asked. 'My men will need to be in peak condition. We can't afford anything which might impair their performance in any way.'

The doctor smiled. 'There will be none, I assure you. Now, if you would be so good as to line up, I will administer the injections.'

Hailsham considered the matter for several more seconds. Finally, he shrugged, slipped off his jacket and began to roll up his shirt sleeve, volunteering himself as the guinea pig. A muted babble of conversation broke out as the rest of the men fell into a ragged line behind him.

'Jesus Christ, Thinker, you've gone as white as a bloody sheet,' Jimmy observed.

The burly Mancunian tried hard to raise a scornful grin, but failed miserably. He chewed at his bottom lip nervously, fighting to control the irrational phobia which had haunted him since childhood and was still one of the few things which could reduce him to a quivering jelly. As someone so self-contained, it bothered him greatly that he had a weakness, something he could not control. Some men feared being trapped in confined spaces, others had a morbid fear of snakes, or spiders. The Thinker was terrified of hypodermic needles.

Jimmy could see the big man's hands trembling, but he found it hard to accept the evidence of his own eyes. This was the man he had watched single-handedly charge up a rocky hill towards an Argentinian machine-gun nest at Goose Green, the M16 in his hands spitting furiously as a fusillade of 9mm slugs chewed up the ground around his feet. This was the man who could slog on through the roughest, toughest route march, his step sure and solid when others around him were beginning to turn to jelly at the knees. And now here was that same man reduced to a nervous wreck at the sight of a tiny silver needle.

The Glaswegian was about to turn to the rest of the men and make a joke at the Thinker's expense, but something stopped him. It was not just the warning, baleful glare in the corporal's eyes. It was the sudden, somewhat frightening realization that they were all, in one way or another, vulnerable.

Instead, he nudged the Mancunian gently in the ribs, winking at him. 'Don't worry, Thinker,' he muttered quietly. 'It's only a little prick, after all. A bit like Trooper Naughton, really.'

The Thinker flashed him a sheepish grin, which bore more than a trace of gratitude. 'I just hate bloody injections,' he murmured, getting back a little of his self-assurance from the shared joke. Nevertheless, he averted his eyes when it came to his turn, still unable to actually watch the needle sliding into his flesh.

Typically, Tweedledum found a source of ribald humour in the situation, grinning up at Dr Su with brazen familiarity as she dabbed his arm with an antiseptic wipe. 'Hope this is good for the clap as well, darlin'. I've never been too sure about those standard-issue condoms.'

The woman's face was a flat mask of oriental inscrutability as she inserted the needle. Nevertheless, it seemed to Tweedledum that she gave it a quite pronounced and unnecessary jerk as she pulled it out again. He was not grinning quite so broadly when he walked away from the table to rejoin his companions.

The unexpected medical treatment dispensed with, Dr Su packed her bag again and left the room. General Chang turned to Major Hailsham.

'The first thing I have to tell you is that the mission will be going ahead virtually as we have planned,' he announced. 'Transport has been arranged and is waiting outside the hotel to take you all directly to a Chinese Air Force base just outside Wuchow. From there you will be airlifted to Tacheng, where you will pick up your arms and equipment.'

The man's delivery was bland, but Hailsham had already picked up on that one little word – 'virtually'.

'Do I take it there has been a change of plan?' he asked.

Chang smiled thinly. 'You are very astute, Major. I compliment you. Yes, as you so rightly assume, we have had to modify our original plans slightly in the light of some recent developments.'

Hailsham's face was grave. He looked at the tall Chinaman darkly, making no attempt to disguise his annoyance. The very essence of all SAS operations was meticulous planning and preparation. Last-minute changes were not only unwelcome – they were dangerous. Nevertheless, he tried to be as polite as possible. 'Perhaps you would care to explain, General,' he suggested.

'Our latest intelligence reports tell us that guerrilla activity in the area has increased far more than expected in recent weeks,' Chang informed him. 'As a result, official Republican forces have also built up considerably. My superiors now feel that our original plan of inserting you and your men over the border by helicopter is unwise, both from your point of view and from ours. We think it much safer to parachute you in at night, from a transport plane flying at commercial altitude. HALO, I believe you call it, if our understanding of your procedures is correct.'

'You've done your homework, General,' Hailsham muttered, returning the man's earlier compliment. 'In which case you should be aware that we use modified parachutes, work with our own RAF Special Forces Flight and drop from an open rear ramp on a Hercules C-130. I take it you have none of these things.'

General Chang seemed to take this observation as a personal affront. His body stiffened, his Mongoloid eyes narrowing even further. 'The Chinese People's Air Force is also highly trained, Major. We have modified Iluyshin bombers with a side-opening door which your men would find more than adequate. Our own special forces seem to have little trouble in utilizing similar techniques to those of your own.'

Hailsham met the man's eyes directly, facing the challenge. His gut reaction was to rise to the bait, but he resisted, shaking his head slowly. 'I'm sorry. General, but I'm not prepared to make that decision without consulting my men. In private, if you don't mind.'

Chang's expression had hardened to obvious rage now, mixed with the faintest trace of incredulity. 'Consult your men?' he demanded angrily. 'Do you not just give them orders? May I remind you, Major Hailsham, that this joint mission was requested and planned at government level?'

Hailsham remained calm and polite in the face of the implied threat. 'I'm afraid we do things a little differently in the SAS,

General. We call it democracy. Now, if you would be so good as to give me a couple of minutes alone with my men.'

For a moment, the Chinaman held his ground, muscles working nervously beneath the flattened contours of his face. Then, clenching his fists into tight knots, he turned stiffly and strode towards the door, nodding curtly towards Captain Leng Pui to follow him.

Hailsham waited until the door had closed behind them before addressing the men. 'Well, I suppose you all heard that. So, what do we think about it?'

Andrew threw it straight back at him. 'What's your opinion, boss?'

Hailsham thought for a second. 'My instinctive reaction is to say scrub the mission,' he admitted. 'But perhaps I'm overreacting.'

'It'd certainly scrub your chances of getting on this year's honours list, boss,' Cyclops put in. 'I reckon they'd have you cleaning out the latrines with a toothbrush a week after we got back.'

'Aye, and it'd be your own fucking toothbrush as well,' Jimmy added, for emphasis.

Hailsham let the ripple of nervous laughter die away. 'Seriously, though, we're not in the business of taking uncalculated risks. And that's exactly what we're being asked to do. A night drop, over unknown territory, from an unfamiliar aircraft and with 'chutes of dubious performance. That's a lot of rogue equations all in one go.'

'On the other hand, we've all done side exits,' Andrew cut in. 'And we could raise our canopy height a few hundred feet to give us all that extra margin of safety.'

'And we could show that Chinky bastard a thing or two about the finest regiment in the world,' the Thinker muttered, gingerly rubbing the bruise on his arm, which was still smarting. He was not at all happy about the thought of having gone through his ordeal for nothing.

Hailsham looked at them all with a sense of pride. 'So the general concensus is that we go for it?' he asked, although he already knew the answer.

Andrew nodded, his ebony face splitting into a grin. 'Who dares wins, eh, boss?'

The matter was closed, the decision made. With a final nod of approval, Hailsham strode to the door and opened it to let the two Chinese officers back into the room.

'We've decided to go along with your change of plan,' he announced stiffly. 'But with one proviso. We do a dummy run over neutral territory to familiarize ourselves with your procedures and equipment.'

General Chang looked relieved. Perhaps *too* relieved, Hailsham thought. 'That can be arranged,' the Chinaman said, once again stony-faced. 'Now, if you are ready, I will escort you and your men to the transport.'

Hailsham fell back slightly, closing in on Andrew as the men filed out of the room and through the hotel lobby towards the twelve-seater minibus which was parked outside.

'What's up, boss?' Andrew asked Hailsham. It was obvious that the major had something on his mind, and wanted to talk.

Hailsham shook his head uncertainly. 'I don't know. Maybe it's nothing,' he replied. 'It's just that I can't help wondering if these slitty-eyed little bastards have any more surprises up their sleeves.'

# 9

Major Hailsham sat in the training seat of the Shenyang F-9 fighter plane, gazing out through the perspex canopy at the sheer grandeur of the panorama spread out some 20,000 feet below him.

To his left, the soaring, jagged and snow-capped peaks of the Tien Shan range competed for his attention with the twisted gullies and canyons of the Turfan Depression almost immediately below. Tearing his eyes away to look to the right, he could see the flat, featureless expanse of the Mongolian Plateau and the vast reaches of the Gobi Desert beyond.

It all looked so barren, so utterly hostile, he thought. Yet the desolate and virtually worthless terrain had been the prize in a history of bloodshed and battle which stretched back over 400 years, the most recent change of ownership coming at the turn of the nineteenth century when the Soviet Union had managed to annex some fifty million square miles of territory from their Chinese neighbours. Right up to the present day, it had remained the scene of countless secret wars and border skirmishes between the two communist giants. No one in the West had the faintest notion of how many lives had been claimed over the years, and it was more than probable that no one really cared, either.

The plane was safely inside Chinese territory, flying north-eastwards along the line of the Sinkiang-Kazakhstan border towards the roughly triangular confluence with Mongolia. Hailsham had insisted on the reconnaissance flight, even though the practice drop over the lower foothills of the Tien Shan mountains earlier that morning had been an unqualified success. Retrieved almost immediately by helicopter, he and his men had been safely back at the Tacheng airbase in good time for lunch. Despite his earlier misgivings, Hailsham had no complaints so far about Chinese efficiency or their good intentions to make the mission a success.

But there was not much to be seen from inside the belly of a modified Iluyshin 28 bomber, and not much chance to study the scenery below when one was free-falling from 38,000 feet and concentrating on getting one's canopy timing right. So Hailsham had requested a personal inspection flight closer to the actual target area and, surprisingly, General Chang had agreed without the slightest hesitation.

They were clear of the Tien Shan range now, flying along the line of the long valley plain between the Tarbagaty range to port and the Altai Mountains to starboard. Ahead in the distance, Hailsham could just make out the towering 15,000-foot peak of Mount Belukha beyond the Kazakhstan border, and knew that they were rapidly running out of airspace which could be considered fully 'safe' in broad daylight. It took just one over-zealous rebel with a SAM-7 at his disposal to make a slight miscalculation of distance, and there would be two more statistics on the list of secret casualties. Hailsham leaned forward, tapping the Chinese pilot lightly on the shoulder and making a circular motion in the air with his forefinger. Nodding, the pilot banked the Shenyang into a long, raking curve and settled the fighter into a straight course which would take them back to Tacheng.

So everything appeared to check out, Hailsham mused to himself. There seemed to be no point in hanging on any longer than necessary. They would go in tonight, an hour or two before dawn. That would give them time to establish a hide and observation post for the following day. Such an OP would give them a vantage point from which they could recce the immediate area and perhaps establish enemy positions from the glow of camp-fires by night. In the early morning light, Hailsham planned to send out the first patrol, led by Sergeant Winston, to set up the first RV point before moving on into the lower foothills. It was normal practice for SAS patrols to move only by night, but they had a lot of ground to cover and they were not officially in a combat situation. Hailsham was counting on any guerrilla groups conducting a basically unsophisticated technique of ambush and sneak attack on their already known enemies. They would already have those established positions, and would hardly be expecting a new force to be literally dropping into their laps. In addition, the small size of the operation, and the high degree of natural cover they could expect once they got into the mountains, gave them an excellent chance of making daylight progress without being spotted. There was also one other factor in their favour. Their main brief was to evade other forces, not to stalk them. And although it was not a normal SAS tactic, running and hiding was an easier option than going in on the attack. As in chess, the defensive player tends to control the play – at least until the endgame.

It was not, perhaps, the most satisfying of strategies, but Hailsham felt confident that it would foot the bill. It had to, since there was no longer any time to come up with any better plan of action.

Just let it be clean, he thought to himself. They were good men who had all risked their lives fighting against their country's real enemies. They most certainly did not deserve to die in a hastily conceived and half-baked operation such as this one. Hailsham's silent plea was something just short of an actual prayer. He had been a professional soldier for too long to retain much belief in a wise and benevolent God.

In Hereford, it was eight-thirty in the morning as Barney Davies tapped out the Foreign Secretary's private, 'hot' number. The call went directly through, bypassing the ears of the whole entourage of personal assistants and secretarial staff, although it was probably monitored by one or other of the British security services.

Davies's message was brief and to the point. 'They're going in tonight,' he said simply. 'At 03.00 hours, local time.'

'Thank you, Lieutenant-Colonel Davies,' the Foreign Secretary said quietly. 'You will of course keep me informed as to developments.' He hung up without waiting for an answer.

'Correct me if I'm wrong, but haven't we already done this once today?' Cyclops asked as they filed into the converted bomb bay of the Iluyshin 28.

'Nah, you must have been having one of your recurring wet dreams,' Tweedledee told him. Turning to the rest of the men, he warmed to his theme. 'Did Cyclops ever tell you he gets a hard-on from heights? That's why he can't go up ladders. Every time he gets near the top, his old man pops out and pushes him off again.'

'He'd have to be fucking close to the wall,' Jimmy threw in. 'What he's got's only good enough for diddling sparrows.'

'Should suit you down to the ground, then,' Tweedledum ventured. 'We all know that the Scots have notoriously tight arses.'

The big Glaswegian growled, shaking a ham-like fist in the younger man's direction. 'I'll see you, Jimmy,' he threatened good-naturedly, parodying his own stereotype.

A high-pitched bleeping cut through the bullshit, indicating that the side hatch was about to close. With a faint metallic squeal, the heavy steel door swung into position, then drew in and locked tight. The aircraft began to throb as the Chinese pilot throttled up the twin Soloviev D-30KP engines, which had previously been purring at idling speed.

'Well, looks like we're off on our hols, lads,' the Thinker said drily. The observation met with a less than rapturous reception.

Hailsham, sitting alone on the far side on the bomb bay, consulted his watch, squinting slightly in the dull-yellowish light from the plane's rudimentary lighting system. It was 01.00 hours. Two hours to the drop zone and teatime at home. He found himself wondering what his ex-wife had given the kids for their evening meal as the Iluyshin began to lumber up the runway, gathering speed as the engines roared ever louder.

It was at times like these that Andrew liked to compose poetry in his head, or at least draft out the bones of an idea which could be fine-tuned and committed to paper at a later stage. It was something to do with body chemistry, he had always vaguely understood – this in-between time, this hiatus just before a mission when every nerve and fibre was tingling with adrenalin yet the brain was somehow idling, numbed with the delay between thought and deed.

Yet not one original thought would come clear in his head. Instead, snatches and phrases from other poets buzzed around, with varying degrees of relevance or meaning. The opening lines from one of Walt Whitman's poems – one of

Andrew's personal heroes – seemed particularly apt, given the circumstances.

> Come my tan-faced children,
> Follow well in order, get your weapons ready,
> Have you your pistols, have you your sharp-edged axes?
> Pioneers! O pioneers!

With these words running around in his brain, Andrew found himself covertly studying the faces of the men around him, analysing and trying to understand what their expressions betrayed. He caught the Thinker's eyes directly, and it was like suddenly coming across a mirror in a darkened room. He felt inexplicably embarrassed, almost guilty, and smiled sheepishly.

The big Mancunian smiled back, but it was a gesture of reassurance, of a secret shared and understood. Andrew felt relieved, instinctively sensing what the man was communicating to him. A man's thoughts were private, personal – and precious. Especially at a time like this.

They were off the runway now, and climbing steadily. Barry Naughton felt the familiar tingle running through his body. Born partly of a fear of flying and partly of personal pride at having largely conquered it, it was like a little power surge from which he could draw inner reserves. This, and the knowledge that he was about to go into a battle situation, recharged and changed him. He was an equal among equals now. As valued, and as valuable, as any one of his peers.

That was the young trooper's secret – the factor which had led him to seek the Army as a career in the first place, and had steered him towards the SAS in particular. And, in no small measure, it had also been the one thing which had got him through the harsh basic training which had beaten many tougher men.

Out in Civvy Street, even in the barracks, Barry knew that his fellow troopers often saw him as the natural butt of a joke, of a bit of piss-taking. A regular Clark Kent, in fact. But the SAS was his secret telephone box. A set of olive-greens became his Superman costume. It was a good feeling, even if psychologically dubious. It sustained him.

'Well, I reckon it's time to open the beauty parlour,' Jimmy said, pulling out his pair of camouflage sticks. He rolled spittle and phlegm around in his mouth, spat it into the palm of his hand and began to work his base foundation into a sticky, creamy consistency before smearing it over his face and neck with the other hand.

Taking his lead, the rest of the men set about applying the 'cam' cream, taking care to cover all exposed areas, such as ears, chin, throats and the backs of their hands and wrists. With the base coat dulling down the natural sheen of their skin and contours of their faces, they proceeded to compound the effect by stroking wide, diagonal smears of black stick to their faces and foreheads to break up the broad outline of their features. Finally, they each smeared the black make-up thickly over more prominent features such as noses, chins and cheekbones, leaving the natural hollows a much lighter shade.

For Andrew, of course, the procedure was slightly different. Jimmy grinned at him as he drew a white make-up stick across his ebony skin.

'Jesus Christ, Sarge. You look like a fucking zebra,' he pointed out.

Suddenly they all had a target.

'Come on, boss, give us a chorus of *Swannee Ribber*' Tweedledum suggested.

Not to be outdone, Tweedledee joined in the banter. 'Or how about an impression of Larry Parkes?' He waggled his hands in the air while opening and closing his mouth silently.

Andrew grinned good-naturedly. He had heard it all a hundred times before. 'When are you honky bastards going to come up with something original?' he said wearily. 'Anyway, now all you ladies have your warpaint on, how about getting ready to rig up? Or are you planning to float down on your petticoats like a bunch of overweight fairies?'

It was a good point. Watched by their sergeant and Major Hailsham, the men moved naturally into a practice routine, forming themselves into two lines, facing each other. From the carefully stacked bundles of bergens and equipment at one end of the Iluyshin's belly, the primary and reserve 'chutes were retrieved, then passed carefully from hand to hand along the two rows. Each man chose the partner immediately facing him, watching each other as they slipped into their thermal suits, zipped them up to the neck and then began to shrug on their 'chutes. With everything in position, it became a question of checking each other's rig, checking straps for tension and making sure every buckle and ringclip was firmly locked in position.

Finally, it was time for each partner to help the other pull on his heavy bergen, and tuck them up just below the small of the back beneath the main parachute packs.

Andrew finished putting the final touches to his make-up and inspected all six men, making his own final check. Then, turning to Major Hailsham, they set about rigging each other up.

'Now we're ready to party,' Andrew finally announced. With Hailsham's assistance, he busied himself checking the 'chutes for the Controlled Air Delivery System (CADS) which would take down the heavier equipment, guided by radio-control devices in the hands of himself and Hailsham.

The whole make-ready procedure had taken just over an hour. Hailsham checked his watch again, satisfied that they were well ahead of schedule. The converted bomber was still well inside safe airspace, the pilot keeping it in steady and level flight at 15,000 feet. Another half an hour and he would start to climb as they approached the Mongolian border area. Then it would be time for them all to hook into the onboard oxygen supply, before switching to their personal canisters for the actual drop. But for now, there was nothing more to do except wait and try to relax.

In fact, the aircraft began to climb almost immediately, much to Hailsham's surprise. He cast a questioning, sideways glance at Andrew, whose face bore a similar puzzled expression. The sergeant shrugged, having no answer.

The interior temperature began to cool quite markedly. The Thinker flexed his body, stretching his muscles as best he could under the restriction of the enclosing parachute harness and the weight of his equipment. What the hell was going on? he wondered to himself. He had caught the brief and silent exchange between Andrew and Hailsham, and it had been enough to tell him that something was not quite as it should be. None of the others seemed to have noticed, and he figured it was not his place to point it out. He trusted Hailsham implicitly, as they all did. No doubt the CO would keep them all fully informed as and when he saw fit.

The rest of the men had begun to react to the drop in temperature now, despite their thermal suits. As with any ordeal of shared discomfort, it triggered off another little exchange of bullshit.

'Christ, it's colder than a witch's tit,' Barry said, shivering.

Cyclops grinned at him. 'You just wait until you get outside,' he answered. 'Just imagine being bare-arsed naked on a glacier and you'll get a rough idea.'

Barry shivered again. 'I hope for your sake that you remembered to wear a fur-lined jockstrap,' Jimmy told him. 'I've heard of guys on these night drops whose cocks got so stiff with cold on the way down that they just broke off with the shock of landing.'

But Barry was not taking the bait. 'Fuck off!' he said simply, grinning at the big Scot.

'Anyway, you could be in a bit of trouble yourself, Jimmy,' Tweedledum pointed out. 'You didn't have your porridge this morning, did you?'

'Talking of that, what do badgers have for breakfast?' Cyclops asked. He waited for a few seconds of expectant silence before answering his own question. 'Ready-brock.'

It was a lousy joke, but they all smiled anyway.

A sudden loud and insistent bleeping cut through the mood, snapping them all back into alertness. Simultaneously a red warning light began to flash from the ceiling of the bomb bay. They all knew exactly what it signified. The pilot was about to depressurize the interior of the plane.

'What the fuck?' Hailsham blurted out, his face now registering something more serious than mere surprise. He checked his watch again quickly, his mind racing. There was no way that he could be that much out on his calculations. Even allowing for an unexpected tail-wind, they could not possibly have reached the drop zone so long ahead of schedule. There were only two real possibilities: either the Chinese pilot had made a serious miscalculation or he was deliberately planning to drop them short of the DZ. But either one was purely academic now. The temperature was already plummeting as the thin, freezing air outside the plane began to rush in to replace that which was being evacuated. Hailsham could feel a tightness in his chest. They needed oxygen, and they needed it fast.

'Get your masks on – now,' he barked. Adjusting his own, he moved into the centre of the converted bomb bay and connected its flexible plastic hose to the central oxygen supply console on the ceiling.

The flashing red light and warning bleeper went off together as the plane became fully depressurized. In the sudden silence that followed, there was only the faintest residual hiss as the side exit door's hermetic seals were released. Then, with a brief metallic squeal, the heavy door began to pull out and away, revealing the star-spangled blackness of the night sky.

There was no longer any time to worry about what might or what might not have gone wrong with the Chinese planning of the operation. It was all automatic now, Hailsham reflected. Training and instinct took over. As if in some ancient and time-honoured tribal ritual, he moved forward with Andrew, the pair of them dragging the CADS into place between them. Behind that, the rest of the men formed themselves into two short rows in preparation for the jump – one to the left, one to the right.

'Switch to personal oxygen,' Hailsham snapped.

Moving together like the parts of a well-oiled machine, each man disconnected his mask nozzle from the on-board supply and snapped it into position on the bottle he carried on the side webbing of his parachute harness. All eyes lifted to the small red light which glowed like a malevolent eye above the hatch door, which was now fully open. Time seemed to freeze. The men fidgeted nervously as they waited for the red light to wink out. It eventually did, accompanied by a loud buzzing noise. Seconds later, it was replaced by a green one, flashing on and off in a slow, regular cycle.

Hailsham made a final adjustment to his face mask, pressing it more firmly into position. He pulled his passive night goggles down over his eyes – a gesture immediately copied by the rest of the men. The rhythm of the flashing green light was increasing now, building up until it was a constant pulse. Finally, it ceased flickering altogether and remained on. It was time to go.

Behind them, the six troopers followed their lead at spaced intervals, throwing themselves out into the icy blackness in the classic free-fall position. Spread-eagled like featherless birds, they began to plummet towards the ground below, the bitter, rushing air tearing at their bodies like an Arctic blizzard.

Hailsham and Andrew dragged the CADS 'chutes to the lip of the open hatch. Then, with a brief nod at each other, they pulled the heavy equipment container with a concerted effort and launched themselves into space.

It was that moment, Hailsham's brain screamed, that breathless, deathless moment of utter commitment. Falling irrevocably, yet strangely suspended between heaven and earth as if in some drug-induced fantasy in which the spaces between time itself had become distorted.

They were going down.

But where? Hailsham needed to know. For Christ's sake, where?

# 10

It was a desert, Hailsham thought. He was standing in the middle of a bloody desert! With a conscious effort, he pushed aside his initial sense of rage at the Chinese, trying to concentrate on the more immediate and practical problems.

First things first. He busied himself hauling in his chute, gathering the billowing folds of material around his feet. Luckily there was only a faint breeze, which made the job comparatively easy. Stamping the gathered parachute into a lumpy ball, he held it between his feet and released his harness straps. He moved his head slowly from side to side, taking in his surroundings and attempting to locate the rest of his men.

In the eerie, greenish glow of the passive night goggles the surrounding terrain was like a schoolboy's impression of a lunar landscape. OK, so it was not exactly desert, Hailsham told himself as he started to make out a little detail and some sense of his surroundings. It was open steppe country – a vast, flattish area of thin grasses and stunted bush and scrub. In the far distance, virtually making up the horizon, the foothills of the mountain terrain which should have marked the outer perimeter of their original drop zone showed up as a jagged, darker green line.

It was difficult to make an accurate assessment of distance with the PNGs, but Hailsham estimated that the first line of hills was at least eight miles as the crow flies. With first light probably less than two hours away, the immediate problem was obvious. Even if they started out immediately, they would be dangerously exposed long before they could reach cover. What was even more worrying were the half-dozen or so pinpricks of light which he could make out between them and the foothills. Obviously camp-fires, but whether they were of nomadic Kazakh tribesmen or guerrilla forces, there was no way of knowing.

Something moved in Hailsham's peripheral vision – a dark, lumpy shape, bouncing or rolling towards him. As his head whirled to confront the sudden menace, his hand was already flying to his hip, clawing at the holstered Browning.

The tension in his body, and the adrenalin rush which had triggered it, seeped away in relief as the wispy, vaguely spherical object brushed against his legs and stopped. Hailsham reached out to touch its dry and brittle fragility. It was a clump of sage brush, torn loose from its tenuous roots in the dry and dusty steppe soil and bowled along on the breeze. He flicked it away again, and watched it continue its erratic course across the arid plain.

Other dark shapes were approaching him now, but these were identifiable and comfortingly familiar. Andrew loomed up out of the darkness first, like a shadow within a shadow. Behind him, Hailsham could pick out the reassuring bulk of the Thinker and the slightly shorter figure of Jimmy.

Andrew glanced at the Browning, which Hailsham still held in his hand. 'Expecting trouble, boss? Or were you planning to fire off a salute to greet us?'

Hailsham holstered the pistol. 'Where are the others? Did everyone make it down safely?'

The sergeant nodded. 'No problems. They're waiting over by the CADS, about 300 yards that way.' He jerked his thumb back over his shoulder. 'I reckon you must have caught a last-minute updraft or something.'

'It sure as hell wasn't a thermal,' Hailsham muttered, shivering. He reached down to pick up his chute, anxious to start moving. 'I suppose you've already noticed that we have company?' he asked, jerking his head towards the foothills.

'We've also got a few problems,' the Thinker confirmed. 'Cyclops seems to think they'll probably have dogs, and we just happen to be directly downwind right now.'

'Shit!' Hailsham hissed. It was something he had not considered, and the last thing they needed at that particular moment was further complications. He fell into step behind Andrew as he began to lead the way back to the main force.

Barry had already opened the CADS container and broken out a couple of folding shovels. He and Tweedledum were busy digging a trench in which to bury the parachutes. Hailsham tossed his own into the pile.

'So, what's the plan, boss?' Tweedledee asked. 'Do we bed in or are we going to get moving?'

'Damned good question,' Hailsham answered. Under normal circumstances, it would have been standard practice to seek out somewhere to dig a trench hide for the morning. Exposed as they were, they might just as well erect a bloody great flagpole instead. 'Short of us all doing about a dozen four-minute miles in succession, I'd say our choice of options was strictly limited.' He broke off, staring out across the open ground towards the foothills once again. The cluster of camp-fires seemed to be concentrated in one small area. Probably a sheltered gully between two ridges of hills, he guessed. Which meant that the campers, whoever they were, probably

97

had a clear forward view over the plain but restricted vision on either side of them. There seemed only one possibility that offered a fair chance of making progress without being spotted.

'We'll split into our two patrols now,' Hailsham announced. 'It'll mean a pretty lengthy detour, but if we fan out we stand a reasonable chance of getting far enough before daybreak to dig in somewhere that offers at least partial cover from any OP in those hills. With a bit of luck, they'll be shipping out at first light anyway – in which case they'll either have their backs to us or they'll cut straight through between us.'

'And if they don't?' Andrew asked.

Hailsham shrugged. 'Then we'll have them caught in a pincer between us. If they prove to be hostile, we'll at least have a fighting edge. We can hit them from two sides.'

Andrew nodded. It was as good a plan as any, given the circumstances. 'Of course, the good news is that it could just turn out to be a bunch of nomads,' he pointed out. 'In which case, if we're lucky, we'll all get to eat goat stew for breakfast.'

'I liked the sound of baked eagle better,' Cyclops observed. 'Smelly bastards, goats.'

'You ain't gonna reek of violets yourself by the time you've humped all your gear over to those hills,' Andrew pointed out. 'It might be bloody cold, but you'll still work up a sweat under those layers of Gore-tex.'

'It's not as bad as I expected,' Jimmy said brightly. 'I've been in colder places. My old lady's bedroom, for a start.'

'You wait until we get up in those mountains,' Tweedledum warned him. 'Your old lady's bedroom will seem like a Moroccan whorehouse.'

'His old lady's bedroom *is* a Moroccan whorehouse,' Tweedledee put in, raising a good-natured laugh.

Hailsham let the merriment die away. 'Right, we'd better get going,' he said finally. 'And once we *do* get moving, we cut the bullshit, is that understood? All communication will be on a strictly business-only basis. Sound travels a long way in open country like this.'

'I suppose that rules out a nice stirring marching song?' Cyclops ventured.

Hailsham glared at him. 'Trooper, I'll kick your arse if you so much as break wind,' he promised. 'Right, let's do it.'

The men broke naturally into the two agreed patrols – Tweedledee, Tweedledum and Cyclops staying with Hailsham; Jimmy, Barry and the Thinker with Andrew. They busied themselves sharing out the supplies and spare ammunition. Andrew slung the heavy Stinger launcher over his shoulder, forcing a grin in Hailsham's direction as he felt the full weight of his extra burden. 'And, yes, I'm still glad I insisted on bringing it,' he said out loud, in answer to an unspoken question.

Fully laden, the two patrols lined up, facing their objective. Hailsham scanned the far ridge of hills through his PNGs, seeking out a primary RV to meet at if they both managed to evade the encampment successfully. Just above and behind the site of the camp-fires, he could make out a long, flat ridge broken by a single high, rocky outcrop. As a landmark, it was good enough. He pointed it out to Andrew.

'If we make it to the hills safely, we RV there at 10.00 hours tomorrow,' he instructed.

The sergeant nodded. 'We'll be waiting for you,' he promised. 'Any prefences for lunch?'

Hailsham smiled, clapping him on the shoulder. 'Just be there,' he said.

The patrols moved out at a tangent from each other, the laden bergen on each man's back making them look like a small caravan of strange, two-legged dromedaries. There were no farewells. To say goodbye admitted the possibility that you might not see one another again. Fanning apart in a wide 'V, they were soon out of sight of each other, even with the aid of the PNGs.

No, he did not regret bringing the Stinger along, Andrew reminded himself, although the extra 65lb of the launcher and the single missile he carried made him feel like a pack-mule. Even so, he still hoped he would not have to use it in anger. For there was no real enemy. If they were forced to kill, it would be for all the wrong reasons, and there would be no pride, no glory, in that.

The thought depressed him. It was a shit mission, and had been from the start. The only enemy, if there was one at all, was what was lurking in wait for them up at that research complex. An invisible enemy, an unknown threat. And the SAS were soldiers, not bloody Ghostbusters. Andrew sighed, thinking about it. Yes, it was a shit mission all right. And he and his men were being used like pieces of toilet paper.

They had covered no more than about seven miles, and it was already becoming noticeably lighter. To his right, away from the hills, Andrew could see a misty band of lighter green creating a thin stripe between the darkness of the terrain and the sky. He raised his hand to the PNGs, lifting them away from his eyes. The stripe was a faint ochre glow now, sandwiched between two slabs of blackness. In a short time it would begin to glow red, then golden, as the early morning sun pushed its umbra ahead of it.

Andrew's gaze travelled to his left, picking out the twinkling of the camp-fires once again. They were closer now, but they seemed higher than they had appeared from their original position. He snapped the goggles back into place and stopped, raising his hand in the air.

The Thinker closed up on Andrew's right shoulder, lowering his mouth to his ear. 'What's up, boss?' he whispered.

Andrew pointed ahead, slightly over to his right. 'Am I imagining it, or is the terrain sloping down ahead of us?' he asked.

The corporal strained his eyes into the gloom. It was difficult to define contour or elevation, but there did appear to be a shallow but sustained incline ahead of them. 'Yeah, I think you're right,' he agreed. 'But we should be going up, not down, if we're heading towards the hills. What do you reckon?'

Andrew sucked at his teeth. He was not sure, but it was a strong hunch. 'I reckon we might have just found ourselves a little bonus,' he said quietly.

Barry had moved up to join them. Behind him, Jimmy kept his distance, remaining in the Tail-end Charlie position. Andrew waved him forward.

'Listen, I want you to skirt out to the right,' he told the Scot as he finally came near. 'Sweep around in an arc and then rejoin us about 200 yards ahead. Thinker and I reckon there's some sort of depression over there. Check it out, will you?'

'You got it, boss,' Jimmy said, slipping away as Andrew shrugged the heavy Stinger into a more comfortable carrying position and began to move off again.

By the time Jimmy had finished his sweep and moved back to rejoin them again, Andrew could see him coming from a good 200 yards away. It was definitely getting lighter – and rapidly. He hoped that Jimmy was going to confirm his suspicions. He was in luck.

'You were right, boss,' Jimmy whispered. 'It's like a very shallow gully, but it gets steeper as you move down. My guess is that it's a dried-up wadi that's been scoured out by the spring snow-melt coming down from the mountains.'

Andrew could not repress a wry grin. 'I'm impressed, Trooper,' he said. 'Nobody told me that you'd graduated in geology.' Serious again, he added: 'How deep do you reckon it gets? Enough to give us cover?'

But Jimmy was way ahead of him. 'Let's put it this way, boss. I couldn't even see you, let alone that ridge of hills over yonder. Looks like we've just found ourselves a place to hole up for a few hours.'

It was all the confirmation Andrew needed. 'Right, let's go for it,' he hissed, breaking away to the right. 'If we can't see our friends up in the hills, it's a pretty safe bet they won't be able to see us, either. The sooner we get dug in, the better.'

Following his lead, the patrol began to move slowly back down the path taken by the Glaswegian. A few minutes later, the last of the camp-fire lights winked out of view as they dropped down below the lip of the shallow ridge and continued their descent.

Major Hailsham had also been acutely aware of the imminent approach of dawn and the urgent need to find some sort of cover. He scanned the bleak terrain ahead with increasing frustration. There was nothing that could be turned to their favour, not even a shallow dip in the ground. It was beginning to look as though they would have to do it the hard away.

He slipped off his PNGs and turned to face the rising sun. A broad band of reddish-gold light was now visible over the horizon. He estimated that they probably had less than three-quarters of an hour before they would be illuminated against the barren background of the steppe like flies on fly-paper.

Time, then, was of the essence – and location seemed not to make much difference. Hailsham brought the patrol to a halt, summoning in Cyclops from 'Charlie' position. 'Looks like we're going to have to dig in here,' he told the men flatly. 'It's not exactly summer camp, but it's going to have to do.'

They all knew what to do. Tweedledum and Tweedledee took a pair of shovels and began to dig out a long, narrow trench. In true SAS tradition, Hailsham dropped his bergen and knelt down to help, scratching at the earth with his bare hands. Cyclops, showing the sort of initiative which had earned him more than one official accolade in the past, sat down on his behind and began to scrape away soil with the heels of his boots.

It was a tough and laborious job. The red, dry and crumbly earth was more like coarse sand, sliding back down the sides of the trench almost as fast as they could scoop it out. Eventually, however, they had managed to gouge out a rough V-shaped slit in the ground, about six feet deep at its lowest point and about five feet wide. It was not much, but for the next few hours, at least, it would be home. Now all they needed was something to cover the top once they were inside. Hailsham remembered his alarming encounter with the rolling clump of sage brush. Where there was one, there could be others, he rationalized. Leaving the three troopers to finish off the slit-trench as best they could, he went in search of further roving herbage.

He returned some ten minutes later, dragging four wispy balls behind him. With the laces from his boots, he lashed them loosely together and held them down with one foot as he rummaged through his bergen for a coil of climbing rope. Finally, after weighing the balls down with his bergen, he ushered the men into the hastily improvised hide and waited for them to settle down as comfortably as was possible. The three men chose to arrange themselves like a rowing team, each sitting behind the other's back with his knees pulled up.

Hailsham found himself thinking of the games of 'Sardines' he had played as a child, and it made him smile. Scrambling down into the single space left, he pulled his bergen in on top of him and arranged the sage brush above his head until it virtually covered the top of the trench. With luck, from the outside it would just look like a clump of drifting grasses which had bunched themselves together. As long as no one decided to take a closer look, it should suffice.

Hailsham tapped Tweedledee lightly on the shoulder. 'You and Tweedledum try and grab an hour's kip,' he hissed in the trooper's ear. 'Cyclops and I will keep watch until daybreak, and if our friends don't move on, we'll have to think again.'

Tweedledee nodded silently, and passed the message on to his mate. The two troopers lolled sideways against the side of the trench hopefully, although the chances of getting any real sleep were minimal. They both fully realized how exposed they all really were. The situation was hardly conducive to relaxation. At best, the next few hours would be a tense and tedious waiting game.

# 11

It was the sort of morning that had inspired countless writers and poets over the centuries, Andrew Winston among them. In other circumstances, he would have seen it as the start to a beautiful day. Lines from one of his own early efforts ran through his head as he surveyed the blood-red orb of the dawn sun beginning to lift away from the knife-edge of the horizon.

Morning
And the blood-streaked labour pains of light
Striate
Across the swollen belly of the dawn.

He smiled ruefully. One day he would finish that particular poem, equating the sunrise to a new birth. Right now, more urgent problems occupied his thoughts.

He slithered out of the hollow which he and his men had scooped out of the side of the gully and began to crawl up its sloping side on his belly. Reaching the top, he peered cautiously over the lip, bringing a pair of powerful non-reflective binoculars up to his eyes.

Despite the earliness of the hour, the encampment was already a hive of bustling activity. The camp-fires had been doused, and Andrew could make out individual figures scurrying about, packing up their blankets and equipment. He nodded to himself, smiling. It looked as though Hailsham had been right: they were preparing to move out.

They were a motley bunch, perhaps forty to fifty strong. Some wore vaguely military-style uniforms or camouflaged fatigues, while others were clearly dressed as civilians, swathed in brightly striped *khalats*, topped by turbans or embroidered skullcaps. With a slight sense of shock, Andrew noticed that there were also several women and children in the party.

The Thinker had slithered up the side of the ridge to join him. 'Friend or foe, boss?' he whispered in the sergeant's ear.

Andrew handed him the binoculars. 'Take a look for yourself,' he murmured, waiting silently while the other man scanned the encampment.

Finally lowering them again, the Thinker glanced sideways with a faint shrug. 'At a guess, I'd say they were a bunch of refugees with an armed escort,' he volunteered.

'That's what I thought,' said Andrew, nodding. 'But not very well armed, from the look of things. All I saw were a few old breech-loading rifles. No heavy guns, no mortars, as far as I could see.' He took back the binoculars, raising them to his eyes once again. 'From the way they're gathering their stuff together, I'd say they were getting ready to move up further into the hills.'

'Damn,' the Thinker hissed under his breath. 'That means they're going to stay ahead of us. That'll give them the advantage of the high ground and all the cover they need to spring an ambush if they feel like it.'

Andrew nodded morosely. Those had been his thoughts exactly.

'So, what do you reckon?' the Thinker asked.

'About the only thing we can do is to give them enough headstart so we stay outside the range of those rifles,' Andrew replied with a sigh. 'But if they do decide to set an ambush, we're not going to know about it until the shooting starts. And even if they have only got a few rifles, that gives them one hell of an edge.'

'In short, a bit of a bastard,' the corporal observed. 'Looks like we got hold of the shitty end of the stick, boss.'

It was an understatement. 'And those fucking Chinks handed it to us,' Andrew said bitterly. 'What the fuck were they playing at?'

The Thinker was silent for a few seconds, pondering. Finally, he said: 'Maybe they knew something we don't.'

Andrew grunted. 'Yeah, and something they maybe didn't want us to know, either.' He stiffened suddenly, raising one hand for silence. Holding his breath, he looked up, his eyes scanning the sky. 'Can you hear what I hear?'

The other soldier strained his ears. Sure enough, echoing down from the hills, he could hear a distant, faint, but unmistakable sound. Both men waited with bated breath as the muted *pocka-pocka-pocka* of a helicopter became gradually louder.

The chopper appeared from nowhere. One moment it was just a distant sound, and the next it was in clear view, rising from behind a high ridge of hills to the far right of the refugee encampment. Andrew snatched up his binoculars again, training them on the black shape silhouetted against the golden sky.

'Soviet-built Mil Mi-24 Hind-A,' he muttered, identifying the craft almost at once.

'Christ,' the Thinker spat out, realizing the implications at once. The Hind-A was strictly an assault helicopter, invariably armed with a large-calibre machine-gun in the nose, three other guns on each of the auxiliary wings and four underwing pods equipped with up to thirty-two 57mm rockets. The Soviets had used them extensively during the Afghanistan conflict, to devastating effect. Their destructive capability and sheer fire-power were awesome. One thing was certain, the Thinker realized: it sure as hell was not on a reconnaissance mission.

The noise from the helicopter's engines was over-powering now, wiping out the need to whisper. Andrew whistled loudly through his teeth. 'Christ Almighty – so *that's* what the fucking Chinks wanted to keep quiet about,' he exploded. 'It looks like Republican forces are gunning these bloody hills as a matter of course.'

The noise of the helicopter had brought Jimmy and Barry scrambling up the side of the gully.

'Heard we had company, boss,' Jimmy said. 'Want us to break out a gimpy, just in case?'

Andrew shook his head. 'We've got to remember – this isn't our bloody war,' he reminded them. 'You heard the orders – we stay out of trouble unless it comes looking for us.'

The other trooper looked up at the Hind-A as it began to curve round on a banking sweep, losing height rapidly. 'Well that bastard's not looking for a couple of pals to play with, I can tell you that for nothing,' he said sardonically. 'And if one of them's not trouble, I don't know what is.'

'Yeah, you're probably right,' Andrew agreed, keeping a wary eye on the flight path of the chopper as he spoke. It was completing its turn now, and beginning to drop straight down into the narrow pass between the two ridges of hills where the refugees were. 'And I've got a nasty feeling that it's just found exactly what it's looking for.'

Even as he spoke, they all saw the flashes of flame spit out from the nose and the wings of the helicopter. A split second later, the staccato crackle of heavy gunfire echoed out across the steppe, rolling off the sides of the hills like thunder.

'Jesus wept,' Andrew blurted out, snatching up the binoculars and training them on the tiny camp. 'Those poor bastards don't stand a chance.'

Andrew watched panicking figures running everywhere, desperately trying to seek some sort of cover as the helicopter's blanket fire-power chewed up the dusty soil all around them, creating what looked like a small-scale sandstorm. He saw several of the fleeing figures tossed aside like rag dolls as heavy-calibre slugs from the chopper's nose-gun tore into their bodies. Others just dropped where they stood, as armour-piercing bullets passed straight through them. There was no attempt to return fire. It was a strictly one-way massacre.

Perhaps half the victims of the attack died in the first few blistering seconds of the aerial assault. Through the binoculars, Andrew could see at least three women among the dead. Then, suddenly, the bodies were all there was to be seen, as the survivors disappeared behind rocks and found fissures in the hillside to hide in.

The sounds of heavy gunfire ceased abruptly and the Hind-A climbed away from the gully, circling round until its pilot had a side view of what had been the encampment. As the helicopter hovered like a malevolent insect, Andrew watched the nose drop and the tail section come up until it resembled a scorpion about to strike.

And strike it did. Four bursts of flame and streaking smoke trails presaged the rapid descent of rockets into the rocky foothills, where they exploded like short, sharp thunderclaps.

'Fuck this for a game of soldiers,' Andrew screamed suddenly. He threw himself back down the gully into the dug-out, emerging a moment later with the Stinger launcher and two missiles tucked under his arm. Grunting with exertion, he hauled them back up to the lip of the ridge and began to make the launcher ready for combat.

'I thought you said this wasn't our war?' the Thinker said laconically, as Andrew slipped a missile canister into the rear end of the launcher and hefted it into position over his shoulder.

The sergeant clapped his eyes to the optical sight. 'This isn't war, it's sheer fucking slaughter,' he grunted, his fingers tightening around the stock and trigger. Bypassing the optional IFF 'friend or foe' identification transponder, he lined up the Hind-A in the sights straight away and locked on.

The launcher bucked in his hands as he squeezed the firing mechanism, launching the infrared missile. As if in slow motion, the warhead streaked unerringly towards its target, homing in on the hot exhaust gases from the twin Isotov turboshaft engines mounted above the helicopter's cabin.

The Hind-A exploded in a red and orange ball of fire, spewing down shattered and smoking pieces of scrap metal in a deadly rain. Then it was gone, with only a few oily black streamers of smoke to mark the fact that there had ever been an aircraft in that particular patch of the sky.

Andrew lowered the launcher to the ground, glancing sideways at Jimmy, Barry and the Thinker with an unspoken question in his eyes. The satisfied smiles on their faces answered him more than adequately. They were all equally glad that the phoney, invisible war was over at last. Now they had a real fight on their hands, with a real and clearly identifiable enemy. They were soldiers again, doing what they were trained to do, and what they did best.

The sergeant grinned broadly at all of them, sharing their relief. 'I think you might say we just chose sides,' he said. 'Let's just hope we chose the right one.'

Two miles away, Major Hailsham watched the last smoking fragments of the Hind-A snaking to the ground and felt a similar sense of elation. He could not fault Sergeant Winston's decision to shoot down the helicopter. Under the circumstances he would have done exactly the same – on purely tactical if not humanitarian grounds. Sooner or later, the pilot would have tired of shooting fish in a barrel and gone looking for other targets. The war would have come to them anyway – Winston had merely pre-empted the fact.

Hailsham reviewed his next move in light of the development. It was extremely unlikely that the pilot or crew had had time to send any sort of message to base. From the moment their on-board sensors had registered a missile locked on to them to the moment of impact had been less than five seconds. Allowing for at least three seconds of surprise and confusion at the completely unexpected attack, the helicopter crew would have been dead before any of them could push the panic button, let alone relay any information.

Hailsham's thoughts turned to the people in the hills, whoever they were. The fact that there had been no attempt to return fire during the attack suggested that they were only lightly armed, if at all. And Hailsham guessed that by now they would either be retreating higher into the hills or digging into cover to tend their wounded. They might be confused, even worried about the source and nature of the sudden new players in the game, although such considerations would not be foremost in their thoughts. Tactically then, Hailsham reckoned, it was as good a time as any to make a forward move, and he automatically made the assumption that his sergeant would think exactly the same way. All things being equal, they would simply RV earlier than planned.

He stretched himself luxuriously, throwing back the crude sage-brush roof of the hide. 'Well, gentlemen, I think it's time to bug out and head for the hills,' he announced breezily.

Tweedledum, Tweedledee and Cyclops scrambled to their feet gratefully, relieved to be able to stretch their cramped bodies. 'Reckon there are any more of those things about, boss?' Cyclops asked.

Hailsham shrugged, although personally he doubted it. All the intelligence information he had received at the secondary briefing indicated that the official Kazakh Republican forces were stretched pretty thinly, trying to cover a vast area in which multiple and sporadic outbreaks of guerrilla activity and ethnic clashes kept them constantly on the hop. It seemed more than likely that the Hind-A had been a lone bird on a simple search-and-destroy mission, probably from a safe base well inside the border, such as Leninogorsk or Blisk. If that assumption was correct, then the helicopter would not be due back at base for at least an hour and a half, so it would be a minimum of two hours before anything else could be sent to the area to find out what had happened to it.

But this was pure speculation, and Hailsham was not going to swear to it under oath. 'Let's just put it this way,' he said. 'The easiest way to find out would be to hang around here waiting.'

It was a good point. Cyclops set about helping Tweedledum and Tweedledee unload their equipment from the trench hide, after which they hastily filled it in again and covered all traces of its existence as best they could. There was no point in giving the enemy an obvious point from which to track them.

Finally packed up and ready to march, they assembled behind Hailsham as he scanned the lowest foothills, searching for the best route to their destination. The obvious, and the easiest, path was the most direct – straight across the steppe towards the gully where the refugees had made camp. Such a route had clear advantages. First, it represented the shortest possible distance between them and the cover of the hills, and secondly it would save a considerable amount of climbing through difficult terrain.

But the obvious solution to a problem is not necessarily the best, and the SAS had never been noted for taking the easy option. The attractions of the route were balanced by the potential dangers, Hailsham realized. He was only assuming that the group already in the hills had limited weaponry. They may have deliberately chosen not to return fire upon the helicopter to conceal their true strength, he reflected. Equally, they may simply not have had enough time to prepare an adequate defence against the attack. So they remained a largely unknown quantity.

With all these factors in mind, Hailsham struck out on a path which would take them well to the left of the encampment and into a stair-like series of rising hills towards the mountains proper. It was a circuitous route, but he reckoned that, with the initial climbing done, it should be possible to cut across what appeared to be a fairly easy plateau towards the RV. He could only hope that his sergeant was making a similar decision.

# 12

In fact, Andrew's decision was much more straight-forward and easy to make. Daylight had revealed that the shallow gully which had afforded them protection would also offer a straight and easy route directly into the mountains.

It appeared that Jimmy's initial assessment of the geological oddity had been correct. The gully was a natural channel scoured out of the plain by the annual spring floods of melt water which had poured down out of the mountains over thousands, perhaps millions of years. Now down into its deepest part, Andrew gazed along the floor of the depression to where it began to incline into the foothills with a smile of satisfaction on his black face.

'Looks like Mother Nature's given us our own private motorway,' he said to the Thinker.

'Pity she didn't think to put in a couple of rest stops,' the big Mancunian muttered. 'I'm bloody starving.'

'Stop worrying about your belly,' Jimmy grunted, humping his heavy bergen up on to his broad back. 'Let's just get the hell out of here before the fucking Russkies come to find out what's happened to their nice whirlybird.'

'Bloody good idea,' Barry Naughton agreed. 'We can worry

about scran when we're off this fucking plain. Anyway, there's bound to be a McDonald's sooner or later. There always is.'

The Thinker did not appreciate the humour. He glowered at the trooper. 'Yeah, bloody dream on,' he growled, but set about loading up his own equipment with a new sense of urgency. He held back as the others began to move out, taking his turn as Tail-end Charlie.

They had covered less than a mile, but Hailsham was sweating profusely under his multiple layers of thermal clothing. The sun was still low in the sky, but the wide difference between daytime and night-time temperatures was already apparent. The major stopped, holding up his hand to bring the patrol to a halt.

'I think we ought to strip off a couple of layers,' he suggested, dropping his bergen to the ground.

The suggestion was gratefully received by everyone, as was the chance of a brief rest while they were complying with it. And, of course, it provided a natural break for another bout of the inevitable bullshit.

'I reckon we'll all have a bloody good dose of crotch-rot before we get out of this weird fucking country,' Tweedledum complained. 'One minute it's trying to freeze your bollocks off, next minute it's trying to cook 'em.'

Cyclops grinned at him. 'You're not supposed to still have any. Somebody back at Training Wing must have fucked up.' He glanced over at Hailsham. 'Ain't that right, boss?'

Hailsham finished packing the garments he had taken off back into his bergen. After glancing at Tweedledum and Tweedledee, he smiled at Cyclops. 'Well, I was promised a pair of bollockless bastards,' he agreed. 'And so far I've had no cause to complain.'

Caught in a trap of his own making, Tweedledum was uncharacteristically silent, temporarily stumped for a suitable rejoinder. Grinning sheepishly, he shrugged on his heavy pack once again and turned to face the foothills.

The four-man patrol set out again to trudge the last two miles across the steppe.

In the Chinese operations room back in Tacheng, General Chang had a satisfied smile on his face as he replaced the telephone receiver. He glanced across at Leng Pui, who was eyeing him quizzically.

'Yes, that was the British authorities,' he confirmed with a nod. 'They were requesting an update on the operation.'

'And what did you tell them?' Leng Pui asked.

Chang shrugged. 'What should I tell them? That everything is proceeding according to plan.' He broke off, to leer at his fellow officer. 'But our plan, of course – not theirs. No point in mentioning that.'

'No point at all,' Leng Pui agreed, echoing Chang's devious smile. 'I think perhaps they might not be too pleased if they knew we were using their precious SAS as pawns in our own game. I must commend you, General. This scheme of yours seems to be working remarkably well.'

Chang preened himself. He was not one for false modesty. 'As I knew it would,' he said. 'This business with the Russian research facility was an unexpected gift from the gods. I could not let it pass without turning it to our advantage. We have everything to gain, and nothing to lose.'

'And if the SAS soldiers survive?' Leng Pui asked.

Chang affected a careless shrug. 'Unlikely,' he said quietly. 'But even if they do, what will they know, and what can they prove?' He shook his head, smiling even more confidently.

'No, the cards are firmly stacked in our favour, my dear Captain. The British SAS are merely playing out the game to my rules. The outcome does not really matter one way or the other. We shall have achieved our objective.'

Leng Pui regarded his superior with a look of frank admiration. 'You should have been a diplomat, not a soldier,' he ventured.

'In these changing times, it is perhaps most prudent to be both,' Chang observed, nodding thoughtfully.

Andrew's reference to the wadi as a motorway was proving to be strangely accurate, for the further they progressed along the dried-out watercourse the clearer it became that it had served as a major route for others in the past. The patrol had already passed several long-abandoned camp-sites, and caches of dumped waste and discarded equipment. They had also noted at least two sites in which loosely piled mounds of rocks and stones suggested makeshift graves. Andrew had assumed them to be civilian, probably marking the passage of nomadic tribesmen or goatherds down to the sparse grazing of the plain during the summer months.

The latest find, however, looked considerably more recent, and was definitely more military in nature. Andrew pulled up the patrol, gazing around at the obvious signs of a recent battleground. One side of the gully bore unmistakable signs of entrenched positions, and there were several patches of scorched and blackened earth where it was clear that mortars had been positioned. The surface of the ground was littered with spent cartridge and shell cases. This had been no band of refugees with a few rifles, Andrew thought. The site betrayed the fairly recent presence of a very well-armed and well-trained fighting unit.

The Thinker had broken away from the patrol to do a little private investigation of the discarded hardware. In the back of his mind, there was the faintest hope of finding the odd tin of rations which had been overlooked. He dropped to his knees beside the shattered remains of a mortar which had been fired just once too often. Beside it, the reddish soil was still stained a dark brown with the blood of its unfortunate operator.

The Thinker looked up and gestured to Andrew. 'Here, boss, I think you ought to come and take a look at this,' he called out. There was something in his tone which put the sergeant on his guard. He moved across cautiously, finally kneeling beside the man.

'What is it?'

The Thinker held up part of the mortar base plate and two shell cases for his inspection. 'Notice anything unusual about these?' he asked.

Andrew was not sure what he was supposed to be looking for. He weighed the objects in his hands for a few seconds, peering at them closely without noticing anything amiss. Then, suddenly, he realized that the armaments were all of Chinese manufacture. He whistled through his teeth and said: 'You reckon this could have been a Chinese force? This far inside the border?'

The Thinker shrugged. 'Either that or the Chinks are deliberately arming rebel guerrilla groups against the official Republican forces. Whichever way you look at it, our slit-eyed friends appear to be playing a double game here. Which rather makes me wonder about our position in the scheme of things.'

Andrew nodded. The man had a good point, and one worth thinking about. 'Maybe that's why they dropped us short of the original target zone,' he mused, eventually. 'It could be this was something they were trying to hide.' He paused, racking his brains for a more simple and understandable explanation, before finally finding one. 'Of course, it could be that a rebel group just happened to get hold of some Chinese ammunition. These guerrilla factions aren't usually too fussy who and where they get their arms from.'

The Thinker looked doubtful. 'Yeah, you could be right – but I reckon something smells,' he muttered firmly. 'There's been something fishy about this whole operation right from the start, if you ask me. I reckon we're the bloody patsies in this little set-up.'

Andrew was not convinced, but he decided it was something to keep in the back of his mind. Certainly he shared at least some of his companion's misgivings. Their situation was complicated enough as it was, without any further unknown quantities. It was not a comforting feeling. He dropped the two shell cases to the ground and straightened up. 'Well, there's not much we can do about it now, anyway,' he said resignedly. 'We've got a rendezvous to keep.' As an afterthought, he bent down again and scooped up one of the shell cases.

'Souvenir?' the Thinker asked. 'Or are you thinking of going into the recycled brass business?'

Andrew grinned, tucking the case into his already overladen bergen. 'I suppose the old man ought to take a look at this,' he murmured thoughtfully. 'Maybe he can make a bit more sense out of what's going on.'

They turned their backs on the scene of battle and began to make their way up the steepening incline of the wadi once again. Another half an hour of steady marching brought them to the first line of real hills, which rose in a series of rocky waves above them.

'Well, so much for the after-dinner stroll,' Andrew grunted. 'Now we all start really working for a living.'

Major Hailsham and his group had also left the steppe behind them and begun their ascent into the mountains. He reviewed the route ahead with a sense of satisfaction, knowing that his choice had been a good one. The foothills rose ahead of them in an irregular, stair-like progression of crags and clefts and, although initially presenting a sharp and fairly steep climb, soon gave way to the jagged line of a natural fissure which would provide good footholds and a relatively easy way to gain height quickly.

'Nice one, boss,' Cyclops complimented him, following Hailsham's eyes up towards the soaring, snowcapped peaks which were their final destination. 'Now all we've got to do is make like mountain goats and we're home and dry.'

Hailsham raised his eyes to the rapidly darkening sky above them. Thick, black clouds of cumulus were beginning to build up, sweeping in from the north over the top of the mountain range. What had been clearly defined snowlines on the higher peaks only an hour before were now misty and out of focus as high-altitude winds whipped up the loose snow and carried it out from the sides of the mountains in thin, airborne drifts. Even down here in the shelter of the lower hills, Hailsham could feel the break-up of the fairly still air pattern which had been a feature of the plains. At the moment, it registered merely as faint, swirling gusts of cooler air. But once they got a few hundred feet higher, it would be a different matter, Hailsham knew. All in all, the imminent change in the weather suggested that Cyclops was being more than a little optimistic in his predictions.

'I wouldn't count on the "dry" bit, if I were you,' Hailsham warned him. 'In fact, given this sort of terrain, I wouldn't count on anything at all.'

The corporal belittled the warning with a carefree grin. 'Listen, boss, I'm prepared for anything,' he said with mock confidence. 'It can't be any worse than the Lake District.'

Hailsham laughed out loud. 'If you found a pile of shit in your Christmas stocking, you'd think Santa Claus had brought you a racehorse,' he said.

Marvelling yet again at the sheer good humour and resilience of the men he had had the privilege of commanding for most of his career, Hailsham strode briskly forward to begin the arduous climb.

# 13

Just as Hailsham had figured, just under two hours of hard climbing brought them to a long, flattish ridge of bare rock forming a narrow plateau between the central massif of the mountain range and its band of lower foothills. Dragging himself on to the shelf, which was at this point about as wide as a three-lane motorway, he sought the temporary shelter of a low, rocky overhang, grateful for the chance to take some relief from the biting wind – and to rest.

The cold air scoured his lungs as he drew in long, shuddering gasps of breath. Age was beginning to show its hoary head, Hailsham thought, ruefully. Or perhaps he was just getting soft. He drew himself closer into the rock face, making room for the others to bunch up beside him, huddling together for extra warmth. Slowly, his breathing returned almost to normal, and he began to shiver.

The threat of a storm seemed to have passed – at least for the time being. Throughout their climb the wind had increased steadily, sweeping away the black clouds but adding a considerable chill factor to the air temperature. The temporary break would give them all a chance to replace their previously discarded thermal clothing – a move which was well overdue,

Hailsham realized. And, if temperatures were likely to fall much lower, it would soon be time to start thinking about stripping down their weapons and removing all excess oil and grease from everywhere except the camming surface of the bolt mechanisms. The techniques of keeping weapons in working order in such extreme cold had been learned by bitter experience. In unusually cold conditions, all lubricants tended to thicken, heightening the chances of sluggish action or even jams. Even spare ammunition had to be wiped regularly, to prevent any build-up of oil, ice or condensation. But conditions were not yet that extreme, Hailsham decided. The operation could safely wait until they reached their rendezvous point. First things first: cold-weather protection for the outside and a quick calorie boost for the inside.

Stripping off his heavy bergen, Hailsham clawed at it with stiff fingers, pulling out the two extra layers of Gore-tex body-suiting and a bar of chocolate. Shrugging on the extra clothing again, he bit into the chocolate and crunched it between his teeth before swallowing it greedily. A couple of swigs from his water canteen completed the hurried snack, after which he scrambled to his feet again.

The others were still nibbling at their chocolate bars in an almost leisurely fashion. Hailsham scowled down at them. 'Come on, you lazy load of buggers. What do you think this is – a bloody Sunday school picnic? We need to get off this exposed ridge before this wind gets any higher.'

Cyclops looked up at him with a pained expression. 'Christ, boss, I thought we were going to spend a bit of time enjoying the view,' he muttered. He popped the last chunk of chocolate into his mouth and scrambled to his feet, checking his watch. 'At this rate, we're going to be early for our date,' he said. 'I do hope Andrew isn't going to stand us up.'

'He'll be there,' Hailsham replied confidently. 'And if I know the stubborn bugger at all, he'll still have the Stinger with him.'

Waiting a few more moments until Tweedledum and Tweedledee deigned to join the party again, Hailsham set out across the flat expanse of the plateau at a stiff pace. There was another, equally good reason for getting off the ridge as soon as possible, he thought. They were exposed not only to the elements, but also to an aerial observer – and it could not be long now before someone came looking for a chopper which had failed to return to base.

In fact, the subject was at that very moment being discussed at top level back in the Kazakh Republican State department in Alma-Ata. Premier Andrei Kuloschow was a worried man. For months now, the reports of civil unrest and ethnic violence in rural areas had been increasing almost daily. Both militarily and in diplomatic circles, the Birlik, as the Uzbek Popular Front was popularly known, were seen to be gaining in power and prestige. Though they were not yet strong enough to pose an open challenge to the official Republican Party of Kazakhstan, such reports of gathering strength were enough to embolden Birlik members, and other dissenters, into ever more frequent shows of defiance which had now spread into major urban areas. In Alma-Ata itself, there had been three food riots and half a dozen demonstrations in the past week alone. The problems were getting too close to home for comfort, and what had started as merely sporadic outbreaks of guerrilla activity was rapidly escalating into civil war.

And now, it seemed, another heavily armed military helicopter had been wiped out of the sky while on what should have been a routine mission. The first, of course, could have been simply down to bad weather. At least two of his military advisers had warned him against the mission to the unknown research facility in the Sailyukem Mountains, but Kuloschow had overridden them for reasons of his own. In his parlous political state, he considered it more than prudent to curry favour with the Communist Old Guard, who still wielded considerable power behind the scenes back in Moscow if not actually in the Kremlin. So he had complied with the discreet request to send a surveillance helicopter to the remote complex, despite the adverse weather reports at the time. It had not returned, and there had been no further communication. Perhaps, when the weather cleared, he would send another to find out what had happened.

But that was another matter. The loss of the second helicopter, reported only a few minutes ago, was a lot more worrying. Quite apart from the loss to the increasingly stretched and cash-starved military, the propaganda value of this latest development was potentially devastating. If news, or even a rumour, got out that a rag-tag band of guerrillas had managed to get hold of sophisticated anti-aircraft weapons, it would raise the stakes dramatically and demoralize his own troops.

Kuloschow looked up at Major Osipov, who had just brought him the news.

'So there's no doubt that it was shot down? No other explanation?'

Osipov shook his head gravely. 'None, comrade. Air control definitely monitored an automatic distress call from the helicopter's computers seconds before it disappeared off the screens. A missile was locked on and closing.'

Kuloschow frowned, placing his elbows on his desk and locking his hands together in a tight knot. Forming a steeple with his two forefingers, he tapped them against his chin thoughtfully.

'Your recommendations, Major?'

Osipov regarded the Premier with barely disguised contempt. The man was weak, with the impressionable, vacillating mind of a politician. And these were times for strength, for making military, not diplomatic decisions.

'I think you know my recommendations,' he replied. 'Although you choose to largely ignore them.' Osipov's tone was both mocking and censorious. He had not forgiven the other man for the loss of the first helicopter.

Kuloschow felt the waves of antagonism emanating from his chief military adviser and let them wash over him. The last thing he could afford was to offer open defiance; his hold on power was too tenuous. He desperately needed the support of the military, if not its respect. The threat of a military coup against his shaky government was real enough as it was, without provoking it further.

As ever, the best the Premier could do was offer the man a sop, a vague promise.

'Your views are, as you say, quite clear to me, Major,' he said. 'But so are mine to you. I regard your solution as the final option, to be resorted to only when all others have been exhausted. I will not sanction genocide while the eyes of the world are upon us.'

Osipov shrugged dismissively. He had heard the objection a dozen times before, and had his own answer to it. 'Then we make the world look away,' he said simply. 'We turn their eyes elsewhere. The Western powers need a new common enemy now that the Iron Curtain is down. Give them one. Give them the Chinese.'

Kuloschow felt himself shrink inside, a tightening knot of insecurity and fear deep in his belly. Such talk was above and beyond his abilities and comprehension, he knew. Before the formation of the Republican Party in 1991, and the decision to secede from the Russian Federation, he had been a simple Party official, a regional administrator – nothing more. Fate had thrust power upon him, but had neglected to prepare him for it. He was used to local decision-making, the politics of internal and strictly local power. To even consider becoming involved in national, let alone international, politics made him terrifyingly aware of his limitations.

Struggling to keep such fears from Osipov, he tried to bring the discussion back to a level that he felt reasonably comfortable with.

'But right now, this minute. What do you suggest we do about this missile threat?'

Osipov allowed himself to smile contemptuously, having the measure of the man and wanting to show it. 'There's not much we can do, for a few hours at least. Those guerrillas will have scattered back into the mountains and the weather is closing in. Until it clears again, we can't safely send in another helicopter. And an air strike would be both expensive and largely futile. Basically, we have to wait until they come out again – and then be ready for them.'

Kuloschow nodded, feeling oddly relieved. To have no choice at all took away the burden of decision. It was at least a respite from pressures, albeit a temporary one.

'Then we wait,' he said.

Having reached the rendezvous point, Hailsham and his team also had nothing to do except wait. His prediction that Andrew and the others would be there waiting for them had proved to be unduly optimistic. He could only assume that they had not been quite so fortunate in finding a reasonably direct route up through the hills.

'Well, you were wrong about the black man, boss,' Cyclops observed, somewhat superfluously. 'Maybe I should have taken a bet.'

'Except I wasn't offering one,' Hailsham retorted. He fished out his high-powered binoculars, handing them to Cyclops and nodding up to the craggy pinnacle of rock above them. 'Instead you've won the chance to shin up there and take a look-see.'

'Thanks a lot, boss,' the corporal groaned sarcastically as he slung the binoculars over his neck and scrambled off with good grace.

Hailsham watched him clamber up the steep rock face until he reached a deep fissure which ran around to the far side of the outcrop. Traversing it as easily as if he were on a child's climbing frame, Cyclops disappeared from view.

Time to grab some scran, boss?' Tweedledee asked.

Hailsham nodded. 'Be my guest,' he said, generously. 'Have yourselves a full-scale banquet if you like.' He grinned wickedly, knowing that all any of them had were the meagre but sustaining high-calorie ration packs they carried in their escape belts.

The major likewise thought about eating, then rejected the idea. Taking a swig of water from his canteen instead, he looked up again just as Cyclops swung into view again round the side of the crag. Coming down only marginally faster than he had gone up, the man dropped back on to the ledge and grinned triumphantly. 'Back in time for tea, I notice,' he said brightly.

'Well?' Hailsham grunted.

Cyclops paused only to take a couple of deep breaths. 'They're coming,' he announced happily. 'I reckon they're still about 400 feet below us, but they seem to have found some sort of path. From the look of it, I'd say it links up the site of that camp we saw earlier and another little gully over the far side of this ridge. Could be a goat track or something.'

Hailsham thought about this before asking: 'Any sign of the natives?'

Cyclops shook his head. 'If they're there, then they're well hidden – but then you'd expect them to be. Anyway, I didn't hang around for too long, just in case.' He paused, drawing in a few more breaths and allowing his body to relax. 'Mind if I make a suggestion, boss?' he said eventually.

'I'm listening.'

'Just something else I noticed from up there,' the corporal went on. 'The path that Winston's on forks off about a quarter of a mile away. It could provide the best route forward, for all of us.'

Hailsham digested this information. 'So you reckon we ought to go down and intercept them?' he asked.

'It might save time,' Cyclops confirmed with a nod. 'If we wait until they get here, we'll have to make a choice whether to go through the gully or to backtrack. And if there *are* any guerrillas in there . . .'

He did not bother to finish, for Hailsham had clearly got the message. The man was right, the major reflected. If they chose to go through the gully, it would be ideal terrain for an ambush. And eight troopers together stood a better chance than four. There was also another consideration. The biting wind sliced along the exposed ridge like an icy razor. Being on the other side of the crag might offer a little more protection – and at least being on the move would help to keep their body temperatures up. Staying still and waiting would only weaken them.

It was this last factor which made up Hailsham's mind. He clapped Cyclops on the shoulder with one hand. 'Yes, good thinking, Corporal,' he said. He looked over at Tweedledum and Tweedledee, who had already consumed their scant meal. 'Well, if you gentlemen have finished washing up the silverware, we'll press on,' he announced.

In truth, both men were grateful for the chance to get moving again, but it would have been out of character to accept the news without a token protest.

'Aw, boss, I need time to let my dinner go down,' Tweedledum complained. 'I've got a real delicate digestion, you know?'

'Yeah, and he'll fart all the way up the bloody mountain just to prove it,' Tweedledee put in. 'Just make sure you're not the poor bastard behind him.'

Hailsham grinned. 'That won't be my problem. It'll be yours. It's your turn to be Charlie.' He turned to Cyclops, nodding up at the climb ahead. 'Is it worth roping up?'

Cyclops shook his head dismissively. 'Nah – piece of piss, even for an old man like you, boss.'

'Cheeky bastard,' Hailsham grunted, but he was smiling. Nevertheless, he was quite content to let the younger man lead the way. No point in pushing it, he thought. Age and rank still brought some degree of privilege – even in the SAS.

He reached the fissure easily enough, feeling a nice, comforting pressure against both sides of his boot as he jabbed his toes into the crevice and began to edge his way around to the blind side of the crag behind Cyclops. Then, suddenly, he felt a cold knot in his guts as he saw the one little feature of the traverse which Cyclops had neglected to mention. Just ahead of them, a rocky outcrop jutted out from the main body of the pinnacle, forming a two- or three-foot overhang.

'Shit,' Hailsham hissed. He braced himself against the almost inevitable feeling of weakness in his legs as he prepared to face his own personal nightmare.

Cyclops still appeared totally confident. Reaching out, he hooked his fingers over the rim of the outcrop and tensed his arms before swinging his body out into space. Rocking himself from side to side, he let himself sway like a pendulum until he could kick out and lock his boot into a firm toehold. Having inched his fingers along the remainder of the overhang until he could shift his body weight into balance, Cyclops pushed himself away and locked both hands over a knobbly, potato-sized projection, pressing himself against the rock face like a gecko. Changing his foothold from right to left, he completed the tricky manoeuvre and began to climb steadily again.

Hailsham let him get well clear before setting out himself. Sucking in a deep, slow breath, he fought to calm his fears. It was stupid to allow himself ever to get into this state, he told himself. It was just a lump of rock, nothing more. He had negotiated worse obstacles than this a hundred times before, and would probably cope with a few more before he finally hung up his boots. Besides, he could not afford to let Tweedledum see his fear. Reaching up to the rim, he dug his fingers into the cold rock and tensed himself to spring clear from the fissure.

As ever, the terrifying certainty that he was going to fall tore at Hailsham's mind and body for a few seconds. Then he was hanging out over the 200-foot drop below him, his body being buffeted from side to side like a rag doll by the swirling winds. Just one step this side of panic, he kicked out wildly at the main body of the rock face, the toe of his boot scraping against it ineffectually as he tried to locate a firm hold. The weight of his body on his fingers seemed impossible to bear. Every fibre of his being screamed that he was trapped now, and would hang suspended above certain death until those fingers gave up the struggle.

'Up a bit, boss,' came Tweedledum's voice from behind him. 'You're reaching too low. Bring your foot up about another nine inches.'

Hailsham did as he was told, making what felt to him like his last desperate kick out for salvation. His boot scraped against smooth rock for a few more seconds, then caught on something. Feeling like sobbing with relief, he turned his foot, digging his toe deep into the welcome crevice and taking the strain off his arms.

Weak but triumphant, he followed Cyclops up the remaining hundred feet of the rock face and finally collapsed beside him on another small plateau.

'All right, boss?' Cyclops asked, grinning.

It took a lot of doing, but Hailsham managed to fix an idiotic grin on his face as he looked up. 'Piece of piss,' he said breathlessly, not quite sure whether Cyclops believed him or not.

As Tweedledum and Tweedledee finally joined them, Hailsham scrambled to his feet and brought his binoculars up to his eyes. Cyclops pointed to the other patrol's position with his finger.

Hailsham had to concur with the corporal's initial assessment. The path they were following certainly seemed to be a regular passageway through the lower hills of the mountain range, probably following a fault line. But there were definite areas where it was clear that natural features had been modified or adapted for the passage of human feet. Places where piles of small boulders had been rolled or dragged aside and the natural line of the path widened were dead giveaways.

Having identified Andrew's patrol, who were making good progress up a particularly steep and winding section of the path, Hailsham swung the binoculars slowly to the left, picking up the fork which Cyclops had mentioned. Again, he could not fault the man's reading of the situation. It definitely appeared to be a secondary track which carved a circuitous but accessible route around the side of another small peak. The general direction was certainly right. It would appear to be their best route forward, just as Cyclops had surmised.

Hailsham lowered the binoculars, nodding thoughtfully. 'We'll intercept them at the fork,' he announced. 'Anyone have a better idea?'

The others shook their heads. 'We're with you, boss,' Tweedledee said. 'You're the sherpa.'

It sounded like a good, democratic decision. Hailsham took the lead, stepping out on a downward course which would take them into the other patrol's line of vision within a few minutes. Although he trusted his men implicitly, Hailsham firmly believed in a modicum of caution. With potentially hostile forces known to be somewhere in the surrounding hills, the sooner they were seen and identified the better, just in case anyone below them was feeling a bit jumpy. As an extra precaution, he unstrapped his SA-80 and held it out in both arms across his chest to signal non-hostile intent.

'We got company, boss,' the Thinker announced, as Hailsham and his patrol came into view over the top of a ridge. The big Mancunian was already dropping to his belly even as he spoke, his hands swinging the Enfield into a businesslike position.

Andrew hit the ground a split second behind him, bringing his binoculars up and training them on the advancing quartet. He began to scramble to his feet again. 'Relax, fellers,' he called out softly. 'It looks like the old man's coming down to meet us.'

'Maybe he wants to offer one of us a piggyback,' Jimmy suggested hopefully. 'Or perhaps he's just pissed off with the whole thing and has decided it's time to pack up and go home.'

'I keep telling you, Trooper – you're too much of a bloody optimist for this game,' Andrew said, grinning.

Jimmy shrugged. 'I'm just a naturally lucky bastard. It started the day me mam decided to breast-feed me.'

The sudden, sharp crack of a rifle shot echoed around the sides of the enclosing hills. His instincts honed by the finest and most intensive combat training in the world, Andrew dropped back to the ground like a stone, his head whipping sideways to check his men.

'Anybody hit?' he screamed.

With equally fast reactions, Jimmy, the Thinker and Barry all barked out a denial. Andrew swung his binoculars back to his eyes, training them on the other patrol's position.

Hailsham, Tweedledee and Cyclops were already down on the ground in defensive positions, having rolled into whatever scant cover they could find. Only Tweedledum remained on his feet, his face twisted into a mask of pain and shock and his left hand clasped tightly around his throat from where blood spurted out through his fingers. For perhaps three full seconds, he continued to stand stock-still until he lurched slightly sideways like a drunken man, his legs seeming to buckle under him. Almost as if in slow motion, he dropped to his knees and then toppled sideways. His body rolled down the rocky side of the hill for several yards before finally coming to a stop against a large boulder.

Andrew's teeth were clenched tightly together as he slowly lowered the binoculars to the ground.

'Oh, shit!' he groaned. 'Holy fucking shit!'

# 14

With his face pressed close against the rocky ground, Hailsham watched Tweedledum's body roll away down the slope in front of him. Raising his head slightly, he tried to pinpoint the source of the single shot, but there was nothing to give any sort of a clue. He could only assume that it had come from somewhere higher in the hills to the left of them.

He glanced to either side of him, locating the other men and making a candid assessment of their position. It was not good. Only Tweedledee had found anything which could be described as cover, having rolled into a shallow depression in which a few stalky tufts of grass had found a tenuous foothold. Both he and Cyclops were laying on bare and open ground, with no more than a few fist-sized rocks scattered between them and the foot of the hill.

Hailsham's heart was pounding in his chest as the seconds seemed to tick away a slow eternity. Why was there no more fire? he wondered. Even a lone sniper, or a rear-guard lookout must see that they were totally exposed. So why was he not even now just casually picking them off like fish in a barrel?

The question immediately begged another. If his guess as to the gunman's position was anywhere near correct, then he must also have had the other patrol in clear view for some considerable time. Why then had he not shot at them? It made no sense. Unless . . .

A wild thought came into Hailsham's head; wild – but in this bizarre situation the only one which provided a rational explanation. Could it possibly be that the sniper had been protecting Winston and his men? That he had perceived the approach of Hailsham's patrol as an attack, and only now had started to doubt that judgement? Hailsham looked down the hill again, to where Tweedledum's body lay huddled against the boulder.

He glanced over his shoulder at Cyclops. 'Listen – I'm going down,' he announced curtly. 'Be ready to give me covering fire if you have to, but don't open fire unless you're fired at first. Got that?'

'You got it, boss,' Cyclops hissed back. 'But what the fuck's going on?'

Hailsham did not bother to try to answer him at that point. He was not even sure if he *had* an answer, although the next few minutes might conceivably provide one. Rolling on to his back, he slipped the catch of his SA-80 into the safe position and cradled the weapon tightly against his belly and chest. Then, taking a deep breath, he threw himself down the hill towards Tweedledum's position. Rocks and stones tore at his body as he rolled over and over down the slope with increasing speed, but Hailsham hardly noticed. His brain was more concerned with the sudden and sharper agony of a bullet tearing into his flesh. Compared with that, a few bruises were nothing. Finally, miraculously, he was lying beside the stricken man in the welcome cover of the large boulder.

Tweedledum was unconscious, but still breathing. Judging from the position of his head against the boulder, Hailsham reckoned, he had probably knocked himself out on impact. The first task was to ensure that the airway was open and clear. Hailsham slipped his fingers cautiously around the sides of Tweedledum's head, probing gently for any tell-tale signs of sponginess which might indicate a skull fracture. The cranium seemed solid enough, Hailsham thought with a sense of relief, and there were no signs of fluid or blood seeping from his nose or ears to suggest internal brain damage. He could only hope that there was no damage to the neck or spine. Not that it really mattered, he reflected on noticing the amount of blood which had already soaked into the ground. If he could not manage to get to the wound and staunch the bleeding, then Tweedledum's clock would run out soon enough anyway. Gently, Hailsham turned the wounded man's face to the side in the normal recovery position and pulled an emergency field dressing pack from his escape belt.

Once exposed, the wound looked better than he could have dared to hope. The bullet appeared to have entered the side of the throat, just under the jaw. Miraculously, it had missed the jugular by centimetres, ploughing on in a downward path until it encountered the firmer tissue of the shoulder muscles. There was no sign of an exit wound, so it was probably still lodged there.

Hailsham wiped away as much blood as he could and pressed the dressing into position over the wound, wedging it in place with a couple of handy stones. It was all he could do for the moment. From now on, Hailsham reflected, Tweedledum's life depended on their all surviving the next few minutes.

Edging his way around the boulder, he called down to Andrew: 'Listen, Winston – I got a theory that these guys think they're on your team.'

Andrew's voice came back immediately. 'Yeah, I'd thought of that myself, boss. They could have taken a pop at us anytime for the last five minutes or so. So what do you reckon?'

'Feel like putting it to the test?'

This time there was just a momentary hesitation before Andrew replied. 'I'm willing if you are, boss. So far it's been looking like a good week for me,' he called back.

'Then let's do it,' Hailsham shouted. He began to rise slowly to his feet, stepping out from behind the safety of the boulder. His heart in his mouth, he started to walk slowly down the rest of the hill as Andrew likewise left his cover and stood waiting to meet him.

The 300 yards which still separated them seemed like as many miles. Hailsham continued to walk down the hill at a steady, apparently casual pace, even though every instinct in his highly trained mind told him it was against all the rules of survival. Oddly, he found himself thinking of an old black and white film he had once seen, called *The Long Walk*. That particular walk had been the route of a condemned man from his cell to the gallows. Or had it been the electric chair? Hailsham could not exactly remember which, but his present situation was chillingly similar.

Seconds dragged into minutes, and still no sound came down from the high ground above him other than the roaring of the wind through the gullies between the hills. Then suddenly it was over and Hailsham was standing at Andrew's side, once more daring to hope that he had been right.

The sergeant's face betrayed his own tension, but he managed to raise a faint smile. 'Looks like we might have guessed this one right, boss. Either that, or our chummy up there is taking a fucking long time to reload.'

Hailsham let out a nervous, tension-relieving laugh – almost a giggle. 'The only problem is I didn't work out the next move yet. What do we do now – stand here like a couple of bloody lemons until the Seventh Cavalry gets here?'

'I got news for you. They ain't coming,' Andrew said gravely. 'Seems like they had a previous engagement or something. What say we show these guys what a friendly pair of bastards we are?'

As he spoke, the sergeant was unhitching his SA-80 very gingerly. Bending down extremely slowly, he laid the weapon out on the ground in front of him and stepped back a couple of paces. It seemed like a sensible gesture, Hailsham thought, following suit.

The two men stood together in silence for several moments, both scanning the hills above them for the faintest sign of movement. Finally, Andrew had to voice the question which had been struggling to surface for the past five minutes.

'What about Tweedledum, boss?'

Hailsham bit at his lower lip and sighed. 'He could make it,' he said quietly. 'But he needs better medical attention than we can give him out here in the open.'

'Bandit,' Andrew hissed suddenly. 'Top of the second ridge, about two o'clock.'

Hailsham's eyes had been scanning the left side of the hills above them. They flicked quickly to the right.

'Yeah, got him,' he confirmed, quickly picking out the turbaned head which had just become visible above a small outcrop of rocks. Even as he looked, two or three more figures appeared out of nowhere.

'These guys are good,' Andrew muttered in grudging admiration.

Hailsham shrugged faintly. 'Well it *is* their turf,' he said almost defensively, although he too was quite impressed. From the top of the hill he had just come down, he would have sworn that the area was clear.

Eventually, some half a dozen people were in plain view, staring down expectantly at the two men. It seemed that they too were unsure of the next move. There was only one way to end the stand-off, Hailsham decided.

'I'm going up,' he announced quietly. 'Let's hope my Russian is up to the local dialect. Otherwise it's sign language.'

'Want me to come with you, boss?' Andrew asked.

Hailsham shook his head. 'No sense in both of us putting our heads in the noose. They've seen that we're friends now. Let's hope that's enough to convince them.'

'Hearts and minds, boss?'

Hailsham grinned. 'This one's more like balls and arses. Ours,' he said as he moved forwards, beginning the steep climb up to the rebel position. Andrew's eyes were on him every step of the way, until he reached the first of the waiting figures, paused briefly and then melted out of vision.

Nearly a quarter of an hour passed before Hailsham reappeared again at the top of the escarpment. He was alone. He picked his way down the slope until he was in prominent view and paused. Raising both hands in the air, he made clear signs for everybody to join him.

Andrew allowed himself a sigh of relief and then turned back to his men, still deep in cover, and said: 'Looks like it's party time, fellers.' He glanced up the hill to his left, noting that Tweedledee and Cyclops had already risen to their feet and were scrambling down towards Tweedledum. Nodding in their direction, he said to the Thinker, who had just reached his side: 'Go and give them a hand – they could probably use it.'

'You got it, boss,' the Thinker shot back before striking off at a tangent up the hill to help pick up and transport the wounded trooper.

Looking more like a bunch of battle-worn stragglers than an élite fighting troop, they all started to make their way up the hill to where Hailsham was waiting for them.

'So, what's the deal?' Andrew asked, when he had got his breath back.

Hailsham smiled at him and said: 'Looks like you're the flavour of the month. Shooting down that chopper had made you a national hero.' He paused for a moment. 'They're Uzbek, mostly refugees from a Kazakh massacre about five days ago. They find it almost impossible to believe that anyone would want to help them. The fact is, they're almost universally feared and despised by both the native Kazakhs and the immigrant White Russians. It seems they have a reputation for overbreeding. The men are supposed to be super-potent and the women oversexed.'

Andrew nodded knowingly. 'Yeah, and I bet they all like loud music and have a natural sense of rhythm,' he said sarcastically. Somehow, it was a story he seemed to have heard before.

Hailsham let the comment pass. 'Anyway, they want to do whatever they can to help us in return. If nothing else, they can probably give us the best route through the higher mountains and provide some valuable intelligence on known rebel positions.'

'What about Tweedledum?' Andrew asked. 'Anyone up there with any medical skills?'

Hailsham shrugged. 'Probably not much above the witch-doctor level,' he admitted. 'Folk medicine, a few herbal remedies, that sort of thing. But at least it will give us a chance to dig that bullet out and patch him up as best we can. This way he's got a fighting chance, at least.'

The major turned back up the hill and began to lead the way to the temporary camp. Some twenty or thirty swarthy, beaming faces greeted them as they climbed over the top of the escarpment and started to descend into the gully below it.

Andrew looked around, whistling faintly through his teeth. 'Not bad for a bunch of refugees,' he said.

The set-up was impressive, considering the nature of the terrain and the people who had created it. In less than a couple of hours the Uzbeks had managed to build a small-scale mountain fortress out of bare rock and earth which would have done credit to a trained military outfit. Apparently using their bare hands, men and women alike had scooped out miniature caverns beneath the larger rock formations and established four protected lookout positions built of rocks, stones and piled earth which gave them panoramic views over the full 180 degrees of the surrounding hills and the valley below. One natural rock fissure had been cleared of loose stones and shale and built up into a fireplace fully protected from the biting wind. Although there was no sign of even the most stunted scrub or brush in the immediate area, they had somehow managed to gather enough wood to create a more than adequate supply of fuel, and a small but welcoming fire was already crackling away merrily.

'Looks like these guys could teach us a thing or two,' Andrew conceded.

Several of the Uzbek women scurried to help the Thinker, Tweedledee and Cyclops as they carried the wounded Tweedledum into the camp. With frantic hand signals and a great deal of fuss, they managed to guide the impromptu stretcher party to a sheltered area near the fire and hastily created a makeshift bed with blankets and animal skins. It was probably not the most hygienic of places to lay a wounded man, but at least it looked comfortable.

Hailsham glanced aside at Andrew as an elderly Uzbek approached them, with a clearly worried younger man trailing miserably in his wake.

'Oh, perhaps I ought to explain something,' Hailsham whispered quickly. 'Rank and uniform don't appear to mean too much to these people. So as far as they're concerned, you're the boss because you're the one with the weapon which can knock helicopters out of the sky. I'm just the interpreter.'

Andrew regarded his superior warily. 'Why do I get this feeling that you're trying to prepare me for something?' he asked. 'Who are these two guys coming over, anyway?'

Hailsham smiled thinly. 'The old fellow is called Mukhtar. He's sort of the head man around here,' he explained. 'As for the younger chap – well, you'll find out about him in a second. Basically, I think you're going to have an executive decision to make.'

There was no time for further explanation, even if it had been forthcoming. Hailsham turned to face the older man, muttering a greeting in Russian. The Uzbek nodded in Andrew's direction, then pointed to his companion before rattling off what seemed to be an impassioned speech.

'What's he saying?' Andrew hissed.

Hailsham translated for him. 'He says you are a good friend,' he explained. 'And he bitterly regrets that one of your men has been shot. However, he is quite prepared to make reparation.'

'What sort of reparation?' Andrew asked.

Hailsham grinned. 'That's the decision you're going to have to make. The young man is Safar. He's the one who opened fire. Without putting too fine a point on it, Mukhtar wants to know if you would like him shot.'

'Christ Almighty, boss,' Andrew exploded. 'What the fuck am I supposed to say?'

Hailsham continued to grin infuriatingly. 'Yes or no, basically.'

Andrew looked relieved. 'Then tell him no, for Christ's sake. Tell him I forgive him . . . it was an accident. Tell him anything.'

Hailsham turned back to the old man and spoke rapidly. Finally, Mukhtar nodded sagely, and Safar looked relieved. With curt, almost formal nods, both men walked away again.

'You bastard,' Andrew growled, though now grinning at last. 'You knew that was coming, didn't you?'

'Just thought I'd let you glory in the power of command for once,' Hailsham said over his shoulder as he strode towards Tweedledum.

The young trooper had regained consciousness and was looking weakly up at Tweedledee, who hovered anxiously over him, looking almost embarrassed at his concern. Hailsham dropped to his knees beside the improvised bed and examined the man's wound more carefully. Most of the bleeding had stopped, and the amount of caked and dried gore on Tweedledum's throat and clothing did not seem quite as much as Hailsham had initially feared.

Tweedledum's eyelids fluttered weakly as he recognized the major. An apologetic smile formed on his pale lips. 'Sorry about this, boss,' he managed to whisper. 'I guess I should have ducked.' The smile faded, to be replaced by a plea in Tweedledum's watery blue eyes. 'How bad is it, boss?' he asked anxiously.

'Don't try to talk,' Hailsham urged him. 'Just try to relax. You're going to be all right.'

Tweedledum's eyes flickered uncertainly. He wanted to believe, but he knew the form. 'You ain't bullshitting me, boss?'

Hailsham forced what he thought to be a suitably reassuring smile. 'I'm not bullshitting you, Trooper,' he promised. 'Once we get that slug out of you, you're going to be as right as rain.'

Suddenly, feeling an insistent nudging in his ribs, Hailsham glanced up and saw a young Uzbek woman standing over him, a small cooking pot filled with boiling water swinging from one hand. With the other, she was doing the nudging, while babbling away in a dialect which Hailsham did not recognize. However, it did not require a great deal of translation to realize that she was telling him to get out of the way. He moved aside and the woman knelt down and began to attend to Tweedledum, washing away the dried blood around the wound with a piece of surprisingly clean-looking fabric. She knew what she was doing, Hailsham thought, noticing her gentle and careful strokes. Clearly these people were more than used to dealing with bullet wounds. Rising to his feet, he strode away in search of Mukhtar to elicit more information.

The woman, it seemed, had been a nurse before the troubles started. Forced by ethnic hatred out of the city hospital where she had worked, she had returned to her native village. There, circumstances had quickly elevated her to the position of doctor, anaesthetist and chief surgeon all rolled into one. Only there was no anaesthetic left, Mukhtar explained apologetically. There had been no drugs at all for some months now.

It was certainly one step up from the witch-doctor he had predicted, Hailsham reflected. At least the woman had some clinical skill, and an understanding of basic hygiene. Even as he returned to watch, she had produced an old but still serviceable scalpel and was attempting to sterilize it with a burning brand from the camp-fire. When the steel blade was glowing a dull red, she immersed it in a fresh pot of boiling water and set it aside on a flat stone to cool. Producing another piece of clean cloth, she rolled it into a thick sausage and thrust it between Tweedledum's teeth, gesturing for Tweedledee to hold it in place.

Hailsham did not stay around for the actual operation – not because he was squeamish, but because there were more important matters to attend to. He sought out Andrew, who was being feted by a small group of younger Uzbek freedom fighters, including Safar, who seemed to have adopted him as a father figure.

'So, how's the national hero business?' Hailsham asked, jokingly.

Andrew looked embarrassed. 'How do you say "no thanks" in this lingo?' he asked. 'These guys have virtually nothing, yet they keep on trying to give me presents. Blankets, bullets, all sorts of stuff.'

Hailsham taught the big Barbadian a polite refusal and waited patiently until he had repeated it to his assembled group of admirers. He began to walk away slowly as Andrew finally got himself free and fell into step beside him, with Safar trotting happily on his heels.

'You're very honoured,' Hailsham said, impressed. 'What they're offering you is their most precious possessions. Life or death, in fact.'

Andrew nodded. 'Yeah, I sort of got that idea myself.' He paused thoughtfully. 'I suppose there's nothing else we can really do for them, is there, boss?'

Hailsham stopped in his tracks, eyeing Andrew warily. The sergeant was thinking about leaving the Stinger with them, he could tell. He shook his head, firmly yet with a trace of regret. 'We've already interfered enough,' he pointed out. 'Our orders were not to get involved, remember?'

'Yeah,' Andrew sighed, nodding faintly. 'Just like Captain Kirk and the crew of the *Enterprise*. Prime Directive and all that.'

'Something like that,' Hailsham confirmed, smiling. 'I didn't know you were a Trekkie.'

Andrew grinned. 'There's a lot you don't know about me, boss.'

'There's a lot I don't know about a lot of things,' Hailsham said. 'That's what makes life interesting.' He led the way over to the rest of the men, who were huddled near the fire, guarding the equipment.

'Looks like we're going to get some hot scran,' the Thinker said hopefully, nodding towards two Uzbek women who were busy cooking something up in a couple of large pots.

'There you are – I told you we'd find a McDonald's,' Barry put in. 'Anybody fancy a Big Mac?'

'More likely a Big Rat,' Jimmy snorted, bringing them all down to earth.

There was a sudden silence as Tweedledee slowly walked over to join them. He sat down moodily, ignoring them all, obeying the conventions. It was not done to talk about either the dead or the wounded. Nevertheless, Hailsham was aware of the man's eyes on him, a mute plea underlying the sadness in them. He understood. Although they were all comrades, the two Tweedles shared a special relationship. Saying nothing, Hailsham climbed to his feet and went to speak to the nurse to get some sort of prognosis.

They were definitely guests of honour, Hailsham realized, noting that the food had been prepared for them alone. He felt slightly guilty as the Uzbek women served them small bowls of a thick, pungent stew, for he was aware that it probably represented half their meagre rations for the week. But it would have been churlish to refuse their hospitality, and he and his men had their own food supply problems to worry about.

Following their example, Hailsham tucked into the meal gratefully, ignoring the strong smell and rather unusual taste. He scooped up the thick stew with pieces of dry, biscuit-like bread, and when that ran out, he used his fingers. Regardless of the taste, it was hot and nourishing, with plentiful lumps of a chewy, whitish and unidentifiable meat, along with roots and brown rice to give it body, and the flavouring of various steppe herbs, which lent a strong and aromatic bouquet. The meal finished, Hailsham was not sure if it was considered good form to belch, as in some Arabic cultures, so he restrained himself. As it happened, the Thinker did it for him, albeit from a natural tendency rather than ethnic etiquette. Two of the Uzbek women smiled proudly, Hailsham noticed, so the gesture was obviously appreciated.

Having put down his bowl, Hailsham sidled over to Tweedledee, who was still picking somewhat halfheartedly at his own portion.

'He's going to be all right,' he assured the trooper. It was more than just optimism, for Hailsham had been greatly impressed by the young Uzbek nurse's handiwork, and she had seemed in no doubt that her patient would make a rapid recovery.

Tweedledee's face brightened, momentarily, before falling again. 'We're going to have to leave him behind, aren't we, boss?' he asked.

Hailsham nodded. 'But we'll be leaving him in good hands,' he pointed out. 'As soon as he's fit enough to move on his own, Mukhtar assures me, they'll show him the way to the Mongolian border, where he should be treated fairly. So far, the Mongolians have refused to get involved in any of this. Once we get home, we can initiate diplomatic moves to get him out safely. There shouldn't be a problem.'

Hailsham was not absolutely sure about the latter part of this information, but managed to sound convincing. Tweedledee brightened up again, returning to his stew with renewed enthusiasm. Hailsham rose and tapped Andrew on the shoulder, urging him to his feet. He led the way across the camp to where Mukhtar and several of the younger Uzbeks were holding some sort of parley. As ever, Safar stuck to Andrew like a shadow, loping along at his heels.

They were warmly welcomed into the group. Hailsham and Andrew squatted down on two blankets which were laid out for them. From underneath the folds of his *khalat*, Mukhtar produced a bottle of vodka, which he offered proudly to Andrew. After taking a swig of the fiery liquid, the sergeant passed the bottle around the group as Hailsham engaged in a conversation in which there was much pointing up into the mountains and much worried shaking of heads. Even though the language went above his head, Andrew was left in do doubt that the Uzbeks did not approve of their final destination.

He nudged Hailsham in the ribs as discreetly as he could. 'What are they saying, boss?' he whispered.

'They know of the region we're headed for,' Hailsham said quietly. 'They say it's a bad place. Animals, and men, die up there. There is a curse, they believe.'

Andrew pondered this information. It all tied in with their own intelligence. Sudden and inexplicable death would certainly seem like a curse to simple and uneducated minds. They would know nothing of chemical or biological poisons, radiation sickness or any of the other possible dangers which might be lurking in the high mountains.

'So basically they're warning us not to go on?' Andrew said.

'In a nutshell, yes,' Hailsham replied. 'But if we are really determined, then Safar will go with us part of the way as a guide. Mukhtar says we will never make it without help to find safe routes and passes through the mountains.'

Hailsham returned to the negotiations, which were shortly brought to a conclusion by the draining of the vodka bottle and a round of handshakes.

'I take it we've accepted their offer?' Andrew said.

Hailsham shrugged. 'There didn't seem to be much choice,' he said wearily. 'Mukhtar painted a pretty bleak picture of the terrain ahead of us, although how much of it was a chance to boast about their own prowess and bravery, I don't know.'

Andrew glanced over his shoulder at Safar, hovering behind him. 'They don't need to boast about their bravery,' he pointed out. 'That poor bastard is probably scared shitless, yet he's willing to go with us.'

Hailsham shrugged. 'Like us, I don't think he has a great deal of choice in the matter. He owes you his life. Tribal ethics mean he's more or less committed to you until he repays that debt. To refuse would be to invite being totally ostracized by his fellow tribesmen. The Uzbeks clearly set great store by honour.'

'Probably another reason why they're feared by many of the other groups,' Andrew said. 'People seem to find it hard to accept any culture which stays true to itself, retaining its own values. In the thirties it was the Jews. Now it's the Asians and blacks.'

Hailsham smiled gently. 'Philosopher as well as poet. You continue to surprise me, Andrew.'

'Fuck it, I surprise myself sometimes, boss,' Andrew blurted out, struggling to assert a more macho image and failing.

Hailsham stared up into the high mountains above them, noting the plumes of snow which were being whipped off the higher peaks by the swirling winds. 'Weather's getting worse up there,' he announced. 'Time to get moving.'

Andrew understood the man's reasoning well enough. Making ground into really bad weather minimized the chances of any unwelcome helicopter surveillance. It would also put them in country where any airborne drop of pursuit troops would be virtually impossible. Even so, it was a far from pleasant prospect. He nodded his assent, adding: 'I'll go and tell the men we're ready to move out. I'm sure they'll be thrilled.'

'Positively ecstatic,' Hailsham agreed, with a cynical smile. He turned to look over at Tweedledum. 'I suppose I'd better go and explain the position. Tell the men they're welcome to come and say goodbye to him if they want to.' He began to walk over towards the stricken trooper.

Despite obvious pain and trauma from his recent surgery, Tweedledum had managed to stay conscious and even forced a weak smile as Hailsham stood over him. The major felt even more confident about the young nurse's prediction that he would pull through safely.

'Hi, boss,' Tweedledum said weakly. 'I don't suppose you've come to offer me a piggyback.'

Hailsham smiled back, realizing that Tweedledum was well aware of the score. 'You've got some sick leave coming, Trooper. Won't it be nice to spend it with such friendly people?' He explained briefly the arrangements for getting him over the Mongolian border. 'You're going to be OK,' he said firmly.

Forgetting his wound for a moment, Tweedledum tried to nod, wincing with the sudden pain. He gritted his teeth, fighting to keep the brave smile on his face. 'Have a drink waiting for me in the Paludrine Club, will you?'

Hailsham nodded. 'You got it. Mind you, you might not want to come home at all. Mukhtar, the head man, tells me he's going to lend you one of his wives to keep you warm at night. And for anything else you might need, once you get your strength back.'

'And here's the even better news,' came Tweedledee's voice from behind him. 'The rest of the boys have agreed to leave you their entire condom ration as a going-away present.'

Hailsham turned, to see the men all hovering behind him, waiting to say their goodbyes. It was time to make a discreet exit, he decided.

Just as Cyclops had originally suggested, the best way forward was the fork off the pathway which Andrew's patrol had followed. Safar pointed to it as they all heaved on their bergens once again and prepared to move out.

Mukhtar and a small delegation of the Uzbek men and women had come to see them off.

'*Shchisliva*,' said the head man. 'Good luck to you.' There was no attempt at a formal handshake.

Hailsham bowed his head ceremoniously. '*Daragoy drook*,' he replied. 'Dear friend.'

One of the women stepped forward, holding out a stick on which were impaled several small skinned and fire-seared animal carcasses. It was obviously a parting gift of food, Hailsham thought, accepting it with a suitable look of gratitude. Turning away, he followed Safar down the hill away from the camp.

The Thinker looked at the distinctly unappetizing string of charred bodies with a look of distaste on his face. 'What the bloody hell are those?'

'Probably marmots,' Hailsham told him.

The corporal looked even more disgusted. 'Bloody hell,' he repeated.

Cyclops grinned at him. 'Don't turn your nose up, Thinker. What the hell do you think was in that stew you enjoyed so much?'

'Aw, Christ,' the Thinker exploded. 'Do you mean I've been eating bloody monkeys?'

Cyclops shot him a pitying look. 'You daft prat,' he said witheringly. 'You're thinking of marmosets. Marmots are burrowing rodents – sort of a cross between a squirrel and a rabbit.'

The pained look on the Thinker's face told Cyclops that he found the fine distinction no more appetizing. 'Well all I can say is I'm bloody looking forward to that fucking eagle,' the Thinker muttered thickly.

Cyclops grinned again. 'I've got to shoot the bastard first.'

They all fell silent, concentrating on keeping their balance as they started to descend the steepest part of the hill.

# 15

General Chang was in a rare complimentary mood. Used as he was to almost total subservience and efficiency, he habitually took excellence for the norm and questioned the slightest deviation from perfection. There might be some areas in which the great communist system occasionally broke down, but the military machine ran with smooth and well-oiled precision.

He regarded San Hung with a benevolent smile. 'You have done well,' he said generously, studying the report which the young lieutenant from military intelligence had just brought to his attention. 'I shall make it my business to see that a commendation goes on your record.'

San Hung did not linger to bask in this uncharacteristic warmth. Past experience had taught him that General Chang's moods could change as rapidly as a pattern of fallen leaves in the wind. With an obsequious bow, he excused himself and backed out of the room.

Chang thumbed the intercom on his desk, summoning Leng Pui, who appeared from one of the interconnecting offices as though he had been primed and waiting for the call. He, too, could not help but notice the rather smug and self-satisfied smile on his superior's face.

'You look pleased, General. Your plans continue to go well?'

Chang allowed himself a patronizing nod. 'With a bit of help from our SAS friends,' he conceded. 'They seem to be playing the game even more enthusiastically than I had hoped.' He picked up the typewritten intelligence report and handed it to the other man.

Leng Pui read the document carefully. It seemed almost trivial – merely an intercepted emergency distress call sent to the Kazakh military base in Alma-Ata some hours earlier. Under normal circumstances it might well have been filed away with dozens of other monitored messages and scraps of intelligence, but it was clear from Chang's attitude that this particular message had some special significance.

His failure to grasp that significance straight away placed Leng Pui in a somewhat awkward and vulnerable situation. Chang was obviously in a mood for praise and self-congratulation. To disappoint him by showing ignorance would not be wise.

Improvising with the sort of devious cunning he had learned from his superior, Leng Pui assumed an approving smile. 'This is excellent news,' he said, with forced enthusiasm. 'And you think the SAS are responsible?'

Chang shrugged. 'Who else could it be? Nothing we have learned has ever suggested that these mountain guerrilla groups possess a SAM capability – and we certainly have not supplied them with such. Mortars, shells and guns, yes – but nothing on this scale. Yet this distress call definitely establishes that a Kazakh military helicopter was brought down by a missile strike. Quite obviously, the SAS have chosen sides, as I fully expected them to do sooner or later.'

'But sooner being better?' Leng Pui said slyly, beginning to catch on at last.

Chang beamed at him. 'Exactly.'

'And now?' Leng Pui asked.

'And now we initiate the next move in the game,' Chang answered. 'We make sure that this information gets leaked to the appropriate Kazakh authorities. Knowing that they have a new enemy to contend with will confuse and disorientate them. Whatever moves they make to deal with it will inevitably split their already overtaxed military capabilities and weaken them.'

'Making it that much easier for our own troops to continue fomenting trouble in the border areas,' Leng Pui said, now fully appraising the situation. 'And we gain a bonus, of course. Giving them the British as a scapegoat will provide a possible explanation of why the rebel factions have been able to arm themselves so well in recent months – and, indeed, to inflict such damage.'

'You miss the most subtle, but perhaps the most important factor,' Chang pointed out, annoyed that Leng Pui had not picked it up and congratulated him. 'Creating bad relations with the British will have severe diplomatic, as well as military, repercussions. It will almost certainly affect any Russian attemps to gain economic aid and trade agreements with the European Community. So they will continue to be weak on two fronts – at the very time when our own economy is going from strength to strength. The face of war has changed, Leng Pui. Today the banknote is as formidable a weapon as the bomb.'

'But if the British should find out . . .' Leng Pui left the awful thought unspoken.

'We must ensure that they don't,' Chang said with a chilling smile. 'Whatever happens, we must appear to be completely innocent in all this. Which is why the SAS must never return from this mission alive.

'And if they do?'

'Then we shall have to kill them ourselves,' said Chang with a shrug. 'A helicopter or transport-aircraft crash on the way back to the Tacheng base. A tragic accident – or even better, some suggestion of a Kazakh attack – might suit our purpose best.'

Chang looked directly into Leng Pui's eyes, seeking admiration and finding it. His expansive mood bordered on euphoria. 'I shall entrust you with the task of leaking this disinformation to Kazakh sources,' he said, as though he were offering the man some rare and precious gift. 'But you must be discreet, and extremely subtle. I have no wish to see my plans fail now because of clumsiness.'

Leng Pui nodded deferentially. 'You can count on me, General,' he promised.

Chang allowed himself a thin smile. 'Yes, I'm sure I can,' he murmured, knowing that his second-in-command had also walked into his intricately spun web of deceit. Now, even if the unthinkable happened and things went wrong, he had an underling to blame. It was another comforting safety-net to have beneath him now that he was walking such a high and dangerous tightrope on the world stage.

What had started out as an open mountain path had now closed in to form a tight and narrow ravine as Safar led the SAS team up into the higher mountains. Although steep, with a fairly steady incline of about thirty-five degrees, the floor of the ravine continued to be reasonably even and obstacle-free, suggesting that they were still following a regular route which was well trodden during the spring and summer months. The directness and comparative accessibility of the path had allowed them to make good and steady progress, gaining considerable distance and height in the past three hours.

But this bonus was more than balanced by a single disadvantage. The narrow ravine faced almost directly north, and acted as a natural funnel for the savage winds tearing down from the wastes of the Siberian plains. It was like trying to climb along a wind-tunnel, but with the added problem that this wind carried a body- and mind-numbing chill factor which reduced the ambient temperature to well below zero. It tore through every square inch of their protective clothing, sucking out the precious body heat created by their physical exertion.

Every yard gained was a triumph over physical torture, and there was a mental penalty to be paid as well. Like the rest, Hailsham was fully and constantly aware that it could only get progressively worse the higher they went. This knowledge clawed constantly at a man's bodily strength and mental resolve, sapping both.

With savage humour, Hailsham made a mental note to mention the place to a couple of the guys in Training Wing when they got back to Stirling Lines. It might appeal to their more sadistic inclinations. Certainly it made the 'Fan Dance' – the 40-mile endurance march up Pen-y-Fan which marked the final phase of SAS recruitment selection – seem like a summer afternoon stroll. And in terms of a 'sickener', or testing ordeal, climbing up an icy wind-tunnel was one innovation which had yet to occur to someone's nasty little mind.

It was certainly God-forsaken terrain, Hailsham thought, staring ahead of him up the seemingly endless climb towards the snowcapped mountains. He could only admire the sheer tenacity of the rugged semi-nomadic tribespeople who called this country home and found it worth fighting, even dying, for. This admiration focused on the figure of Safar 20 yards ahead of him, trudging steadily onwards with hardly a break in his step and never a backward glance. Clad in a goatskin jacket and a few tattered blankets and with only a small skull-cap to cover his head, he seemed oblivious to the cold which chilled Hailsham to the bone even through the protection of his high-tech thermal gear. Perhaps it was simply a matter of growing acclimatized, Hailsham reflected. Or maybe it was a genetic thing – generations of survival in such extreme conditions producing a thickening of the blood, or some bodily capacity to produce extra heat.

The thought depressed Hailsham, sapping his resolve to go on. They should not be here, a silent voice screamed in his brain. They did not belong in these mountains, in this country, in this stupid, logic-defying situation. He tore his eyes away from the little Uzbek guide, staring down instead at his next step, and the step after that. How many had he already taken, he wondered. How many more would he take before they reached their objective? How much longer could his body continue to dredge up new reserves of strength?

It came as almost a shock to Hailsham to suddenly realize that his mind had locked into a cyclic chain of depression and defeat. 'Stupid bastard,' he cursed himself under his breath. It was not physical strength he needed most now – it was mental stamina. He was forgetting the most basic rules of endurance survival. More importantly, he was forgetting his men, and their psychological needs. They must be suffering the same mental and physical anguish, and indeed it was probably worse for the youngsters like Barry and Tweedledee. He fought to clear all negative thoughts from his head, concentrating on the positive aspects of what they had achieved so far. Positive reinforcement – that was the key phrase that the psychology boys liked to use a lot when they were discussing continuation and cross-training exercises.

Hailsham broke step, coming to an abrupt halt and turning to look back down the steep incline behind him. The steppe was far below and behind them now, their original drop point an invisible spot beyond the horizon. His men were strung out at irregular intervals back along the ravine, looking isolated, fatigued and every bit as dispirited as he himself had been. It was time, he decided, to give the men an opportunity to recharge their mental and physical batteries with a short rest and the chance of some comradeship and shared humour. He held his ground as Cyclops, the Thinker and Tweedledee trudged wearily to join him. Barry and Jimmy were still a good 50 yards behind them, with Andrew the straggling backmarker, still encumbered by the crippling weight of the Stinger on top of his formidable personal burden.

The major waited until they were all clustered around him again, and then faced forwards to check on Safar. The Uzbek guide had got the message now, and had come to a halt about 60 yards ahead of them. Realizing that a rest had been called, he started to backtrack slowly to join them.

'Tea break, boss?' Cyclops asked. 'I could do with a nice hot cuppa. Hope somebody remembered to bring the fucking kettle.'

'Dunno about the kettle, but the poor old sarge looks like he's carrying the bleeding kitchen sink,' Jimmy observed as Andrew finally staggered in to join them.

It was Hailsham's cue to tap the heavy missile launcher slung across Andrew's broad back. 'Time to ditch it, Andrew,' he murmured. 'We said the lower foothills, remember?'

Andrew put on a brave face. 'It's all right, boss. I can manage it for a while longer,' he insisted.

'We could take turns,' the Thinker suggested. 'It's been a pretty handy little tool to have along, so far.'

Hailsham gave the idea only fleeting consideration, finally shaking his head. The climb ahead of them could only get more demanding, the weather conditions worse. It was important for the men's morale that they perceive the task ahead of them as getting easier, not ever harder. Shedding excess weight now would help to give them all that much-needed boost.

The decision made, Hailsham was adamant. 'The Stinger stays here,' he said firmly. 'We'll cache it, along with all the spare missiles the rest of you are carrying and any other non-essentials.'

'Christ, boss, we're travelling bloody light as it is,' the Thinker pointed out. 'There ain't much else we can ditch, is there?'

Hailsham shrugged, conceding that the corporal had a point. 'Maybe not,' he agreed. 'But shed what you can. We're going to need to be as light-footed as mountain goats in another day or so. The less energy we waste now, the easier it will be when the going really gets tough.'

To start the ball rolling, Hailsham stripped off his own bergen and rummaged through his basic equipment, discarding what few bits and pieces he considered reasonably expendable. The others followed suit, and in a few minutes there was a small pile at the side of the ravine.

'Wonder what the bye-laws round here are like for littering?' Jimmy said. 'We don't want to upset the locals, do we?'

'I expect they're already pissed off, what with all those bits of junk from the helicopter scattered all over their nice clean mountains,' answered Barry, raising a smile. 'And talking of dumping stuff, how do we have a crap without freezing our arses off?'

'Do it in your pants,' Jimmy suggested. 'It might help to keep your balls warm. Only stay downwind from me, that's all.'

'Wouldn't have thought it would bother you,' Barry retorted. 'You're full of crap already.'

Hailsham smiled to himself as the lavatorial humour served its traditional purpose of lightening the men's spirits. The rest break was obviously having its intended effect. He busied himself dragging all the bergens into a pile across the width of the narrow footpath. Heaped one on top of the other, they made a partially effective windbreak. Hailsham squatted down behind it, grateful for its shelter.

'Why don't we all sit down and have a cosy little cuddle?' he said with a leer. 'And if you're all really good boys I'll tell you the story about the whore and the donkey in Kuwait City.'

'Which one did you fancy then, boss?' Jimmy shot back. But he took Hailsham's suggestion at face value, sitting down and pressing himself up against his superior officer in the lee of the makeshift windbreak. The idea caught on quickly. Tweedledee, Andrew, Barry, Cyclops and the Thinker joined them gratefully, squatting down in a tight little circle and huddling together to pool their precious body warmth.

Nobody thought of inviting Safar, who seemed content to sit on his own in the teeth of the wind, studying them with a faintly pitying smile.

# 16

It was with mixed feelings that Major Osipov studied the latest piece of intelligence intercepted by the Alma-Ata military base. While on the surface it appeared to offer him a perfect chance to act on his own initiative, he was all too aware of the possible dangers of sticking his neck out. Premier Kuloschow might be weak as a politician, and lacking any vestige of respect within the military, but he still had strong Party connections, some of whom still wielded considerable power behind the scenes. The time and circumstances for a military coup were rapidly ripening, but had yet to reach their best season for plucking. To bite too deeply, too soon, could be to taste the hard sourness of unripened fruit instead of the soft succulence of sweet flesh.

Osipov made a mental effort to control the impetuosity which fuelled his boundless ambition. For once, it would do no harm to err on the side of caution, bide his time until he had more pieces of the strange jigsaw puzzle which had been thrown down in front of him. For if, as the coded message suggested, the British SAS had now become involved, then he would need to be very sure of his ground before making any move at all. It was not even certain that the information was genuine. Perhaps it was nothing more than a deliberately leaked piece of disinformation put out by the Chinese for reasons of their own. Certainly that would not be a new trick, or a ruse which had not succeeded in the past. Much as Osipov despised the Chinese, he had a healthy respect for their cunning. In truth, they were a worthy enemy, which only sweetened the game.

Osipov considered the matter objectively. It was clear that he needed more answers, which, paradoxically, meant that he first needed more questions. But who to ask? Where to start looking? His whole body tensed with the sheer frustration of it all. For Kuloschow was probably nearer to the essential information than anyone, even though he was probably still unaware of it. And to give the politician the slightest hint that the mysterious research facility in the Sailyukem Mountains might be the key to something of international importance would be to show his own hand prematurely, and lose the initiative which he had now gained.

That the research station *was* the key to the mystery, Osipov no longer had any doubts. Whether the Chinese message was genuine or not made little difference. The fact remained that a military assault helicopter had been destroyed while on a routine surveillance mission – and that made it a military matter demanding a military response. And in that response lay the means to achieve his own ends – simple, direct and myopically brutal. For given a credible pretext, Osipov felt sure that he could justify an all-out genocidal war against the Birlik and any of the other rebel factions which threatened the fragile status quo. It would be a move which would at once restore the morale and the ambition of the military hierarchy who even now were poised for a return to the power and the glories of the old regime. And Major Yuri

Osipov would be at the head of that power, the triumphant returning warrior in whose face all that glory was reflected.

That, in essence, was the crux of Osipov's grandiose but essentially simple plan. It also incorporated his essential weakness, his own personal blind spot. For his thinking was strictly conditioned by the limitations of his military training and background. There had never been anything else. He saw everything in direct and simplistic terms. The roots of power lay in strength and control, and the only reference point was the strength of the old and familiar past. His conditioning, both by his military upbringing and his political convictions, left little room for any understanding of diplomacy, certainly not any acceptance of its possible role in the scheme of things. The major was ill-equipped to deal with even the basic politics of a simple and authoritarian regime, let alone the increasingly complex, fragmented and subtle influences now at work within an embryonic democracy. So he simply ignored them. It was a philosophy which, up till now, had always worked well enough.

Osipov returned his full attention to the business of the intelligence report and how he was going to use it to his best advantage. It was decided, then, that he would keep the information from Premier Kuloschow, at least for the time being. With that as a starting point, his primary task seemed clear enough. Somehow he had to find out more about the suddenly important Phoenix Project and what might possibly lie behind the wall of secrecy which surrounded it. Until he had some answers on that score, any questions as to the reasons behind the involvement of the British SAS were superfluous.

Which brought him back to his original problem: where to start looking. Someone must have access to the information he needed. His own military intelligence seemed to be the most logical place to initiate the search. It was, after all, inconceivable that the secretive structure of his own system could work against him. Surely the slave could never be turned against the master – even in these turbulent times. Secure in this conviction, Osipov applied himself to the task in hand.

The storm seemed to fall down from the overhanging mountains with the sudden ferocity of a surprise mortar attack. One moment Hailsham and his men were huddled together against the icy blast of a strong but steady wind. The next they were engulfed by elemental forces of unbelievable fury. The wind no longer seemed to have a definite direction. It wheeled and whirled above them like a demonic, crazed, living thing – out of control and seemingly hell-bent on destroying any other form of life which dared to defy it. Swirling, cyclonic gusts approaching eighty miles an hour ripped first along the length of the narrow ravine and then quartered to roar across its width, creating within the trench a temporary vacuum which sucked the very breath out of their mouths and lungs as it scoured the ravine floor and drew up grit and small rocks with the force of missiles.

Rolling waves of thick black cloud gathered from nowhere to hang like a blanket over their heads. Day was suddenly night, but a night which was pierced every few seconds by the blinding glare of sheet and streak lightning raging both above and between the higher mountains. Each flash was almost immediately followed by the deafening clap of thunder and the rolling echoes which followed it, confirming that they were in the very eye of the storm.

Hailsham's limited knowledge of meteorology told him that the storm was caused by a sudden and severe temperature inversion and not uncommon to mountainous regions. This piece of information led inevitably to two further conclusions – one good, one bad. Although among the most violent and destructive of all weather extremes, such storms were essentially short-lived, sometimes lasting only a few minutes. But they were almost certain to lead to a further temperature inversion, bringing savage cold and the strong likelihood of blizzard conditions in their wake. With the reasonable expectancy that the fierce winds would persist for several hours after the actual storm had subsided, the wind-chill factor would be horrendous, and heavy snow and drifting could soon turn the mountain path which had been their friend into a new and terrible enemy. Already the bucketing mix of hail, sleet and freezing rain was beginning to churn up the floor of the ravine, threatening to turn the steep incline ahead of them into one vast mud-slide.

To stand up and remain upright for more than a few seconds would have been virtually impossible, so Hailsham did not even try. With considerable effort, he managed to drag himself towards Safar on his hands and knees, his body rocked from side to side by the buffeting winds. The little Uzbek had dropped from his exposed position on a large flat rock at the first sight of the looming clouds, and was now curled, foetus-like, beneath its scant shelter.

Hailsham curled up beside him. Normal conversation, even shouting, was out of the question above the roar of the wind and the now almost continuous thunder. Cupping his hands around the man's ear, Hailsham used them as a megaphone.

'We've got to get out of here,' he shouted in Russian. 'Can we make it to anywhere more sheltered?'

Safar appeared to think for a few moments, finally nodding his head. Mutely, he pointed further up along the ravine in the direction they had been travelling and then closed and opened both hands, extending all his fingers stiffly. It was a gesture which was obviously meant to convey the number ten, Hailsham realized. But whether the man meant ten kilometres, ten miles or ten minutes' travelling time was unclear. He shouted again into Safar's ear: 'I don't understand.'

The young man uncurled himself, copying Hailsham's improvised ear-trumpet technique. 'There is a cave. Perhaps ten minutes from here. But we will have to climb to it. It will not be easy.'

Whipping hailstones stung Hailsham's face like shotgun pellets. He could almost feel the air temperature dropping again, as the expected inversion started to take place. Soon the hail and sleet would start to give way to driving snow and they would all be trapped in a total white-out. There was really no choice: they had to make a move and they had to make it now. He jabbed one finger up the ravine, nodding his head. Turning, he began to scramble back towards the huddled knot of his men as Safar attempted to push himself to his feet.

Heads bowed, the tight circle of troopers looked for all the world like a bunch of Buddhist monks crouched in prayer. Only Jimmy dared to look up as Hailsham slithered into the group. Teeth gritted against the rasping wind and the sting of hail, the Scot tried to contort his face into a grin.

'Fucking hell, boss – and I thought the weather in the Highlands was changeable,' he screamed out at the top of his voice, but the words were snatched away on the teeth of the wind.

Hailsham made no attempt to shout, merely signalling the intention to move out with a complicated series of hand gestures which would have put a mime artist to shame. They served their purpose well enough. With a series of shoves and nudges, the message was passed around the huddled circle and the men started to struggle to their feet and retrieve their stacked bergens.

Picking up the heavy and unwieldy backpacks was one thing; trying to put them on again was something else. The men might just as well have been attempting to light cigarettes under water. As fast as a man managed to hook his bergen over one shoulder, a blast of wind would catch against it and either sweep it over his head or throw man and backpack to the ground together. It might have been funny in a silent film; here it was merely a useless and painful waste of energy. As was so often the case in times of shared difficulty, the only answer lay in teamwork. Sorting themselves into twos and threes, the men helped each other to shrug on their backpacks and equipment until they were all fully laden again and ready to move out.

Hailsham had hoped that the additional weight of the bergens would give them all a little more stability. Instead they created a larger area of wind resistance, and the two opposing forces more or less cancelled each other out. Crouched over like a small band of misshapen dwarves, the men fell into a ragged line behind Hailsham and began to shamble up the increasingly treacherous floor of the ravine path. Virtually no one managed to remain on both feet for more than a few moments at a time. Before they had covered a quarter of a mile, all were caked in thick mud, soaked through and bruised from frequent and painful contact with the ground, the rocky sides of the ravine, or each other. Their senses numbed by the ear-splitting crashes of thunder and the roaring wind, and physically exhausted by the uphill struggle and the constant battle for a decent lungful of air, they had only the harshness of their survival training to drive them on in conditions where lesser men might have given up any hopes of survival.

Not that similar thoughts did not occur to them, training or no training. Perhaps for the third time in as many minutes, Hailsham considered calling a halt to the agonizingly slow forward march and huddling down again in the hopes of sitting out the storm. But common sense and a dogged determination to survive prevailed each time, and he forced his unwilling feet to shuffle on, one leaden step at a time. Apart from the physical difficulty of forward movement, the element of mental frustration was itself challenging. He might take ten or so forward steps before one foot slipped on a patch of icy mud, or a savage gust of wind from an unexpected quarter knocked him sideways. Then it would be a question of scrabbling with hands and fingernails against the slippery floor of the ravine, trying to arrest the downhill and backward slide which would rob him of the few precious feet he had gained. But slowly progress was made, and the small party dragged itself on towards its unknown goal as the storm continued to rage about them.

The mountain path began to widen out, the enclosing walls of the ravine becoming less high. With this diminishing protection came a new challenge which seemed wildly out of proportion to the comparatively minor change in the surrounding terrain. The wind assaulted them now with renewed fury, forming an invisible wall across their path. Ahead of him, Hailsham could see the slight figure of Safar pressed forward at a seemingly impossible angle, as though he were a puppet suspended on wires. Straining into the teeth of the gale, his feet scrabbling along the slimy floor of the path, he looked like a mime artist telling the tale of a man suddenly confronted with a huge but imaginary plate-glass window. Only when the fierce wind abruptly dropped, or veered off in another direction for a split second, was it possible for the little Uzbek to make any forward movement at all – and that would only be in clumsy, lurching steps which might take him all of three or four feet before the invisible obstacle returned to block his progress once again.

It was obvious that Safar was finding the task beyond him. Crouching down even lower and pushing his broad shoulders into the wall of wind like a rugby player scrumming down, Hailsham threw himself forward with dredged-up reserves of energy, gradually closing the gap between them. Motioning over his back with one arm, Hailsham urged the rest of the men to close ranks behind him, tightening up from a strung-out, ragged line into a physically connected knot of brawn, muscle and sinew. Their combined weight and force seemed to make quite a difference. Rather like a tug-of-war team in reverse, they began to make steady forward progress once again, pushing the blanket-clad Safar out in front of them like a colourful standard.

Another seven or eight minutes of struggling along in this concerted fashion brought them to a place where the path opened out even wider, dipping down to form a shallow bowl at the base of a massive and towering pinnacle of rock. Grateful for the limited amount of shelter it provided, the entire party collapsed weakly in the lee of the cliff-like rock to regain some strength.

The raging eye of the storm seemed to have passed over them now. Hailsham found himself counting off the seconds between lightning flashes and the thunderclaps which followed, applying the old formula of five seconds to a mile. The interval between light and sound was clearly noticeable now, and extending rapidly. Hailsham estimated that the centre of the storm was now at least three-quarters of a mile behind them, and moving away at a speed of around forty miles an hour. Conversation was now possible again, provided it was conducted at fairly close range in short, shouted bursts.

'Where now?' he yelled to Safar.

The man's swarthy face cracked into the semblance of a grin. Glancing upwards, he jabbed one finger vertically into the air along the line of the almost sheer rock face towering over their heads.

'Jesus Christ!'

Hailsham's explosive curse was delivered for his own benefit, but for some reason it seemed to increase Safar's sense of amusement. Grinning like a monkey, he shook his head from side to side as if to offer Hailsham some welcome reassurance.

'Easy,' the Uzbek blurted out. 'I show you easy way.' He pressed his back against the rocky wall behind him and began to push himself to his feet again. Beckoning for Hailsham to follow him, he started to edge along the base of the pinnacle to where it disappeared behind a couple of huge, weather-worn boulders.

The base of the rock face began to curve to the right. Following Safar around it, Hailsham finally saw the reason for the guide's enthusiasm: a giant jagged cleft in the main structure of the massif which cleaved almost vertically upwards. The effect was to create a vast chimney which was more than generously provided with craggy outcrops forming a crude but negotiable stairway. Looking up it, Hailsham tried to estimate its height – a calculation somewhat complicated by the fact that the cleft tapered towards the top, distorting the natural sense of perspective which would have allowed a true assessment. He guessed that the main fissure rose a good three hundred feet before narrowing into little more than a split in the rock. Seen from this level, the last thirty feet or so looked like being a rather tight squeeze for an average-sized man. Hailsham could not help feeling slightly dubious, particularly when he considered the Thinker's bulky frame.

He gestured up towards the top, shouting to Safar. 'How wide?' he asked, moving his outspread hands in from arm's length to just over a foot apart.

Safar held out his hands about eighteen inches apart. 'Is easy,' he insisted again. 'Even for big man.'

The Uzbek seemed to be confident enough, Hailsham decided. No doubt he had used the chimney before, either as an emergency escape route or a temporary bolt-hole. Assuming he was right, even the Thinker or Andrew should have no trouble in squeezing through the narrow gap, although they would all have to take off their bergens and equipment before starting the climb.

Jimmy had slithered up to join them. He looked up, following Hailsham's point of view to the top of the cleft and smiling happily. 'Stairway to Heaven,' he shouted almost exultantly.

Hailsham failed to understand the Scot's obvious enthusiasm for a moment, finally remembering that rock climbing and mountaineering were his favourite forms of leisure pursuit. On his periods of leave, he did this sort of thing for fun. There was no accounting for taste.

'You crazy bastard,' Hailsham yelled at him. 'You're actually going to enjoy this, aren't you?'

Jimmy nodded, his eyes gleaming. 'Want me to lead?' It was a request rather than an offer.

'Too bloody right,' Hailsham screamed back. 'Only let Safar up first. He will be at the top by the time we get our bergens roped up. Each man will have to pull them through behind him, but it shouldn't be too much of a problem.'

'I'll go back and get the others organized,' Jimmy shouted, turning and beginning to edge back round the rock face. Hailsham turned his attention to Safar, jerking his head upwards in a clear gesture for him to start climbing. Stepping into the wide base of the fissure, the little Uzbek jumped onto the first flat ledge of protruding outcrop and began to clamber up the chimney. Hailsham watched him progress steadily with almost primate-like agility, marvelling yet again at the man's apparent ability to tap new reserves of energy.

The major began stripping off his assault rifle and bergen, opening it to take out a coil of thin but tough nylon cord. He secured the SA-80 butt upwards and then slung the heavy bergen beneath it. The rope was only two hundred feet long, but each man carried his own coil. Any two of them tied together should be more than enough for the job, Hailsham figured. By working on the chain principle, adding a new length every time someone retrieved their equipment, they would be able to hoist all the equipment up without facing the problem of how to lower a flaccid rope back down through the convoluted and craggy sides of the chimney.

Jimmy reappeared round the curve of the rock face, leading the rest of the men. He lashed his own rope to the end of Hailsham's, then secured the free end tightly around his waist. Waiting only for a curt nod of approval from the major, he followed Safar's lead and started the ascent.

Although physically demanding, the climb was not technically difficult. Even the final stage, which required a certain amount of bodily contortion to get through the narrowest of the crevices, was not beyond the ability of a reasonably fit man with a head for heights. To the SAS troopers, their bodies hardened to peak fitness, it was little more than a routine exercise.

Cyclops, the last man to come up, hauled up his gun and bergen and untied them both, deftly coiling his rope again and returning it to its allotted place. Hailsham considered their new situation. Somewhere on the way up, what had looked like a single and isolated pinnacle of rock at the bottom had merged into the next ridge of mountain behind it. The top of the chimney had opened out onto a wide, flat ledge, which in turn gave way to a narrow pass which seemed to have been slashed out of the mountain with a horizontal, scythe-like sweep. It was an odd-looking formation, and Hailsham could not even guess at the geological forces which could have created it.

Now that they were clear of the chimney, they were all fully exposed to the full force of the elements once again, whose fury showed no signs of diminishing. Although the thunder and lightning had all but ceased, the winds were as savage as ever, and the ambient temperature had dropped dramatically. Obviously the secondary temperature inversion was well under way. All of a sudden the downpour of sleet and rain ceased, to be replaced by a swirling white blanket of fat, sticky snowflakes. Within seconds, it was virtually impossible to pick out any feature more than a few feet away. Hailsham could only hope that Safar knew the terrain intimately, for any further progress now would be almost blind.

The men all pressed themselves in to the deepest part of the ledge, uncomfortably and acutely aware that any one of the violent and unpredictable gusts of wind which constantly clawed along the ledge could suck them from it at any moment and toss them back down the express route of the three-hundred-foot climb they had just negotiated. With knowledge like that, having his back to a solid wall of rock gave a man some degree of consolation.

In view of the dangers, Hailsham thought about ordering the men to rope themselves together, then decided that would be equally risky. Any safety factor was likely to be outweighed by the fact that they were all physically weak from the exertion of the recent climb and their senses dulled by the constant onslaught of the weather. If one man went off the edge, it was more than possible that the next one in line would simply have neither the strength to absorb the sudden strain nor the speed of reaction to do the right thing in the first vital second. In that case, there was every chance that they would all plunge to their deaths without a prayer. All in all, it was probably better that every man took his own chances, Hailsham decided. He had sufficient faith in each one of them to know that they were as much aware of the potential dangers as he was.

Wet snow plastered Hailsham's face mask and goggles, obscuring his vision completely. He clawed at the tinted plastic covering his eyes, managing to improve his immediate field of vision to a misty yellowish blur in which he could just about see nearby shapes. Safar's blanket-swathed form appeared as a vaguely ovoid patch of brighter colour against the general dull ochre. Very gingerly, Hailsham picked his way past two other figures, which he took to be Andrew and Jimmy, and pressed his mouth to the side of Safar's face as it finally came into rough focus.

'How far to this cave?' he yelled.

'Very near,' came the shouted reply. 'Perhaps thirty yards, no more. I will lead the way.'

Hailsham shook his head violently. 'No,' he shouted, emphatically. Reaching up, he pressed Safar's head with his fingers, turning it in the direction of Jimmy, standing next to them. 'You follow him, as close as you can.'

Meekly, Safar nodded his head in assent, without understanding Hailsham's reasoning, which was essentially simple. The Uzbek guide, being the smallest and lightest of any of them, was the most vulnerable, Hailsham figured. And Jimmy was the most experienced mountaineer in the party. It seemed only logical that he should lead.

The Scot, having overheard the shouted exchange, slipped neatly into his role. Keeping his back still firmly pressed against the rock face, he began to move along the ledge, testing each step with a cautious probe of his left foot before transferring his weight to it. Safar, followed by Andrew and then Hailsham, moved in his wake, their arms outstretched against the rock behind them so that their fingertips were almost touching. Only the sheer size of the blurry figure next to him told Hailsham that the Thinker was the next man on his immediate right. He had no idea of the order of the rest of the men following, although it was really of no importance. Perhaps exercising more caution than was strictly necessary, the windswept party made slow but steady progress along the ledge.

A sudden yell from Jimmy came out of the swirling white fog for a brief second before the sound was snatched away on the wind: 'I think I see something.'

Even as Hailsham turned sideways, a sudden and particularly fierce gust struck him full in the face as the wind changed direction again and blew directly against the main rock face. The immediate after-effect was to cause a strong back-draught which temporarily sucked the blinding snow away from the ledge like a giant vacuum cleaner. In a few moments of comparatively clear vision, Hailsham was able to see the mouth of the cave as a dark gash against the overall greyish-white of the mountain. He could even make out the look of triumph on Jimmy's face as he stepped in front of the cave's mouth and began to turn towards it.

Above the howl of the roaring winds, the staccato burst of gunfire from a Russian AK-47 hit them all with almost physical shock. For the merest fraction of a second before the blizzard closed back again, Hailsham saw Jimmy's body lifted clear off its feet by the force of the dozen or so slugs which chewed into his upper torso and threw him backwards over the lip of the ledge. The screaming wind drowned out the faint sounds of the trooper's body bouncing off a series of rocky outcrops on its way to the ground below.

Shock might well have frozen another man in his tracks. For Hailsham, it merely triggered off the lightning responses which had been programmed and reinforced by a lifetime of training. He reacted instantly. No longer concerned with caution, he threw himself past the still figures of Andrew and Safar, rolling his body along the rock face until he was a matter of inches from the mouth of the cave. His fingers were already clawing at his webbing, deftly unhooking a stun grenade and transferring it to his right hand, where he pulled the pin. Counting off the vital seconds, he jumped momentarily into the entrance of the cave and tossed the 'flash-bang' in, rolling back against the shelter of the solid rock face again in one smooth, fluid movement.

Even in such a moment of sudden and terrible crisis, Hailsham's mind was still making rational decisions. He could have chosen a fragmentation grenade, or he could have simply unhooked the nearest one, not knowing or caring which type it was. But the stun grenade was a deliberate choice. Jimmy's death was something which was over and done with. It was not an act which immediately cried for vengeance. One trooper was dead – but six remained alive. Hailsham's responsibility was to them now. Whoever was in the cave, he needed them alive, not dead, for it was impossible to get information from a corpse.

The grenade exploded with an echoing roar. The mouth of the cave belched light and smoke, the force of the explosion clearing a dark vortex in the blizzard. Hailsham swung his SA-80 into position and threw himself into the cave, his keen eyes sweeping the interior. The dull, greenish glow of a chemical light aided him as he made a lightning assessment. Even as Andrew jumped in behind him ready to provide covering fire, he had identified the position and harmlessness of the two occupants and was moving towards them, his finger on the trigger.

The two men, both natives, lay sprawled and motionless on the floor of the cave, temporarily concussed by the effects of the grenade. Hailsham jumped forward, kicking away the AK-47 and the much older PPS-43 which lay beside their bodies.

He waved the business end of the SA-80 menacingly as the first man groaned faintly and began to stir. His finger positively itched against the cold metal of the trigger. Now that the moment of crisis had passed, and his cold logic had been followed through, a wave of pure emotion swept through his body: anger, and sorrow, at the sheer tragedy and futility of Jimmy's death tore at his guts and brain. An eye for an eye, a tooth for a tooth. The compulsion to pull the trigger and rip both men to bloody shreds of flesh and bone was so strong that it threatened to overwhelm him completely.

Strangely, it was the sound of the rest of the troopers pouring into the cave behind him and the massed click of cocked weapons which helped him to remain calm.

'Hold your fire,' Hailsham heard himself bark. His finger eased off on the trigger as the second man began to revive and pull himself up into a sitting position, staring up at the sudden invaders with a look of sheer terror in his eyes.

'Who the hell are they?' Andrew asked, the question tailing off into a faint sigh of despair.

'Kazakh,' Safar spat out, total hatred and venom in his voice. He rattled off a short and highly impassioned speech in Russian which caught Hailsham unawares. Long before he had managed an effective translation, the little Uzbek had thrown himself forward and was reaching under the folds of his blankets.

Too late, Hailsham realized his intention. In a matter of seconds Safar had produced a wicked-looking knife and had dropped to his knees in front of the two captives. With two savage, sweeping strokes, he had slit both their throats.

The Uzbek climbed to his feet again, turning towards Hailsham and Andrew with a happy smile on his face. It was an expression which begged gratitude and admiration, much like a young puppy who has just taken his first crap outside the house. His sparkling eyes clouded with confusion at the major's look of hopeless anger.

With a heavy sigh, Hailsham let his weapon droop towards the ground. He turned to glance at Andrew, his teeth gritted in a gesture of utter frustration.

'Goddammit – I wanted them alive,' he muttered helplessly. 'They could have given us valuable intelligence about whatever other guerrilla forces are out there.'

Andrew glanced down dispassionately at the two bloody corpses. 'It appears our little Uzbek friend knew something about them,' he observed.

Hailsham nodded, remembering Safar's brief speech before dispatching the two Kazakhs. 'He seems to think they were part of the raiding party which carried out the massacre in their village recently. This ethnic hatred thing obviously cuts both ways.'

'So what do you think they were doing here on their own?' Andrew mused. 'An advanced scouting party, do you reckon?'

Hailsham grunted. 'Bloody good question. Wish I had the answer. If there are any more of these bastards about, I was hoping to know about it. They obviously shoot first and ask questions afterwards.'

Cyclops was bending over the two bodies, admiring Safar's knifework. He was obviously impressed. 'Sweeney Todd couldn't have done a neater job,' he murmured, turning to the Uzbek. 'Nice one, Safar. If I ever do get to shoot that bloody eagle, you can chop its fucking head off.'

Although he did not understand the words, Safar was quick to pick up the suggestion of praise he had been seeking earlier. He grinned again, for the first time in the last few minutes.

'What shall we do with the bodies, boss?' Cyclops asked. 'They ain't going to be much company if we're staying around for a while.'

Hailsham nodded towards the mouth of the cave. 'Just drag 'em out and drop 'em over the edge,' he replied. 'There's not much else we can do.'

The Thinker stepped forward to help carry the two dead Kazakhs to the edge of the ledge and dispose of them. Afterwards he walked back to the thick pool of blood on the floor and made a vain attempt to cover the gory patch up with dirt with the sole of his boot. Failing, he unzipped himself and pissed over the floor.

Tweedledee let out a low groan of disgust. 'You dirty bastard,' he complained. 'We've probably got to kip in here tonight.'

The Thinker was unrepentant. 'More hygienic,' he muttered, justifying his action. 'One of the bastards might have had AIDS or something.'

Tweedledee was not impressed with this dubious logic. 'So we settle for a dose of the bloody clap instead, do we?' he demanded sarcastically. 'Well I know where *you're* dossing down, that's for bloody sure.'

Normally Hailsham would have let the harmless banter go. This time, however, he responded with unaccustomed edginess. 'All right you two, knock it on the head,' he snapped. He walked quickly to the mouth of the cave and peered out. Even through the white-out of the blizzard, it was clear that the daylight was fading. They had made it to the shelter of the cave just in time. 'OK, so we basha down here for the night,' he announced curtly. 'We'll grab some scran now and then get a decent night's kip. We'll need to be on our toes tomorrow.'

Andrew rummaged through his bergen and fished out the stick of preserved marmot. Only partially cooked, unflavoured and stone cold, it was chewy and barely palatable, but no one complained. Jimmy's death, and Hailsham's sombre mood, had subdued them all. They ate in strained silence. The Scot's name was never mentioned. It was the unspoken law. He would not even exist again for any of them until his name appeared on a clock-tower plaque back in Hereford.

# 17

Major Osipov had not been as discreet as he imagined. More importantly he had overlooked one small thing, in what was to prove a fatal error of judgement. In his contempt for Premier Kuloschow he had failed to grasp the essential nature of the man himself. For while he might be militarily, even diplomatically naïve, Kuloschow was not a fool. And he was at heart a politician, naturally endowed with the devious cunning of that breed.

At best, politics was an exposed and vulnerable profession. Even in the most stable and well established of systems, sudden and dramatic change could sweep up through the levels of power without warning, and with lightning speed. What might begin as a small pebble dropped into a seemingly calm pond had created a huge ripple by the time it reached the shore. And in the chaotic fragility which had followed the break-up of the former Soviet Union, such ripples could easily grow into huge waves which smashed down everything in their path. There could be no defence – only some sort of early-warning system which would detect that first tiny disturbance.

The other fundamental rule of politics was that the man at the top could easily become the most vulnerable – unless he did something to protect himself. The astute politician was aware of that fact and made preparations accordingly. Kuloschow was no exception to this rule. Although raw in actual experience, he was well versed in the theory of political power.

'The buck stops here,' as the Americans liked to say. It was not strictly true, of course, since it presupposed a man being careless or stupid enough to let the buck get that far in the first place. Or lacking the foresight to put in place a series of measures which could deflect that buck from its path.

Major Osipov had failed to grasp any of this. His 'discreet' enquiries through military intelligence into the buried secrets of the Phoenix Project had been the original pebble in the pond. Premier Kuloschow's strategically placed chain of spies and informers had detected the first ripple and passed on a warning. This in turn had set in motion an inexorable series of events which could end only one way.

There was a perfect phrase to describe this phenomenon. The Russian peoples dearly liked to believe that it had originated in the roots of their own colourful language. Roughly translated, that phrase was: the shit's about to hit the fan.

Kuloschow had few illusions about the precise nature of his own position. He was little more than a figure-head, and probably only a temporary one at that. He was premier in name only – a purely titular office in which he danced, puppet-like, to another's hand on the strings. And it was to that hand that Kuloschow now had to turn.

It was ironic, even slightly insane. For all the cataclysmic upheaval which continued to sweep through Eastern Europe, very little had actually changed. Economic reforms, political moves and counter-moves, optimistic talk of democracy and

Western treaties aside, one thing remained constant. The old ideas still ruled, the former regime was still in place and poised to resume its control of power at any time. The old guard had not been dismantled or swept away. They had merely gone undercover, biding their time until the moment was right to re-emerge and assume their former power once again.

Kuloschow was aware of all this, and the knowledge both limited and channelled his possible courses of action. Osipov had unwittingly opened a can of worms, and that action had caused the ripples which had alerted Kuloschow. Now he, in turn, had felt forced to pursue the same delicate matter at a higher level. In this process of escalation, the ripples had become the very waves which Kuloschow recognized and feared. Hidden powers and men with dark secrets foresaw the threat and took steps to pull its teeth. Power put trust in power; strength relied on strength. The hidden men appealed to their oldest ally – the military. Through Major Osipov.

Thus, in a bizarre twist of fate, the snake had taken its own tail between its fangs and bitten it. The circle was closed.

Andrew awoke to the first grey fingers of light creeping into the gloom of the cave. He rose quietly, careful not to disturb any of the other sleepers around him. Stepping gingerly over the bodies huddled closely together for warmth, he walked to the mouth of the cave to survey the new morning.

Although it was still bitterly cold, the storm had completely abated and the winds had dropped to little more than an erratic stiff breeze. A few flakes of snow fluttered down from the leaden sky, but otherwise it promised to be a calm, if not pleasant, day. Andrew luxuriated in a few precious and rare moments of privacy and peace before looking up into the mountains and their final objective, seeing with the eyes of a soldier but the soul of a poet. The soldier saw a forbidding landscape of ravines, crevasses and treacherous, icy gradients which muttered danger and death. The poet saw the grandeur of snow-covered mountains which sang of challenge and human triumph.

Lost in such thoughts, the sergeant was completely unaware of Hailsham stepping up behind him.

'Morning, Andrew. Enjoying the view?'

Andrew turned, with a slight start of surprise. He forced a smile to his lips, masking his sense of disappointment that his private moment was over. 'Something like that,' he replied with a nod. He paused for a while as Hailsham's eyes took in the same panorama. 'What do *you* see out there, boss?'

Hailsham did not even think about the question. 'My job,' he answered simply, but it said more about him than he could possibly have realized. He walked back to his bergen and returned with his binoculars and map. Taking up the binoculars he trained them on the distant mountains again, scanning in a wide sweep until he found the two reference points he was searching for.

'How far now?' Andrew asked. 'Or perhaps more to the point, how long?'

Hailsham shrugged. 'In actual distance, probably no more than fifteen or twenty miles, as the crow flies. Trouble is, we're not crows.'

Andrew grinned weakly, still studying the same snow-capped mountains. 'Maybe just as well,' he observed. 'This is more like penguin country.' He was suddenly serious again. 'Can we make it in the next forty-eight hours, do you reckon? We're starting to get bloody close to our sell-by date.'

Hailsham sighed deeply. He did not really need reminding that they were now a full day behind their planned schedule.

Even though he had incorporated some leeway into his original plans, things were getting uncomfortably tight. Much more delay, and it would become impossible to complete the mission and get back to the rendezvous point with the Chinese in time for safe retrieval. Which would leave him with a difficult decision to make: whether to scrub the mission and beat a hasty retreat, or complete the job they had come to do and risk being stranded. Neither response would be very satisfactory – from either a personal or a professional point of view.

Safar had now woken up and come over to join them. It was perhaps bad timing on his part as Hailsham turned the burning question of the moment on him: 'How much longer?'

At least he was optimistic, Hailsham thought with a slight sense of relief. With his usual irrepressible good humour, the Uzbek could not even see a problem. 'I will take you to the next mountain plateau by evening,' he promised with an easy smile. 'From there you will be able to see the place you seek.'

'And Kazakh guerrilla forces?' Hailsham asked. 'Are we likely to encounter any hostility?'

Safar shrugged. 'If we see them, you will kill them,' he said firmly.

Hailsham was grateful for the young man's blind faith, at least. If nothing else, it went some way to alleviating some of his own doubts. For the moment, he preferred not to even think about the secondary problem of the official Kazakhstan Republican forces. Now that the storm has passed, it was surely only a matter of hours before helicopter patrols would be out looking for them. And Safar's reference to a mountain plateau had been rather disconcerting, suggesting an ideal site from which to launch a search-and-sweep operation. It would not take much military planning to set up a landing and refuelling base in a dangerously short space of time. Just two choppers and a small support team of maintenance engineers would give them the capacity to scour an area of up to fifty square miles within the next two days. The next two *vital* days, a little voice inside his head reminded him, in case he had not already realized.

Hailsham mentioned nothing of these fears to Andrew. Keeping some problems to oneself was one of the responsibilities of command. But his consideration was largely wasted, for the black sergeant had already identified and thought about the problem for himself. He had seen enough of the new morning to know that the weather was lifting fast, the heavy and low cloud cover already beginning to break up and melt away. In an hour or two it would be ideal flying weather. A reconnaissance mission was probably well under way at that very moment, with planes or helicopters already warming up on the tarmac at Alma-Ata. They might even be in the air already.

It was not a pleasant thought to dwell on, Andrew realized suddenly, pulling himself up with a mental jolt. He glanced across at Hailsham. 'So, what's Safar's verdict?' he asked.

The question snapped Hailsham out of his own gloomy thoughts. 'Sorry, I keep forgetting that you don't follow the lingo,' he apologized, quickly passing on a rough précis of Safar's information.

Andrew assimilated it with a curt nod. 'I guess the sooner we get going the better. Someone's going to be coming looking for us – and somehow I don't think they'll be bringing us morning coffee.'

Despite himself, Hailsham smiled. 'You could be right,' he conceded. 'They sure as hell won't be wanting to wish us a nice day, either.'

\* \* \*

In fact, if they had seen the sealed and coded orders which Major Osipov was at that very moment opening, they would have been as surprised and confused as he was.

Osipov read the orders carefully for the second time, just in case there was some room for misunderstanding. There was none. They were as clear and as unambiguous as they were baffling. No matter how he tried to find some hidden rationale, he failed miserably.

In fact, the instructions were so completely bizarre that Osipov might well have suspected some sort of trick. But they carried a top security coding and had come through the correct channels. Only one thing was certain: they had not passed through Premier Kuloschow's hands on the way.

# 18

For breakfast the troopers finished off the remainder of their high-calorie ration packs. It might be the last meal any of them got for some time. From now on they were on a strict survival regime, and would have to live off the barren terrain – a prospect which was not exactly promising. Thinking about it, Hailsham realized that none of them had actually noticed any signs of animal life since landing. Not that they had been specifically looking for it, of course, but it was somewhat disquieting, all the same.

At least water was no problem, Hailsham thought. He supervised the operation of packing freshly fallen snow from the ledge outside into their canteens, replenishing their dwindling reserves. Although several of the men had urinated out through the mouth of the cave before bedding down the previous night, they had all shown the foresight and consideration to aim sideways and piss with the wind behind them. Apart from which, all were sufficiently versed in mountain survival techniques to scoop up only snow which was pristine white. Rule number one, Hailsham thought to himself, recalling the phrase often echoed by ski instructors: Never eat yellow snow.

Finally, they were all packed and ready to move out. The men gathered in a knot at the entrance to the cave, obviously expecting some sort of rallying call from the boss. Hailsham did not disappoint them. He looked at them calmly but firmly.

'All right, let's get ready to move out,' he announced. 'I'm not going to call a full battle order at this point, but I want you all to be ready for a shake-out at any time. Just in case the thought hasn't already occurred to you, our two friends last night were obviously part of a guerrilla combat unit – and these particular natives are far from friendly. Whether they were a scouting unit or just a couple of stragglers, we have no way of knowing. But the strong likelihood is that there will be others in the vicinity, so keep your eyes skinned and your ears open.' Hailsham paused for a second. 'Is that clear?'

'Clear as a virgin's piss,' the Thinker murmured, with a nod. It was a comment which evoked an immediate guffaw of derisive laughter from the rest of the men.

'When the fuck did you ever meet a virgin?' Tweedledee demanded. The Mancunian grinned at him benevolently.

'A bloody sight more times than you,' he countered. 'The difference being that I didn't leave 'em in the same state.'

It was an effective put-down. Tweedledee lapsed into silence, having the good grace to know when he had been bested. He followed the others' lead in shrugging on his bergen and running a final check on his SA-80. All weapons had already been cleaned and wiped free of overnight condensation as a matter of routine.

'OK, let's hit the road,' Hailsham said. 'And watch your steps out on that ledge. I probably don't need to remind you that we had a little bit of snow last night.'

As understatements went, it was a little bit like the guy in the lounge bar of the *Titanic*: 'I know I asked for more ice in my drink, but this is ridiculous.' The previous night's blizzard had brought down well over fifteen inches of thickly packed snow. Although the high winds had blasted most of it over the side of the ledge, there were several places where an outcrop of rock, or a fissure, had provided somewhere for it to stick fast. Once started, heavy drifts had quickly built up, some of them as tall as a man and spread across the full width of the ledge. In fact, looking along the narrow route which they had to negotiate, Hailsham thought the irregular series of white mounds looked like a spaced-out sentry line of headless snowmen performing guard duty on the mountain path.

He pushed such fanciful thoughts from his head, considering the series of snowdrifts as the obstacles they actually were. Although clearing them out of the way should not be too much of a problem, it would be time-consuming and not without risk. The ledge was totally exposed, and well within rifle range of many of the surrounding peaks, and someone equipped with a half-decent telescopic sight would be able to pick them off like ducks in a shooting gallery. If there *were* any more guerrillas in the immediate vicinity, Hailsham could only hope and pray that they did not have a Cyclops among their ranks. Or indeed that their armaments did not extend to the latest laser-sighted hardware.

He was slightly surprised when Safar stepped outside the cave and turned back in the direction they had come from the previous night. Although there was no real reason for it, he had somehow expected that their route would be in the opposite direction. Double-checking, Hailsham reluctantly questioned the Uzbek guide's sense of direction.

'Why are we backtracking?'

Safar pointed along the ledge in the opposite direction and shook his head violently. 'No way on,' he explained. 'That way leads only to a sheer rock face. Impossible to climb. We must go back.'

He seemed pretty certain, Hailsham thought. With a faintly resigned shrug, he fell into step behind the guide and began to pick his way carefully over the more obvious patches of ice and snow which glistened in the diffused light of the pale morning sun. Even though the ledge was well over two feet wide at this point, it was still hazardous and nerve-racking going. Some of the frozen patches were not apparent until the men actually trod on them. Two or three times in the first twenty yards, Hailsham felt one of his feet slide out on an invisible section of black ice, or skid on some loose shale beneath the snow which had been blown down from the main face by the savage winds. At such times, he could only recover himself, shrink back into the inner part of the ledge and marvel at the fact that they had ever made it through the full fury of the storm.

Finally they reached the widest section of the ledge at the top of the chimney. Hailsham relaxed slightly, tensing again only when he glanced down the plunging fissure which they had previously climbed. In the cold light of morning, and in the aftermath of the blizzard, it was no longer a negotiable stairway between the two levels of this part of the mountain. Overnight, driven and packed snow had completely filled in the open section, turning it into a gleaming white chute in which all footholds had been totally obscured. It reminded Hailsham of a near-vertical bob-sleigh run. He glanced uncertainly at Safar, who was hovering uncomfortably around the mouth of the chimney.

'I hope you're not going to tell me that we have to go back down again,' he muttered thickly.

Much to Hailsham's relief, the little Uzbek shook his head and pointed upwards. Following the line of his finger, Hailsham's eyes took in a short, stiff but negotiable climb towards a long, ridged hog's back which stretched, he estimated, about two miles to the left. Assuming that Safar intended to lead them around it, the route then gave way to a section of rugged and broken hillocks and cols of snow-covered rock and beyond that what appeared to be a sheer rock face. It was this eventual obstacle which gave Hailsham the most cause for concern. It was difficult to judge from this distance and with the naked eye, but at a rough estimate the vertical cliff was anything from seventy to a hundred and twenty feet high and looked treacherously glassy.

Hailsham unslung his binoculars and lifted them to his eyes to take a more detailed look. It was not immediately encouraging. Seen in greater detail, the vertical rock face was indeed well over a hundred feet high, and as smooth as if it had been cleaved out with a single blow of some mighty axe. Apparently devoid of suitable hand or footholds, it looked impassable.

Hailsham scanned along the wall of rock and ice to the east, eventually identifying another one of the odd, slashed-out ledges which seemed to be a fairly common feature of this stretch of mountain. It ran horizontally for perhaps half a mile or so, then started to slope up at an increasingly steep gradient, eventually forming a small pass which led around the end of a blind ridge. Beyond that, it was impossible to even guess what lay ahead, but Safar had spoken of a plateau and Hailsham could only assume that it lay immediately above the sheer rock face. Sudden, cataclysmic subsidence millions of years ago would account for both the cliff-like drop and the broken and rugged crags below it. Satisfied with his schoolboy geology and comforted with the probability of a safe and easily negotiable route, Hailsham lowered the binoculars and glanced across at Safar once again, nodding his agreement.

'It looks OK,' he conceded.

The young man treated him to one of his cheerful grins. 'No fuckin' problem. Piece piss,' he said proudly.

Hailsham smiled to himself. The Uzbek was learning fast, he thought. By the time he got back to his own people, he would probably be able to cuss as fluently as a regular squaddie. Which might well come in useful in the future, since Tweedledum was probably at that very minute teaching the Uzbek women a few choice phrases of his own with which to enrich their native language.

Andrew and Cyclops had moved over to join them. Cyclops jerked his thumb towards the little Uzbek guide. 'Does Sherpa Tenzing here know where we're going?' he asked.

Hailsham was still smiling. 'No fuckin' problem,' he said, mimicking Safar's broken accent.

Cyclops regarded him blankly, failing to understand the humour. 'Ask a bloody silly question,' he muttered to himself moodily, sloping away to rejoin the others.

Andrew looked slightly worried, Hailsham noticed. There was obviously something on his mind. 'Care to share it with me, Andrew?' he said.

The Barbadian looked uncertain for a few moments, finally shrugging. 'I suppose I'm just a bit worried about our little reception committee last night,' he admitted finally. 'If the other direction from the cave is impassable, they can only have come down the route we're about to take up.' He broke off to nod up at the higher mountains. 'And it can't have escaped your attention that there are at least three places in that terrain up ahead which would make damned good positions for an ambush.'

Hailsham's face was suddenly serious again. 'The thought had occurred,' he said candidly. 'But your concern is noted and appreciated. However, I don't see that we have much choice in the matter. Do you? I'm always open to suggestions.'

Andrew's thick lips curled into a rueful smile. 'We could always hop on the first bus home,' he murmured. 'Failing that, I'm afraid I don't have much to offer.'

Having been reminded of the problem, Hailsham was busy thinking it all through again. He was silent for a long time, running as many permutations as he could think of through his head. Finally he spelled out what few conclusions he had come to.

'Everything rather depends on who those two were, where they came from and where they were going,' he announced. 'If they were scouts, then it's a pretty sure bet that there's a larger force somewhere up ahead of us. In which case, the chances of an ambush or an attack will depend on the strength and intentions of that force. And how they perceive us, of course. They might well consider it prudent to go into hiding and let us pass, rather than attack.' Hailsham paused. 'Right so far?'

Andrew nodded. 'Pretty well, I should think. But there's a lot of "ifs" in there, boss.'

Hailsham sucked at his teeth. 'On the other hand, they could have been two stragglers trying to reach a rendezvous point when the storm broke. If so, then the question is: were they going up – or coming down?'

'There is one other possibility,' Andrew put in, just in case Hailsham had overlooked it. 'They could have been loners – either survivors from a group which had been attacked, or a couple of deserters who'd had enough and were going home to their families.'

Hailsham let out a little snort. 'Now who's creating a lot of "ifs",' he replied, a faintly sardonic smile playing about the corners of his mouth.

The entire discussion was basically pointless, Andrew suddenly realized, grinning ruefully. Hailsham was right, of course. In the final analysis, they simply had no choice. No matter what lay ahead of them, or what might possibly happen, there was only one way forward and they had to take it.

The two men looked at each other with sheepish grins on their faces, both suddenly aware of the futility of their conversation.

'You realize that we've just wasted a good five minutes,' Andrew pointed out, rather superfluously.

Hailsham nodded. 'The thought had occurred,' he said, falling back on the phrase which had triggered the discussion in the first place.

They had made good time, covering a good three miles in just over a couple of hours. The men were in good spirits, encouraged by the reasonable ease of the climb and the weather, which could only be described as benign compared with what they had experienced previously. The temperature remained comfortably above zero, keeping the thick blanket of snow on the ground soft and light. Even where it had piled up into drifts which came up to their knees, they had little trouble ploughing through it, the leading man creating a path for the others to follow. Just to spread the strain even more, Hailsham had ordered a change in the marching order every half a mile or so. The last of the heavy cloud cover had melted away now, leaving a high and light mist of cirrus which occasionally allowed the pale, watery sun to shine through for several minutes at a time. Despite the fact that the wind had freshened slightly again, and was blowing against them along the side of the hog's back, it was a pleasant enough day for healthy outdoor activity, and the trek was bracing without being too strenuous. In another time and place, Hailsham might have considered it a jaunt rather than a mission.

Viewed at close quarters, the cliff-like rock face looked even more formidable than Hailsham had supposed. Viewed through the binoculars, which had a slightly foreshortening effect, it had appeared to be vertical, but he saw now that this was not the case. In fact, it actually cantilevered at an angle of about 110 degrees for the first twenty or thirty feet, before returning to the vertical. Great sheets and rivulets of ice festooned various parts of the face, glistening in the weak sunlight. Even the most experienced climber, armed with specialist equipment, would have found it challenging in the extreme. On the plus side, the ledge he had noticed was considerably wider than he had assumed, quickly becoming an open pathway which curved around the side of the mountain.

Hailsham focused his eyes on the spot where the pass disappeared from his line of vision, then scanned the surrounding area. The fears of an ambush he had shared with Andrew now resurfaced. If one was to come at all, that would be the place, he realized, for that particular spot was in a direct line of fire from any one of a dozen locations higher up the surrounding peaks. He found the prospect sufficiently worrying to bring the party to a halt. Outlining the situation in a few well-chosen words, he prepared the men for a heightened state of alert.

'Until we reach the plateau, you're all to consider yourselves under full battle order,' he told them. 'And that means aggressive fire, by the way. These jokers have already shown us how trigger-happy they are, so I don't want anyone playing Mr Nice Guy. If you see anything, shoot first and worry about evasive action afterwards. Is that understood?'

The question was largely rhetorical, but a rattle of cocked and primed weapons gave Hailsham any answer he might have needed. He turned his attention to Safar, who was standing immediately behind him. 'This might be a good place for you to turn back,' he murmured in a gentle but oddly insistent tone. 'You have done more than enough, and we all thank you for it. But now it might be advisable for you to return to your people.'

Hailsham saw the sense of rejection which temporarily clouded the young man's swarthy face and felt slightly guilty. The little Uzbek had understood him on a level which went far beyond the mere translation of another language. For without wanting to spell it out, Hailsham knew that Safar's continued presence was no longer needed, and might even start to become a dangerous liability. The men had taken to him almost like a favourite pet, or a mascot. In a crisis situation any one of them might act instinctively rather than rationally to protect him, thus endangering their own lives and that of the others. It was not a risk Hailsham cared to take.

There was another factor, of course. Clad in his colourful swathing of blankets, Safar made a rather tempting target. If, as with many Arabic cultures, the pattern of those blankets carried some clue to ethnic identity, then parading Safar in their midst would be like a red rag to a bull. Hailsham had already seen enough evidence of the blind and instinctive hatred between the Uzbeks and the Kazakhs to know that Safar's presence was inviting attack. Without him, the possibility that the Kazakh forces would choose to leave them alone was increased.

With the instinctive racial knowledge of one whose people had been spurned and despised for generations, Safar could tell all this from Hailsham's apologetic eyes. There was no attempt at argument. With a brief, deferential nod of his head, the little Uzbek complied meekly.

'I will leave you now,' he murmured simply. 'Just follow this path.'

He turned away without another word and began to walk past the file of men, who looked at him with fond, almost sorrowful expressions on their faces. The Thinker stepped out into the little Uzbek's path, holding out the AK-47 which he had picked up from the dead Kazakh in the cave, and thrust it into his hands. 'You might find this will come in useful,' he said quietly, even though Safar could not understand the words. It hardly mattered. It was a gesture which was universal. Safar grasped the weapon, cradling it against his chest with a thin smile on his face. Between friends of any culture, the traditional parting gift was recognized and appreciated.

The men stood in silence and watched him walk away for several seconds. He never turned to look back at them. Finally, their last respects paid, Hailsham called them all back to attention.

'Right, let's get moving,' he said brusquely. 'And keep your bloody eyes open.'

Weapons at the ready, and their senses on full alert, the column of men moved forward onto the ledge and began the gradual ascent to the narrow pass. Each footstep was more cautious now, carrying a new sense of urgency. Hailsham's fears had been communicated all too clearly. Fears which were totally justified, as it was shortly to turn out. For carried on the wind, and echoing through the valleys and ridges between the mountains, the sound of helicopter engines was about to reach their ears.

# 19

Tweedledee, in the Tail-end Charlie position and strung out some fifteen yards behind the main party, heard the sound first. He froze in his tracks, hissing ahead to Andrew, who was next in line.

'Psst. We got company, boss.'

'Jesus Christ,' Andrew spat out, his concern tinged with more than a hint of indignation, as though he took the unwelcome intrusion as a personal affront. 'That's all we bloody need right now.' He shouted a warning ahead to Hailsham, at the front. 'Incoming bandits.'

Hailsham had detected the faint sound of the choppers, and was already considering a suitable reaction. Not that there was much choice, he thought bitterly. Their position could hardly have been worse. Strung out along the ledge, with absolutely no cover at all, they might as well be waving welcome banners. He craned his neck upwards, his eyes sweeping the skies above. There was no visual sign yet, but the sound was definitely growing louder by the second. The helicopters – at least two of them, Hailsham reckoned – were headed in their direction sure enough, and with a particularly irksome sense of timing.

There was a Jewish expression which summed up their position rather succinctly, Hailsham reflected with a sense of irony: 'Caught between a rock and a hard place.' It could have been specially commissioned for this very situation. Basically there were two choices – either make a break forward for the limited cover offered by the pass ahead or stay where they were. Both options were fraught with dangers. To rush forward blindly could be to run straight into an ambush, in which case they would probably be cut to shreds. To remain exposed invited the same fate. Hailsham's sense of frustration was almost like a physical pain inside his head. Indecision tore at him like a terrible guilt.

Then, suddenly, there was no decision to make any more. The matter was taken out of his hands as the two Hind-A choppers cleared a long ridge of hills to the east and came into view. Wheeling in the sky like a pair of scout bees performing a food dance, they homed in inexorably towards the troopers' position. Hailsham studied them stoically, a strange sense of calm creeping through his body like an anaesthetic. His only identifiable feeling was one of mild surprise, he realized. For some obscure reason, he had always expected to die in a hot climate.

These thoughts were not those of a defeatist, but of a realist. Hailsham was a born fighter, and would take a brave stand against whatever odds fate threw at him. But cold logic told him that six lightly armed troopers pinned against a bare rock face stood absolutely no chance of survival against two combat helicopters hell-bent on destroying them. It was as certain as night follows day.

Equally as certain was his duty. Hailsham dropped to one knee on the rocky floor of the ledge, bringing his SA-80 up to his shoulder. He barked what he expected to be his last orders to the rest of the men.

'Fire at will when you think you've got a chance of hitting something worthwhile.'

There was little point in spelling it out any more plainly. Hailsham knew only too well that his men were as aware as he was of the awesome armour-plating specifications of the MIL Mi-24 series of helicopters. They were all tough – but the Hind-A assault version was perhaps the toughest of all. It had few vulnerable points, and it would take a very skilful or a very lucky shot at close range to bring one down.

Trooper Barry Naughton also reflected on the probability of death – but without the equanimity of his commanding officer. It wasn't supposed to be like this, a little voice screamed inside his head. Not so cold, so impersonal . . . so mechanical. All those hours spent in the 'killing house' at Hereford, pitting his brain and physical reflexes against recognizably human enemies, even if they were only cardboard pop-ups. All the months of training, of shared challenges and hardship, inherited foes and adopted friends. Comradeship, both group and individual pride, even the banter and the piss-taking. Everything the Army, and the SAS, had had led Barry to believe that an Army death would be like Army life. A matter of men pitted against men, an intense, close, and essentially living thing, somehow. Not hopelessly confronting two hunks of cold, grey metal in a cold, grey sky.

For the first time in his life, Barry wished that he could be more articulate, if only in his own mind. He would have liked to explain his own thoughts to himself more clearly, sift through his own confusion and make sense of it. Disappointment, tinged with more than a hint of bitterness, crowded in on him. He only knew that this moment was wrong, and perhaps everything else had been wrong, too. Even his very reasons for choosing the Army as a career. Now, too late, he had begun to understand something about himself and his needs, realizing for the first time that the Army could never, and would never, satisfy them.

Barry glanced sideways at his companions in turn, the bitterness spilling out of him as helpless anger.

'Fuck you,' he screamed. 'Fuck you all.' His hand dropped to his hip, drawing his Browning. Raising the handgun to his temple, he shot himself through the head.

Hailsham registered the noise of the single shot, and the sight of the trooper's head exploding sideways in a spray of blood and white bone fragments, almost as subliminal images. They were not real – they were just snatches of somebody else's nightmare.

Reality was the two helicopters hovering like a pair of malevolent dragonflies waiting to close in on their prey. Only they were *not* closing in, Hailsham suddenly realized with a shock. Both craft had assumed and were holding a position immediately above the steeper side of the hog's back the troopers had traversed earlier. Watching and waiting. Hailsham shivered slightly, the sense of quiet menace was so acute.

Seconds ticked away into a minute, and then two. To the men crouched on the exposed ledge, the tension was almost unbearable. Each of them knew that both of the choppers carried at least four 57mm rockets, and were well within range to launch them. Yet they did not fire. What the hell were they waiting for? Hailsham asked himself.

Andrew posed the question out loud. 'What the fuck are they playing at?' he exploded.

Hailsham could only shrug. 'Maybe they're just toying with us,' he suggested. 'Maybe they've radioed back to base and are waiting for specific orders. Who knows?'

'Or maybe they're scared of us,' the Thinker put in, with characteristic sarcasm. It was intended to be a joke, but it gave Hailsham food for serious thought.

'Actually, you might not be too far from the truth,' he muttered eventually, having analysed the situation and made possible sense of it. 'Neither of those pilots has any way of knowing we don't have the Stinger any more. To them, this could seem like a stand-off situation.'

'Which would explain why they're holding a position over that ridge,' Andrew agreed, following Hailsham's chain of thought. 'At the first sign of a missile launch, they can simply drop down behind it like a couple of concrete skylarks.'

At another time, Hailsham might have enjoyed Andrew's colourful imagery, even found it worthy of a smile. But the tension of the situation, and the horror of Naughton's death, had numbed everything except that which had been programmed into his subconscious by a lifetime of training. Several minutes had now passed, and expected death had not materialized. It was time to consider survival again.

'Someone's got to make a move to break this deadlock,' Hailsham said firmly. 'It might as well be us. I suggest we start to make a slow and very cautious bug-out back to the rocks at the base of the cliff. If the bastards let us get that far, we can at least break up and seek individual cover. That is, of course, unless anyone else has a better idea.'

The Thinker spoke for them all. 'Sounds pretty good to me, boss.'

Andrew also nodded his assent. Hailsham rose to his feet, stepping sideways over the dead trooper. Never taking his eyes from the two hovering helicopters, he executed the first of a series of slow, crab-like steps back down the slope of the ledge.

As though they were linked in some strange and invisible way, these small movements were picked up and copied by the two helicopters. Both craft rose perhaps thirty to forty feet higher in the sky, drifting to the left side of the hog's back as though carried on the wind. Hailsham froze; the choppers ceased their lateral movement and dropped back to the ridge again.

'This is fucking crazy,' Hailsham muttered. Galvanizing himself into movement once more, he took another dozen steps.

The two helicopters started to rise again, but this time they did not stop. Hardly daring to believe his own eyes, Hailsham watched the two craft climb steadily to a height of around two hundred feet above the ridge, then peel off and wheel away back in the direction they had come from. In a matter of minutes they had dwindled to gnat-like insignificance in the sky and then out of sight altogether behind the mountains. The chatter of their engines faded to a dim and distant echo, then fell below an audible level. They were gone.

Sheer relief, and a sense of incredulity, hit them all like a punch in the guts.

'Well what the hell do you make of that?' Cyclops asked finally, of no one in particular. He was not really expecting an answer, and was not surprised when none was offered. Now that the immediate threat of the helicopters was past, the men's thoughts were free to dwell on Barry again. They all looked back up the incline to where he lay as he had fallen, his shattered head surrounded by the dark stain of blood already congealing in the cold.

Andrew pulled Hailsham slightly to one side, sighing deeply. 'What a fucking waste,' he murmured. 'What the hell was he thinking?'

Hailsham shrugged helplessly, his face drawn and grim. 'Christ, we think we're so bloody clever, don't we?' he said bitterly. 'We kid ourselves that our selection and training techniques are foolproof – but they're not. Every now and again, some poor bastard like Naughton slips through the net somehow.' He looked at Andrew, his eyes heavy with unjustified guilt. 'Goddammit, Andrew, someone should have picked up that he was likely to crack like a rotten egg under the first crisis situation. The pathetic little bastard should never have been badged.'

Andrew attempted to reassure him. 'That was nothing to do with you, Mike,' he pointed out. 'It's not your fault.'

But Hailsham was not going to be consoled easily. He shook his head slowly from side to side. 'But I picked him for this mission, Andrew. I'm responsible for that.'

'You chose him from a shortlist because he had Arctic training under his belt and he was a good back-up sniper in case anything happened to Cyclops,' Andrew reminded him forcefully. 'On paper he was the right man for the job. Fuck it, Mike – if you want to start apportioning blame, then we all ought to collect our share. Nobody ever really *talked* to the kid, for Chrissake, apart from the bullshit and the piss-taking. Maybe that was the trouble – none of us ever really knew him.'

Hailsham digested this, glancing up at the body on the ledge again. 'The unknown soldier,' he murmured finally, an edge of savage irony in his voice. He looked up into the empty sky again, as if to completely reassure himself that the helicopters were gone.

'Think they'll be back?' Andrew asked, reading his thoughts.

'Christ knows,' Hailsham answered with a shrug. 'But I don't think it's a good idea to wait around here to find out. Let's get moving.'

He moved into point position again, ready to lead them all back up the ledge on their original course. There seemed to be little point in reminding the men about staying on their guard again. They were all as totally primed for action as a she-cat on heat. They passed Naughton's body, leaving it where it lay on the bare ledge. There were not even enough loose rocks around to build a cairn. If scavengers had not already taken it, they would remove the body for proper burial on the way back, Hailsham thought. That was if they got back.

They reached the point where the ledge cut round the side of the mountain into unknown territory. It sliced deeper into the rock face here, creating a sloping overhang of rock above their heads. Rather than walk upright on the outer edge, Hailsham led them deeper into the V-shaped gash – a manoeuvre which necessitated crouching over like a tribe of primitive ape-men. Rounding the bend, Hailsham was slightly dismayed to see that the ledge had largely crumbled away for about twenty feet, leaving only a thin shelf of rock no wider than a man's boot. However, the fissure in the rock face continued, although it now dropped in height to no more than a horizontal slit. There was no real choice but to drop down and slither through the next section on their bellies, pushing their bergens ahead of them.

'I suppose this ain't the best time to tell you about my claustrophobia, is it, boss?' the Thinker said deadpan, imme-diately behind Hailsham. Nevertheless, he followed the major's lead in hitting the deck, although he preferred to progress on his back rather than his stomach.

Hailsham edged his way forwards until the fissure began to open up again. Ahead of him, he could now see that they had come round the edge of the mountain and would shortly be, as he had fully expected, totally exposed to any one of half a dozen vantage points from the other surrounding peaks. He stopped, craning his head around to hiss back to the men behind him.

'We go out singly, at twenty-second intervals. First sign of trouble, you get your heads back under cover, ASAP. Understood?' Raising himself onto his hands and knees, Hailsham crawled forward another few yards until he was able to climb to his feet again. He shrugged into his bergen and checked his SA-80. Now comes the nasty bit, he thought.

Squinting against the sudden shock of stepping out into full daylight again, Hailsham took a breath and moved out from beneath the cover of the overhang. He took in the immediate terrain quickly with practised and wary eyes. The ledge widened and flattened out in front of him, forming an open bowl at the foot of two steep and rocky slopes to his left and right. Both climbed for several hundred feet, at roughly the same sort of gradient, but it was the one on the right which immediately seemed to offer the most promise. Slightly broader than its companion, it faced north-east and so was constantly exposed to both the warmth of the daytime sun and the icy blasts of Arctic winds. Generations of sudden and dramatic temperature change, added to the ferocity of wind, storm and blizzard, had split and eroded the rock face into broken and channelled ridges and fissures which provided an almost stair-like ascent. Climbing it would present little difficulty, Hailsham thought with deep satisfaction. He took another few steps forward, clearing the way for the Thinker to come out behind him.

The sudden, sharp crack of a rifle shot and a small spurt of chipped rock and dust from the ground in front of him made Hailsham react with lightning speed. Without pausing to even consider from which direction the shot had been fired, he threw himself to the ground, scrabbling backwards to regain the cover of the overhang. The Thinker, who had just been climbing to his feet, had no chance to get out of the way as Hailsham backed hurriedly into his legs. Thrown off balance, the corporal stumbled and fell forwards, ending up hunched over his CO's back like a dog mounting a bitch.

'Jesus Christ, boss – we can't go on meeting like this,' he muttered, struggling to pull himself off into a more dignified position. Regaining his hands and knees, he crawled up to Hailsham's side. 'Looks like we've got a problem,' he said with typical understatement.

Hailsham nodded. 'I had a bad feeling about this all along. Don't you just hate it when you're always right?' He twisted his body round, curling into a near-foetal position so that he could call back to the rest of the men still making their way along the fissure. 'Everybody freeze where they are for the moment – only get ready to back off fast if I give the word.'

Andrew's voice echoed up to him. 'You got cover, boss?' There was genuine concern in his voice.

Hailsham looked upwards at the comforting solidity of the rock overhanging his head. They were protected well enough for the present, he reckoned. There was no way anyone outside could have a direct line of fire. In the longer term, however, their safety largely depended on the position, strength and fire-power of their unknown enemy. If they were in a position to get closer, and had a grenade launcher at their disposal, then Hailsham and the rest of his men could be in deep shit.

Hailsham neglected to make this particular point to Andrew as he called back his answer. 'We're OK here, but I need to get out there again to take a look-see at what we're up against.' He glanced aside at the Thinker. 'Reckon you can squeeze up close enough to give me covering fire without shooting me up the backside?'

The Thinker grinned. 'I can try,' he said. 'It largely depends on whether you can keep your arse and your head down at the same time.'

'Point taken,' Hailsham muttered, returning the grin. 'So let's do it.' He crawled forward until he could raise to a crouch and poised himself on the balls of his feet. 'Cover on my left,' he hissed at the Thinker. 'My gut tells me that's where they are.'

'You got it, boss.' Completely serious now, the big man cradled the bullpup in his arms and moved into position behind Hailsham.

'Now,' Hailsham hissed. He threw himself into the open, firing a short burst into the air.

Behind him, and to his left, the Thinker began a longer, raking burst along the top of the eastern ridge, counting off three seconds in his head before pulling back again to make room for Hailsham. Two individual rifle shots cracked out before Hailsham was safely back under the protection of the overhang.

'See anything?' the Thinker asked.

Hailsham nodded. 'I was right. They're up on the left sure enough. The arrogant bastards are so confident they've got us completely pinned down that they're standing right out in the open.'

The Thinker flashed him an apologetic smile. 'They could be right, boss.'

'Yeah,' Hailsham grunted. 'Anyway, go again. I need to get an accurate head count. Give me another three seconds, and concentrate your fire about eleven o'clock. Ready?'

'I'm with you.'

217

The two men poised themselves to repeat the first manoeuvre. This time, the Thinker saw a couple of figures as he opened fire, and had the brief satisfaction of seeing one of them topple sideways before he ducked back into cover.

'And then there were five,' Hailsham murmured as he retreated under the overhang. 'Nice one, Thinker.'

The Mancunian smiled proudly. 'We aim to please, boss. Reckon that's all of 'em?'

Hailsham considered for a few seconds, finally nodding. 'Sounds about right,' he said. 'Six up there, plus the two we encountered earlier. These guerrilla groups rarely operate much into double figures.' He allowed himself a thin smile. 'Encouraging, don't you think? If you look at it from the right perspective, we've already accounted for a third of the buggers.'

The Thinker was not impressed with the philosophical school of thought which said that a half-empty glass of beer was half full. 'You look at it that way if you like,' he said. 'Personally, I'm a half-empty man.' He gave Hailsham a quizzical look. 'So, what do we do now?'

'I think it's time to call a Chinese parliament,' Hailsham said.

# 20

Hailsham outlined their position as simply and as quickly as possible. 'So, gentlemen, that's the situation,' he finished off. 'Please consider yourselves free to make any suggestions.'

'There's the obvious, of course,' the Thinker said. 'We just shoot and scoot.'

'Yes, there's always that possibility,' Hailsham agreed with a nod. 'But that doesn't offer us very good odds. There's just about room for two men at a time out there, and damn-all cover. You were lucky the last time, picking one of them off while they were still out in the open. They'll have learned a lesson from that and taken up good defensive positions. It means we'd be out there, completely exposed and with no targets to shoot at. Sitting ducks. Even at a conservative estimate, I'd reckon our losses would be sixty per cent.'

'Suppose we loaded those odds a bit more in our favour,' Cyclops suggested. 'We could break out a mortar and one man could operate it from under the cover of the overhang. A nice pattern of shells laid down on that mountainside would give the bastards something to think about while the rest made a run for it.'

It was a sensible suggestion, which Hailsham thought about. 'OK, that's a good contender,' he admitted at last. 'The main drawback as far as I can see is that whoever is on the mortar is on a hiding to nothing. Sooner or later, he's going to have to run the gauntlet all on his own.'

'I'd thought about that, boss,' Cyclops said. 'Perhaps I didn't make it clear that I was volunteering for the job.'

'Noted and commended, Corporal,' Hailsham replied. 'But I'm still looking for the main chance which is going to get us all out of here in one piece.'

'Look, we don't really want to get into a fight at all, unless we have to,' Andrew pointed out. 'Like someone said before we started out on this crazy mission: this ain't our war. So, isn't it at least possible that these guys might feel the same way?'

'What are you suggesting, boss?' asked Tweedledee. 'We surrender to 'em?'

Andrew ignored the facetious comment, directing his attention to Hailsham. 'Well? Seriously, don't you think we ought to offer them the chance of a truce? What have we got to lose?'

It sounded like an eminently sensible suggestion, Hailsham thought, although he held out faint hopes of it succeeding. Experience so far had shown the guerrilla forces on both sides to be both nervous and trigger-happy. Fortunately for them in the latter case, Hailsham thought gratefully. If the over-eager rifleman had not loosed off that first, erratic shot, they might all now be dead. If the guerrillas had been a bit smarter, they would have waited for the entire patrol to get out into the open, and then picked them all off in one fell swoop.

Hailsham detached the white hood from his Arctic suit and draped it over the barrel of his SA-80. Think this will do for a white flag?' he asked. Without waiting for an answer, he moved out towards the lip of the overhang, holding the gun out at arm's length.

A fusillade of shots gave him the answer he had feared. Returning to the rest of the men, he smiled ruefully. 'Well, it was a nice idea, anyway,' he said to Andrew. 'Pity everyone doesn't share your pacifist inclinations.' He was silent for a few seconds. 'Well, has anyone else got any bright ideas?'

'Suppose we bug out and try to find another way up?' the Thinker put in. 'Maybe even a completely different route.'

There was a long silence during which it became clear that no more suggestions were forthcoming. Rather than let time waste any more, Hailsham decided to sum up the options for them.

'So, basically, we go out all gung-ho like the Light Brigade or we sneak back with our tails between our legs.' He paused for a second, the trace of a sparkle in his eyes. 'Or we go for a combination of the ideas we've already discussed.'

Hailsham had some sort of a plan, Andrew could tell. 'What are you thinking, boss?'

Hailsham did not answer him, turning to Cyclops instead. 'How's your climbing, Corporal? Ever manage to get past the giant-spider phase in the school playground?'

Cyclops shrugged. 'I managed the tree at the bottom of the garden once. Why do you ask?'

'The face at the bottom of this pass,' Hailsham said. 'It's nasty, but not impossible.'

Cyclops looked at him doubtfully. 'Christ, boss, we'd never make that loaded with all our equipment.'

'True,' Hailsham allowed. 'But one man, carrying only a rifle, might stand a bloody good chance.' For the moment, he said no more.

He had no need to, for Cyclops was already ahead of him. 'And if that just happened to be a sniping rifle, and the guy carrying it knew how to use it . . . we could be talking about a whole new game plan,' he finished off for Hailsham.

The major looked him squarely in the eyes. 'That man would have to volunteer, of course,' he murmured. 'He'd also have to be something of a prat to even consider such a hazardous mission.'

Cyclops grinned good-naturedly. 'The sort of prat who would offer to sit out in the open with a mortar, for instance?'

Hailsham nodded. 'Yes, someone like that might do quite nicely. Then, if another prat like myself were to operate the mortar . . .'

He did not bother to finish. It was, after all, a Chinese parliament. The rest of the men had to make their own decisions. Hailsham sat quietly, eyeing them all in turn as they digested the scheme he had outlined.

'It could work,' the Thinker muttered eventually. 'Dammit, boss, it could bloody well work.'

'It *will* work,' Cyclops said quietly. 'I could probably pick off two or even three of those bastards before they even knew what was happening. And once the whole mountainside under their feet starts going up like Guy Fawkes Night, they'll be too bloody busy running like fucking rabbits to worry about you guys.'

'But just in case, you'll be in position to cover the boss when he makes his run,' Andrew put in, his tone reflecting the general air of enthusiasm. 'I like it.'

Perhaps they were all getting a bit *too* carried away, Hailsham reflected. His face more serious, he looked at Cyclops again. 'Seriously, though, the whole thing hangs on you being able to get up that rock face. Can you make it, do you think?'

It was Cyclops's turn to review the whole scheme in the harsh light of reality. There was no point in making rash promises. 'I won't know until I try,' he said with complete honesty. He turned to Andrew. 'How much proper climbing equipment are we carrying?'

The sergeant's face suddenly fell as a terrible thought struck him. In the temporary euphoria, it was something they had all overlooked. 'It ain't good,' he said grimly. 'This whole jaunt was basically underequipped from the start, as you well know. Cutting weight seemed like a good idea at the time.' He paused for a moment, as if unwilling to release the really bad news. 'The trouble is, most of the gear was in Jimmy's bergen. He was our climbing expert.' He paused again, racking his memory for a complete inventory of the limited equipment he had requisitioned. 'We've still got ropes, of course, and there should be a few pitons and perhaps half a dozen spikes in your own pack. That's about it, I'm afraid.'

Cyclops accepted the news with a philosophical shrug. 'Well, I suppose it will have to do,' he said. Stripping off his bergen, he began to rummage through it for the items in question.

'I just had an idea that might help,' the Thinker blurted out suddenly. He began to rummage through his own equipment, finally pulling out a small handful of time fuses and detonator caps. Andrew and Hailsham looked at him with puzzled expressions on their faces. The Thinker grinned back sheepishly. 'Well, they do tell us to improvise,' he said quietly. 'So this is my contribution.' He held out the detonators to Cyclops. 'If you really got stuck, one of these might blast out just enough rock to give you a hand or toe hold in an emergency,' he suggested. 'Only don't blow your own fucking head off, that's all.'

Cyclops accepted the detonators gratefully. The Thinker was right. At a pinch, they might just work. It was worth taking them along, anyway. Every little helped. He unpacked the L96A1 sniper rifle, stroking the green plastic stock with the caress of a lover. He even whispered words of endearment to the sleek killing machine: 'It's just going to be me and you, my beauty. You won't let me down, will you?'

After assembling, carefully cleaning and checking the weapon, Cyclops packed a dozen of the heavy 7.62mm slugs into his escape belt and glanced up at Hailsham. 'Right, I'm ready,' he announced flatly.

Hailsham nodded, glancing at his watch. 'It should take you about twelve minutes to get back down to the face,' he said quietly. 'And hopefully no more than twenty to make the ascent. How long to set up once you reach a decent firing position?'

Cyclops thought over Hailsham's projected timings carefully. They seemed reasonable enough. 'Give me another five minutes on top,' he suggested eventually. 'I'll need a couple of ranging shots to recalibrate the sights after humping this baby up a mountain. No point in blasting off blind if you're not going to hit what you're aiming at.'

Hailsham ran the figures through his head again. 'OK, so forty minutes tops,' he said. 'We'll set up for action well before that, but wait for your first two shots. Exactly thirty seconds after your second shot we'll fire a few bursts up the mountain to bring them out into the open. Then it's down to you. We'll give you exactly five clear shots before we open up with the mortar and make our break for it. If everything goes well, we'll RV with you up on the plateau Safar spoke about.'

For a makeshift plan, it all seemed pretty tight. 'You got it, boss,' Cyclops said, and prepared to move off. It took a certain amount of intricate shuffling and manoeuvring in the narrowest part of the fissure to let him through, but eventually he was clear and on his way. The Thinker and Tweedledee took advantage of the extra room to crowd up into the cover of the overhang, taking it upon themselves to set up the mortar.

'Well, all we have to do now is wait, gentlemen,' Hailsham said, checking his watch again.

There was a long, strained silence before Tweedledee finally piped up. 'You know, boss – you never did get around to telling us that story about the whore and the donkey in Kuwait.'

Hailsham smiled thinly. 'Didn't I?' he replied with mock surprise. 'Well, in that case . . .'

Despite the luridness of the tale, which Hailsham embellished freely for the occasion, it was a long and agonizing wait for all of them. Everyone had seen the rock face on the way past, and was fully aware of the difficulties it posed. Their watches had rarely been used so much in such a short space of time.

Just over half an hour had passed when they heard the first, faint echo of a small explosion. It made them all jump, even though they were already on tenterhooks.

Three pairs of eyes flashed towards Hailsham's, questioningly.

'He can't have made it already,' Andrew murmured, glancing at his watch again for perhaps the twentieth time.

Hailsham shook his head slowly, looking aside at the Thinker. 'Looks like your little idea came in useful after all,' he observed. The sound they had heard had to be one of the detonator caps going off. The firing signature of the Accuracy International was loud, and distinctive. Even from a distance it had a sharp, unique quality.

They settled back to wait again. The allotted forty minutes passed. Hailsham's face was taut with strain as he realized a full hour had elapsed since Cyclops's departure.

'Dammit, he should have made it by now,' he hissed.

There was a pregnant pause; nobody seemed to want to voice the obvious. But somebody had to say it.

'Maybe he didn't make it,' Andrew said flatly at last, letting them all off the hook.

There it was, out in the open. There was almost a sense of relief underneath the depression which settled over them like a black cloud.

'Yeah,' Hailsham grunted, a deep sigh following the single word of resignation. He checked his watch again, his face grim. 'We'll give him another five minutes, and then we'll have to revert to Plan A.'

They all fell silent again, deliberately avoiding each other's gaze as the seconds continued to tick inexorably away.

Finally, reluctantly, Hailsham spoke again. 'It's time to make a move,' he announced gravely. He started to make for the mortar. 'Move out in your own time as soon as I start plastering that mountain. And good luck,' he added, trying vainly not to make it sound like a farewell.

The sudden, sharp report of a heavy-calibre rifle shattered the silence, cracking off the mountains in a series of spitting echoes.

Relief was not the word for the wave of near-exultation which seemed to sweep through the air of gloom like a storm wind charged with electricity. It hit Hailsham like a blow in the chest, driving air from his lungs up into his throat, where it lodged in a painful lump. Andrew felt like Saul on the road to Damascus, or a kid waking up to his first Christmas stocking. Miracles *did* happen, there really was magic in the world. The Thinker let out a loud whoop which was totally out of character.

'He made it. The beautiful bastard made it,' Tweedledee screamed out, the look on his face mirroring the sheer disbelief in his voice.

They all waited, picturing Cyclops's actions and counting off the seconds in their heads. A minor adjustment with thumb and forefinger . . . another squint through the adjusted sights . . . another cartridge slipped into the breech . . . loaded and cocked. Finger on the trigger now . . . taking up the slight pressure of resistance . . . gently squeezing.

The second report was the signal for them all. Hailsham's eyes darted to his watch then back up to Andrew, counting under his breath as the Barbadian tensed himself for action.

Thirty seconds,' he barked. 'Go.'

Andrew was already crouched and poised under the last safe area of cover. On Hailsham's command, he exploded from underneath the overhang, emptying the entire thirty-round magazine up into the mountains in less than three seconds. He was already well back in cover and getting ready to slam a new magazine into the SA-80 when the first of half a dozen rifle slugs chewed into the ground and rock face where he had stood. Almost simultaneously came the louder crack of the Accuracy International L96.

Hailsham dropped to his belly, slithering up to the mortar and sliding the base plate forward until the firing tube pointed clear of the overhang. Four 51mm bombs lay out in a neat line in readiness. Selecting the first, Hailsham cradled it in his hand, waiting for Cyclops's next four shots.

They came with remarkable speed – even for Cyclops. Even knowing the man's legendary skill, Hailsham found it hard to believe that any man could reload, select a target, aim and fire the single shot, bolt-action weapon – so quickly. He could only pray that the shots were as accurate as they were fast. He held the tail fins of the mortar bomb over the open mouth of the firing tube as the last of the five shots cracked out amid the still-reverberating echoes of its predecessor.

First-shot accuracy with the comparatively cheap and simple British 51mm mortar was never easy, and Hailsham was not even really trying. He dropped the first bomb into the tube, merely raking it down a couple of degrees and reloading as the first missile discharged with a dull whoosh. Firing the second shell, he twisted the base plate the merest faction of an inch and dropped in the third just as the first explosion boomed out from the mountainside above.

Hailsham notched the firing tube up again, holding the last missile in position. 'Get going,' he screamed without looking round. He waited perhaps two seconds until Andrew ran past his prone body and then dropped it into the tube.

Then the Thinker and Tweedledee were also past him and gone, breaking out from cover and running at full pelt, firing sideways from the hip. The chatter of three weapons, and the echoing rumble of the rest of the exploding mortar shells created a wall of noise through which it was impossible to pick out the sound of individual rifle fire. Hailsham thought that he heard two more shots from Cyclops's L96, but he could not be sure.

Then, abruptly, there was silence again. Hailsham sucked in a deep breath. So, this was it, he told himself, pushing himself to his feet and staring out into the open. He had estimated a twenty-second run to the bowl at the foot of the two hills. Once upon a time he might have done it in fifteen. Except he was no longer twenty-five, and they were probably already at an altitude of around 13,000 feet.

Neither was a factor that he cared to dwell on, even if there had been time to do so. 'Oh well, shit or bust time, Hailsham,' he told himself out loud, jumping off the balls of his feet and breaking into a run.

A single bullet smacked into the rock face in front of him, but Hailsham kept running. Up ahead, two of the SA-80s opened up in unison from inside the cover of a rock fissure with a couple of short bursts. Three or four single shots came from another location nearby. After that there was silence again. There was no more rifle fire.

Reaching the bowl, Hailsham threw himself into a diving roll and sought the scant cover of a shallow depression. He lay face down, catching his breath for several seconds before glancing up and attempting to get his bearings.

Andrew's grinning black face popped up from behind a long, flat rock to his right. 'Actually, I think we got 'em all, boss – but I'd keeni-meeni over here just to be on the safe side, if I were you.'

Hailsham took the advice to heart, adopting the slithering, snake-like belly crawl which the poached Swahili phrase suggested. Wriggling over to join Andrew, he heaved himself over the top of the rock and dropped into cover beside him.

'You really think we got the lot?' he asked.

Andrew nodded happily. 'Pretty sure,' he said confidently. 'I saw Cyclops take two out as we started running, and Thinker popped one just after we hit the bowl. One of your mortar rounds threw something up in the air that looked remarkably like the bottom two-thirds of a body, and I just hit that last bastard who took a shot at you. If your original head count was right, I figure we're home and dry. He broke off to shrug. 'Not that it really matters, anyway. If there is anyone left up there, Cyclops can pick 'em off while they're still squinting down the sights. So, do you want to move out again?'

Hailsham shook his head. 'No, we'll rest up for five or ten minutes. Just in case there are any stragglers left up on that mountain. By that time they'll have either shown themselves or got the fuck out to safer ground. Don't forget – they don't know we're not coming after them. Besides, we've got a long, hard climb ahead of us, and a poor old bastard like me needs all the rest he can get.'

'Jesus, boss, you hared along that ridge like a bloody nineteen-year-old,' Andrew told him, in what was supposed to be a compliment.

Hailsham laughed cynically. He could still feel his heart pumping in his chest like an antiquated steamhammer. 'Yeah, but a nineteen-year-old what?'

Just as Hailsham's initial recce of the northern slope had suggested, the climbing was hard enough, but not too difficult. It was more like advanced rock climbing than real mountaineering, and by taking it at a restrained but steady pace they could monitor their own progress almost minute by minute. Less than half an hour after leaving the bowl, they were starting to come more or less in line with the top of the face which Cyclops had taken, and were probably slightly over halfway to the summit.

Hailsham's belly was starting to rumble. It was now nearly six hours since their last, meagre meal and they had all burned up a great deal of mental and physical energy. Although he was in no doubt that they could all hold out for a while yet, the need for food would become a priority soon enough, even if the reasonably bearable weather conditions persisted. But if the storms and the icy winds returned, it might be a completely different matter. For nothing drained the body's reserves as efficiently as bitter and sustained cold. Allied to hunger, it could be an equally efficient killer.

The route ahead offered at least some slim hopes, Hailsham thought optimistically, recalling his basic research into the topography of the region before the mission had got under way. The high mountain plateaux were invariably used as summer pasture areas by the semi-nomadic tribespeople of the region. It was more than possible that the droppings of grazing animals had enriched the ground over the years to the extent that it had set up its own limited life-chain. Beetles, insects or worms at the lowest and most unpalatable end of the spectrum, and perhaps small mammals at the more optimistic level. Allowing himself to pursue this line of reasoning to its eventual, if somewhat wishful, conclusion, Hailsham dared to imagine that the plateau areas might even be the source of the ground-burrowing marmots which seemed to make up the basic protein source of the locals.

With this thought in mind, Hailsham suddenly realized that he should have asked Safar for more details about the life-cycle of the creatures and how they were captured. Did they roam free in the winter months, and if so, what was the best way to trap them? Or did they hibernate, and have to be dug up from deep underground burrows? Cursing himself for his oversight, Hailsham reflected that he did not even know if the rodents were diurnal or nocturnal in their habits.

Forcing himself to snap out of a potential chain of negative thoughts again, Hailsham indulged in the most fanciful imaginings, picturing the plateau region populated by stray or abandoned goats which had somehow managed to establish feral colonies and survive the harsh winters. Fantasizing about a fresh goat steak brought the saliva bubbling to his palate and started his stomach rumbling again with renewed vigour. With a conscious effort, Hailsham pushed all thoughts of food from his mind and concentrated on his climbing once again as the going suddenly got tougher.

Dragging himself over the crest of a rocky ridge, Hailsham saw that the terrain immediately ahead changed dramatically. Quite abruptly the crags and crannies which had assisted their passage were no longer in evidence. It was as if a giant bulldozer had run amok down the mountainside at a crazy angle, sweeping away all surface features and leaving only a smooth, tilted plate of rock which was too steep to even retain snow. That had all slipped down the face into massive drifts at the left-hand corner, in depths it was impossible even to guess at.

Hailsham regarded this new obstacle morosely. To attempt a vertical climb of the tilted plane was obviously impractical, since the direct route up represented a gradient of perhaps sixty-five or seventy degrees. The only realistic approach was to traverse it at an obtuse angle, gaining height gradually. The smooth wall of rock stretched ahead for about a mile and a half, actually rising about six hundred feet to the mouth of a rocky gorge which split the next range into two near-vertical faces.

Skirting round the area of more obvious snowdrifts, Hailsham moved warily, checking each step foward with a cautious probe of his foot. Several times his leg sank almost up to the thigh in the soft, powdery snow before encountering something solid beneath it. Acute awareness of the dangers of plunging into a hidden crevasse at any moment made for agonizingly slow and gut-churning progress, and Hailsham was profoundly relieved when he finally reached the bare rock face and hauled himself up onto it. He sat back, watching the rest of his men as they followed his ploughed-out trail through the drifts.

Andrew perched himself on the rock beside Hailsham. 'Where now?'

Hailsham jerked his thumb over his shoulder towards the gorge. 'Hobson's Choice, from the look of things. It won't be easy,' he added, rather stating the obvious.

Andrew took in the daunting traverse across the rock face with a faint nod. 'I'm beginning to think we sent Cyclops up the easy route,' he muttered. 'From here, that looks like a job for Spiderman.'

Hailsham allowed himself a wry smile. 'We're supposed to be supermen – remember? Faster than a speeding bullet . . . clearing tall buildings at a single bound? Nothing's impossible for the SAS.'

Andrew grinned. 'Oh yes, I forgot. Well, that's all right, then.'

'However, as handy telephone boxes around here seem somewhat conspicuous by their absence,' Hailsham went on, 'I suggest a slightly more mortal approach. We'll just take it in very easy stages. Let's call it the Janet and John approach to mountaineering.' He half-turned, running his eyes along the inclined plane of the face and seeking out features which could be used to their advantage. Although there were no obvious fissures or projections, the seemingly smooth face was not uniformly bland. At varying heights and angles all the way up, the main mass of reddish-brown rock was striated by layers of a darker colour, like a multi-layered sponge cake. It was obviously composed of two compressed, but clearly different rock layers. And where two layers met, there was almost sure to be a slight imperfection caused by differing degrees of erosion, Hailsham knew. It might be no more than a few millimetres, but it would probably be enough for a man to get some sort of a grip on. Preferably a man unburdened by heavy equipment.

Hailsham extended one finger, tracing along the fault lines. 'There,' he said, pointing to one such layer. 'And there,' he added, running his finger back, tracing out a zigzag route across and up the face.

233

Andrew followed Hailsham's directions with keen eyes, nodding his approval. 'Yep, that's the way to do it,' he agreed finally. 'It's a bloody long way round to gain comparatively little height, but it's probably our best bet.'

'*My* best bet,' Hailsham corrected him. 'This one's best tackled as a solo. I'll leave my equipment here and take a rope up. Once I reach the mouth of that gully I can secure it and you can all pull yourselves straight up. Then we haul up our gear and we're on our way again.'

'That's if there *is* a way,' Andrew pointed out. 'We don't know what that gully might lead into.'

'Party pooper,' Hailsham shot back. 'Let's face that one when we come to it.'

He began to strip off his bergen. Andrew's hand descended on his arm, restraining him. 'With the greatest respect, boss, have we got the best man for the job here? I'm younger than you.'

'And heavier,' Hailsham pointed out.

Andrew shrugged. 'Well, if age and weight are going to be the chief criteria here, then what about Tweedledee?' he asked.

Hailsham smiled grimly, nodding his head up the wall of rock. 'One slip up there and there's only the fast route down. It's got to be down to you or me, Andrew – and I've got the casting vote on this one.'

It was obvious that Hailsham had made his mind up, Andrew reflected. He was sorry now that he had even mentioned his age. The last thing the man needed at this moment was anything which could sap his confidence. 'Yeah. You're probably right,' he conceded, stepping back as Hailsham finished peeling off his equipment.

Hailsham coiled a length of nylon rope around his waist and secured it. 'Tie on extra lengths as you need them,' he said to Andrew. 'I'll give you a clear signal when it's safe to follow me up. Last man ropes on the excess gear and we can all haul it up together.'

Andrew nodded. 'Good luck, boss.'

Hailsham grinned, exuding more confidence than he really felt. 'I taught Peter Parker his tricks in the first place.'

Andrew did not understand. He looked at Hailsham blankly. 'Peter Parker? Who's Peter Parker?'

Hailsham clucked his teeth in a vaguely reproving gesture. 'Spiderman's alter ego,' he reminded the big Barbadian. 'Good Lord, Andrew, doesn't *anybody* read comic books any more?' He turned away and began to scramble along the sloping side of the rock face with a curious half-slithering, half-hopping motion which made Andrew think of a giant land-crab.

The sergeant watched him progress along the shallowest part of the incline towards the first strata fault, gaining a few precious inches in height for every few lateral feet. As the gradient increased, Hailsham pressed himself tightly against the face, his hands spread out wide and flat, and his feet splayed out at angles to gain the maximum possible amount of friction between his boots and the smooth rock. Every possible square inch of his body was glued against the unyielding surface, as though Hailsham was consciously willing his entire body to melt into the rock, fuse and become part of it.

He looked less like a land-crab now, Andrew thought idly. More like a tree-frog or a gecko.

Hailsham reached the darker layer of rock strata and pulled himself up until it was at eye level. With the side of his face pressed against the cold rock, he examined it carefully. If anything, it was slightly more promising than he had dared to hope. Granular and slightly pitted in texture like coarse sandpaper, it was obviously softer than the smooth and slab-like volcanic basalt trap-rock which had engulfed it a hundred million years ago. The eroding effects of wind and ice over the ages had done their slow but sure work, eating away at the rougher surface until it was distinctly impressed within the overall outer level of the main face. The tiny lip which it created was probably no more than a centimetre at its deepest parts, but it was enough to get a fingerhold against.

Easing himself into position, Hailsham began the tricky business of backtracking along the fault line. His cheek still pressed tightly against the rock face, he dared to turn his head slightly, rolling his eyes upwards. Seen from this perspective, the gradient above appeared almost vertical, although he knew it was not. It just looked that way – and felt that way! Hailsham marvelled at the sheer impossibility of his position. It seemed that his entire body-weight was being suspended on his fingernails alone. He was not sure that his boots had any kind of grip at all, and he did not feel disposed to put it to the test. His fingertips shrieked out with pain and cold as he edged, precariously along his zigzag path to the next strata, which slanted away again to his right.

He was now just over twenty-five feet above the heads of Andrew, Tweedledee and the Thinker, who were following every painful inch of his progress with hypnotic fascination.

'Dammit, boss, if you're going to slip, then do it now for Chrissake,' Andrew found himself saying under his breath. It was not a wish for failure, but a last plea for Hailsham's safety. He could probably survive a fall from this height with no more than a few nasty bruises. In a matter of a few more minutes, the choice would be between broken bones and death. Both probably more or less the same thing, Andrew reflected, given the vulnerability of their position. It would be almost impossible to carry a badly wounded man down out of the mountains again. And if they left him, he would never survive the first night in the cold.

But Hailsham did not slip, against all the odds. Reaching the second layer of pitted rock, he turned himself again and set out back across the face, now climbing about one vertical foot for every four gained sideways.

'He's a human fucking limpet,' the Thinker said, impressed.

Andrew tore his eyes away from the fly-like figure on the rock face and busied himself tying on another length of rope. He could not bear to watch any more.

Maybe he should have worn gloves, Hailsham thought. His fingers were completely numb now, despite the fact that several nails had been broken and torn away from the quick, leaving the sensitive flesh bleeding profusely. He shrugged off the thought, knowing that it was academic anyway. Besides, although gloves might have offered some protection from the cold and the roughness of the stone, they would have provided less grip. He might not have made it this far – and warm hands were not much use to a man with a broken spine lying at the bottom of a mountain. At least the numbness held the pain at bay, Hailsham told himself philosophically. He could only hope that his fingertips actually retained more feeling and sensitivity than his brain was registering. For at least ten minutes now, he had had the strangest feeling that he was clinging to the mountainside by sheer willpower.

Suddenly there was a small but deep vertical fissure in the main rock formation, just above his head to the right. And above that, a definite inward slant to the face, presenting a sloping shelf which culminated in a flat ridge. And that was it. Above that ridge lay an easy scramble over broken and pitted rock to the snow-filled mouth of the gorge. For the first time since starting the ascent, Hailsham actually dared to believe that he might just make it to the top.

Gratefully he reached up and jammed the heel of his hand into the crack, pulling himself up and feeling a sense of relief as the strain of his body-weight was transferred to his wrist and arm. He brought up his left foot, scraping the side of his sole tentatively against the face, feeling for the tell-tale roughness of the granular strata. Finding it, and probing for the support of the thin lip between the two layers, Hailsham poised himself both mentally and physically for the next, critical move.

Everything depended upon the security of that foothold now. It really was shit or bust time. With a silent prayer to a God he did not really believe in, Hailsham pulled his hand out of the fissure and let his weight drop onto his left foot.

It held. Holding his breath lest the slightest bodily movement could upset the delicate balance of things, Hailsham tensed the muscles of his calves and thighs and pushed himself up until he could jam his elbow into the tiny cleft. Another upward heave, and he was free to throw his left arm onto the shelf and drag himself up to the ridge.

Hailsham lay there, face down, for several seconds. He still hardly dared to believe that he had made it. Finally he pushed himself up on to his hands and knees and scrambled to the mouth of the gorge, scooping away the deep drifts of snow until he had uncovered a rocky crag around which to secure the rope. Tying it off, he slithered back down to the ledge on his behind and called over the edge to the men waiting below.

'Come on up,' he yelled. 'The lift's working now.'

It was not much of a joke, but Hailsham found himself dissolving into childish giggles at his own wit.

The gorge ran deeper into the mountains than anyone had imagined. They had already covered at least a quarter of a mile, and although it had begun to narrow to a width of only a few feet, it showed little sign of ending. Equally, it showed little sign of leading to a negotiable pathway to the plateau above. On either side, the sixty-foot walls of rock were smooth and vertical. Their only hope so far, Hailsham thought, was that the ravine would eventually narrow to the extent that they could climb between its two sides like a chimney. In the meantime, they had no choice but to keep moving. Wading through the deep snow which sometimes came up to their chests, the team continued penetrating into the very heart of the mountains.

The gorge ended, eventually opening out into a huge, bowl-like canyon. They were now surrounded on all sides by sheer, unscalable faces of rock which all apparently ended abruptly in a flat rim no more than fifty feet above their heads.

Hailsham brought the party to a halt, swivelling his head around to take in the full panorama with a sinking heart. There was nothing to offer them even the remotest chance of a climb to the top. They had reached a dead-end, and they were trapped. They might as well be at the bottom of a well, Hailsham thought, heavily. He cursed silently, thinking of the plateau just those few tantalizing feet above. So bloody near – yet so bloody far!

Tweedledee put it even more succinctly. 'Now we're *really* fucked,' he groaned. No one argued.

God, but he hated to be beaten, Hailsham thought angrily. He continued to scan the sides of the canyon, convincing

239

himself that there had to be something he had missed, some feasible route up he had overlooked.

He had missed nothing – nor did he miss the brief flash of movement at the rim of the canyon on his right.

It was crazy, impossible. Altitude sickness, Hailsham's brain told him, trying to find some rational explanation for the unexplainable. He was hallucinating. Or maybe it was a bird, a trick of the light, something plucked off the canyon rim by a freak gust of wind.

But a coil of nylon rope was a rare, and particularly bizarre, hallucination. And far too heavy to be carried on the wind. And birds did not drop from the sky like stones, unravelling themselves as they fell.

Andrew had also seen the coiled rope tossed out from the plateau above. With unbelieving eyes, he watched it fall to the canyon floor before looking across at Hailsham and exchanging a glance of total bemusement.

'Cyclops?' he breathed. It was the only possible explanation he could think of.

'Well it sure as hell wasn't God,' Tweedledee put in, as the rope crashed into the snow less than ten feet away from him.

Hailsham's eyes were fixed on the spot where the now dangling rope looped over the edge of the canyon. There was no further sign of movement. He continued staring for nearly a minute, finally realizing that their unknown benefactor was not going to show himself.

'Well, boss, what do we do now?' Andrew asked. 'Somebody up there obviously likes us.'

Hailsham could only shrug helplessly. The entire situation was just too bizarre for words. He trudged over to the dangling rope, seizing it and tugging at it heavily. It was clearly well secured at the top. With another helpless shrug at Andrew, he wedged one foot against the sheer cliff face and began to climb. For some reason, he had the curious feeling that he might disappear in a puff of blue smoke when he reached the end of the rope.

He was wrong. Hauling himself up to eye level with the rim of the canyon, Hailsham was immediately struck by several things. One was that the plateau was much vaster than he had imagined, stretching out in an unbroken white plain all the way to the foothills of the Sailyukem Mountains.

Unbroken, that was, but for the two black shapes of the two Hind-A assault helicopters in the immediate foreground. Nearer still, and more immediately menacing was the line of a dozen soldiers, clad in heavy grey uniforms and greatcoats pensioned off from the Red Army and each cradling a Kalashnikov in his hands.

Hailsham's heart fell through his boots. He was caught like a fly on flypaper and there was nothing he could do about it. Cursing himself for his impetuosity, he finished hauling himself up to the safety of the plateau and stood stiffly, waiting for the next move.

A young man – no more than thirty-five, Hailsham estimated – stepped forward briskly. He wore the insignia of a captain, and was smiling.

'Major Hailsham? We've been expecting you,' he said, in a friendly tone, and in near-flawless English. 'What took you so long?'

Hailsham just could not take it all in. He gazed over towards the helicopters again, where another, smaller group of soldiers had set up tents, an ammunition and equipment dump, and a petrol-fired cooking stove. Cyclops was sitting next to it, basking in its warmth. He was grinning stupidly, and sipping hot soup from a tin mug.

# 21

'What the fuck is going on?' Hailsham demanded. Under the circumstances, he thought he was being rather restrained.

The young officer extended his hand in formal greeting. 'I am Captain Dmitri Yascovar, of the Kazakh Republican Army,' he said quietly. 'Please relax, Major. My men intend you no harm.'

To back up his words, Yascovar raised one hand in the air and clicked his fingers. The armed soldiers stood down at once, dropping their rifles butt down on the ground.

His question remained unanswered. Hailsham repeated it, this time a little more politely. 'Do you mind telling me exactly what is going on, Captain?'

Yascovar smiled warmly. 'All in good time, Major Hailsham. First, I suspect that you and your men could do with some hot food and a drink. If you would care to bring them up, we have a meal waiting for you.'

He stared into Hailsham's eyes, identifying the distrust there.

'But, of course, I am forgetting. You will need some sort of proof of our good intentions. Please forgive me.' Yascovar reached into the inside pocket of his greatcoat, drew out a thin, folded sheet of paper, and handed it across. It was a fax, Hailsham noticed as he unfolded the sheet. His sense of unreality increased. After their days of isolation in some of the wildest country on the face of the earth, it seemed totally incongruous to be receiving a faxed message on the top of a bloody mountain, he thought. Nevertheless, he began to read the single sheet.

It bore the unmistakable seal of the British Foreign Office, albeit slightly smudged by the old-style heat-sensitive paper which the East Europeans were obviously still using in their fax machines. Hailsham initially suspected a forgery, but the coded reference at the top left-hand corner of the sheet was letter-perfect, leaving little doubt that it was the genuine article.

The message was short and to the point:

'Major Hailsham. Until you receive further specific orders by direct radio link, you are expected to cooperate fully with officers of the official Kazakh Republican Army.'

The letter was signed by the Foreign Secretary, and countersigned by Lieutenant-Colonel Barney Davies.

Still no closer to understanding the strange new turn of events, Hailsham handed the letter back like a man in a dream. Only then did he accept Yascovar's proffered handshake, returning it curtly and without warmth. He moved back to the rim of the canyon and shouted over the side.

'Sergeant Winston. Bring the rest of the men up – and don't do anything hasty when you notice the reception committee up here.'

He turned back to Captain Yascovar. 'The letter mentioned a direct radio link to my superior officer. How soon can that be arranged?'

'As soon as you wish, Major,' Yascovar answered politely. 'Our base at Alma-Ata has been in virtually permanent contact for the last five hours. I can patch you through from one of the helicopters as soon as you are ready.'

The young Kazakh officer seemed perfectly sincere, even anxious to please. Despite his initial mistrust, and continued confusion, Hailsham found himself warming to the man. He wondered if Yascovar knew about the helicopter which Andrew had shot down. It seemed improbable that he should not, and yet that made his apparently genuine friendliness even more baffling.

This question, at least, was soon answered as Andrew, Tweedledee and the Thinker finally appeared over the rim of the plateau and assembled into a bemused and dispirited group. After a few meaningful gestures from the armed soldiers and a confirming nod from Hailsham, they dropped their weapons and equipment into an untidy heap in the snow. Yascovar's eyes flashed over the weaponry, betraying the faintest flicker of surprise. 'I was given to understand you were carrying an anti-aircraft missile system, Major. It would appear that I was misinformed.'

Hailsham flashed a quick glance at Andrew, warning him not to show any reaction. Under the circumstances, it seemed safest to give away as little as possible, Hailsham thought. Obviously Yascovar was aware that the helicopter had been shot down, but not totally sure who the culprits were. For the time being at least, that doubt might be best left unresolved.

Their own situation, however, definitely needed clarification.

'Are we to consider ourselves prisoners?' Hailsham asked, returning his attention to Captain Yascovar.

The man shook his head firmly. 'By no means, Major. More like allies. Perhaps unlikely ones, I admit – but allies nevertheless.' He seemed to take pity on Hailsham's continued confusion, and smiled sympathetically.

'I was not briefed to give you any great details, Major, but perhaps I can stretch my orders to at least give you an idea of the broader picture.'

Again Hailsham was struck by the man's sincerity. It seemed like a genuine offer – almost an attempt to establish mutual respect and understanding between two military officers. 'That would be nice,' he muttered.

'In simple terms, it would appear that you have rattled a large stick in a nest of rats,' Yascovar went on. He paused, looking somewhat apologetic. 'But no doubt you have a more descriptive phrase in the English language.'

Hailsham shook his head, smiling despite himself. 'No, I think that covers it quite adequately.'

'Ah, good.' Yascovar looked pleased. 'Anyway, your involvement, and that of the Chinese, has stirred up things which had been buried and forgotten for a long time. This may have been the intention of the Chinese all along, of course – it is often difficult to know how their devious minds work. But now that certain matters are out in the open, it has become clear that they can only be tackled at a diplomatic level. So our two governments are now working together, Major. You and I are mere servants of those governments.'

Hailsham was no nearer to understanding exactly what was going on, but he was beginning to get the general picture. 'Duty calls and no questions asked – is that it?' he asked.

Yascovar smiled. 'We are soldiers, Major Hailsham. Politicians make the wars – we only fight them.'

It was a simplistic view, Hailsham thought. Either that, or it suggested that matters had escalated to a much higher international level than Yascovar was prepared to admit. It was even possible that the Kazakh captain was just as confused as he was. Perhaps he was taking refuge in the position of simply following orders. Or perhaps it was no longer clear where, or from whom, those orders were coming.

'I take it that individual heads are rolling?' he said, probing the man.

Yascovar's smile turned to an open grin. 'The sharks are in a feeding frenzy, Major,' he replied. 'But I really cannot tell you any more. I think I may have already exceeded my authority.'

Hailsham thought that he understood a little better now, but he would know a whole lot more when he spoke to Barney Davies. 'Your frankness is appreciated, Captain,' he said politely. 'But I think I would like to make that call now.'

'Of course,' Yascovar said, nodding. 'But perhaps you and your men would care to join your comrade while I set up the necessary link. I think you will find he is quite complimentary about our hospitality. He certainly seemed to appreciate the food.' He then turned away and began to lead the way across to the camp.

Andrew fell into step beside Hailsham. 'What the hell is this all about, boss?' he hissed in Hailsham's ear.

Hailsham shrugged, lacking an adequate answer. 'For the moment, it appears to be food,' he muttered obliquely.

The smell of hot, spicy stew and freshly brewed thick, black, Turkish-style coffee proved irresistible as they neared the camp. Hailsham allowed himself and his men to be ushered into one of the tents, where they squatted down on a soft carpet of thick army blankets and waited for the food to be served. The interior of the tent was cosy and warm, heated by flexible metal pipes which carried hot water from the petrol stove outside.

It was all very efficient, Hailsham thought – suggesting that the whole operation had been fully equipped and prepared for a full-scale mission. After making sure that they were comfortable, Captain Yascovar made his polite excuses and left, promising to establish the radio link while the meal was being served. The men were left alone, and, glancing outside the tent, Hailsham could see no sign that any sort of guard had been posted. On the face of it, at least, Yascovar's assurance that they were not prisoners seemed to be borne out.

Cyclops came into the tent to join them. He grinned at Hailsham sheepishly. 'I hope you don't think I was collaborating with the enemy, boss, but I was bloody hungry,' he said. 'Anyway, there's been no attempt to interrogate me in any way, and they didn't even insist on taking my handgun.' He patted his holstered Browning High Power to back up the statement. 'So I figured the best way to play it was to just go along with them until you got here. I hope I did the right thing.'

Hailsham nodded, putting the trooper at his ease. 'That's what we're all doing, until I can find out exactly what's going on. They're trying to patch me through to Lieutenant-Colonel Davies at the moment.' He turned to face Andrew and the others. 'So, gentlemen, until I have some hard information, you might as well keep your questions on ice. I suggest you try to relax and make the most of the hospitality which is being offered to us.'

The speech effectively pre-empted the barrage of questions which Hailsham had been expecting – exactly as it was supposed to.

'So what's the bloody grub like?' the Thinker asked Cyclops.

'Just like your mum used to make,' Cyclops assured him.

The Thinker grimaced. 'Shit. My old lady was the worst fucking cook I ever knew. The only reason I joined the bloody army was to get some decent scran.'

It was a wild enough exaggeration to raise a smile all round. The mood was almost jovial by the time two soldiers eventually turned up, bearing trays of hot stew with great chunks of bread, proper eating utensils and a big pot of coffee and tin mugs.

The Thinker regarded the food with obvious relish. 'This is as good as the bloody Ritz,' he muttered. 'Pity about the waitresses, though.'

The soldiers put down the trays and left. Hailsham and his men set about the food voraciously. They had all forgotten how hungry they actually were. The metal plates were all wiped and licked clean by the time Captain Yascovar returned.

'Major Hailsham? Everything is ready for you now,' he announced.

Hailsham jumped to his feet expectantly. At last he might get some answers he would understand, he thought. He followed Yascovar outside and across to the nearest helicopter.

The craft's radio officer handed him a pair of earphones and a mike, then stepped into the background and stayed there. It seemed to Hailsham that he was hovering about not so much to monitor the conversation as to be ready to offer help if it was needed. In any case, he was only a private, and it was unlikely that he understood much English. Not that Hailsham had expected privacy anyway.

Slipping on the headset, Hailsham thumbed the mike button. 'Hello, this is Major Mike Hailsham, 22 SAS. Reporting for briefing as ordered.'

Despite the distance of the radio link, and the fact that it was being patched through at least one intermediate base, Barney Davies's voice was unmistakable.

'Mike? I expect you have a question or two.'

Hailsham laughed cynically. 'That's a fucking understatement, Barney, and you know it,' he said. 'Here's question one
for starters. What the fuck is going on? Question two – is
this supposed to be an open conversation? I have visitors.'

'Don't worry about that, Mike,' Davies assured him. 'This
link is scrambled at this end and patched through GCHQ.
There's full and open cooperation between our government
and the government of the Kazakhstan Republic. Over and
above that, it should be safe from outside ears. As far as
you are concerned, Captain Yascovar is as fully briefed by
his people as you're about to be.' Davies paused for a second.
'Oh, and be nice to him, by the way. He'll probably be a
general by tomorrow.'

'Jesus!' Hailsham hissed, making the obvious inference. 'It
really is the Night of the Long Knives, is it?'

'Now who's dealing in understatements?' Davies asked.
'A three-way hotline between Moscow, Alma-Ata and London
has been buzzing almost continuously for the past thirty-six
hours, the Chinese delegation has stormed out of the Hong
Kong talks and is threatening a total boycott, the Kazakh
Republican military chief Osipov is under close arrest, and
there are some very embarrassing questions being asked in
the House of Commons. Yes, I think one might reasonably
say that the shit has well and truly hit the fan. Does that
answer your question?'

'Eloquently,' Hailsham said. 'So where does that leave us?'

'Surprisingly, smelling of roses,' Davies told him. 'Having
tipped over the slops bucket, the Kazakh authorities seem
quite anxious to have us help clean up the mess. However,
the Foreign Secretary has insisted I point out that you do
have a choice.'

'Choice?' Hailsham queried. He did not quite understand.

'You can abort this mission right now,' Davies said, spelling it out for him. 'If you do decide to pull out, Captain Yascovar will make sure that you are all safely escorted back to Alma-Ata and transferred to a neutral base. No questions asked, no complications. However, if you want to stick around, then the Kazakhs would appreciate your help. They're not too experienced in this sort of situation.' Davies paused for a few seconds to let it all sink in. 'Well?' he demanded eventually. 'Do you want out?'

Hailsham almost exploded into the mike. 'No bloody way,' he said vehemently. 'No way am I prepared to abort this one, Barney. Not now. I've lost three men, and I've dragged the others through hell and out the other side again.'

It was the answer which Lieutenant-Colonel Davies had fully expected. Knowing Hailsham as he did, it could hardly have been otherwise. 'That's what I thought, Mike,' he said. 'But I was asked to give you the choice, and I did.'

'So, when are you going to fill me in with the details?' Hailsham asked, growing impatient. 'How much more do we know about this mountain complex and what we might face up there?'

There was a long pause at the other end as Davies assembled his thoughts. 'Right, are we sitting comfortably?' he asked eventually. 'Then pin your ears back, Mike. This gets kind of complicated.'

Another, shorter pause, and Barney Davies began to launch into a story of horror, intrigue, conspiracy and double-dealing that soon had Hailsham's head spinning.

'Well, now you know as much as I do,' Captain Yascovar said, as they walked back towards the tents from the helicopter. 'It's all rather incredible, don't you think?'

251

Hailsham let out a derisive grunt halfway between a laugh and a snort. 'What I find incredible is that all this could have remained buried for so many years,' he muttered.

'Simply because no one wanted to dig for the truth,' Yascovar pointed out. 'Until your mission stirred things up, nobody had asked any questions. Once they did, of course, the whole thing snowballed.'

'But what the hell were our various governments doing all that time? American intelligence . . . our own security services?'

Yascover shrugged. 'They didn't call it the Cold War for nothing, Major. The Iron Curtain was a lot thicker than many people ever realized. And don't forget that it worked both ways – or would you have me believe that neither British or American scientists were involved in warfare research projects during those thirty years? I don't know if you're aware of it, Major Hailsham, but the rumour still persists throughout the Eastern bloc that AIDS was originally developed by the Americans as a biological weapon for use in Vietnam.'

Hailsham smiled thinly. 'And we thought it was the Russians in Afghanistan.'

'So you see,' Yascovar went on. 'The world continues to hold unpleasant mysteries and secrets. People such as you and I are always the last to know, Major.'

Hailsham nodded. 'You make your point, Captain.' He stopped in mid-stride, turning towards the Kazakh officer. There was a slightly embarrassed look on his face. 'Look, do you think we could start again?' He held out his hand.

It was more than just a conciliatory gesture. Barney Davies had made it clear that they were to work together. Although each officer would be responsible for his own men, the planning and execution of the raid on the Phoenix complex was very much a joint mission. And, in typical SAS fashion, rank was virtually suspended. To all intents and purposes Hailsham and Yascovar were equal.

The Russian took Hailsham's hand in a firm grip. This time, there was real warmth, even friendship, in their handshake.

They began to walk on towards the tents again. 'So, when do we move in?' Hailsham asked after a while.

'Just before first light tomorrow,' Yascovar answered him. 'I thought that the element of surprise might work in our favour. The complex was designed to withstand the full fury of the elements, and it is heavily protected against attack. Breaking into it will not be easy.'

Hailsham nodded.

'Which is why you and I have a busy night ahead of us. There's a lot of planning to be done,' Yascovar added.

Both men were silent again for a while. Finally Yascovar said: 'By the way, what did happen to your SAM system, Major?'

There did not seem much point in trying to lie. 'We had to abandon it,' Hailsham said. He eyed Yascovar cautiously. 'Look, it was unfortunate, but we thought we were under attack.'

Yascovar dismissed the matter with a wave of his hand. 'Such things happen,' he said quietly. 'As I said earlier, Major Hailsham – we are soldiers. We leave politics to the politicians.'

'Yes,' Hailsham murmured thoughtfully. The matter ended there.

# 22

Captain Yascovar seemed to have given himself the shitty end of the stick, Hailsham thought initially. By opting for a frontal assault on the main body of the complex, he was exposing himself and his men to the full fury of the facility's defensive shield. Their actual knowledge of those defences was sketchy, to say the least, but even their limited intelligence suggested that it posed an awesome threat.

The research building itself, built six subterranean levels deep into the very bedrock of the mountain, was constructed of steel-mesh reinforced concrete. The top eight feet which actually showed above the ground was of even more robust construction, a windowless and virtually featureless block of eighteen-inch-thick concrete built around a cage of sheet-metal plating. The only indication that the structure was anything more than a solid and inaccessible monolith was the single access port at ground level, designed like a bank vault door and controlled only by sophisticated electronic coding from deep within the lower levels.

All four sides of the roughly square building were protected by video-sighted 7.62mm heavy machine-guns and the slightly domed roof was virtually bomb-proof. Externally an area of somewhere in the region of thirty square metres in the immediate vicinity of the access port was heavily seeded with electronic proximity mines, controlled by well-protected sensors built into the structure of the roof. Internally the facility boasted a complement of thirty-two well-armed security staff. On paper, the complex seemed impregnable.

Yet that was what Yascovar had set himself and his men up against. Compared with that task, his own job was a doddle, Hailsham told himself. Breaking into buildings was, after all, the SAS's stock in trade.

Seen in this light, Captain Yascovar's plan made logical sense, Hailsham realized. A full-scale frontal assault would give the security forces something to think about while the real invasion took place. It was all about having the right men for the right job – and having them in the right place at the right time.

Curiously enough, it was the very design and structure of the complex which gave it its one weakness. For the sheer size of the subterranean building demanded a vast intake of fresh air which had to be sucked in, filtered and purified and then pumped around the labyrinth of laboratories, offices and corridors. Three massive intake vents higher up in the surrounding mountains took care of this inflow, although all of them were armoured and protected against explosives. Even if access could have been effected, there would still have been no way through the whirling intake turbine blades, or the impassable wall of filtering and pumping machinery.

But air sucked in also has to be pumped out again – and it was here that the original designers had created the single, vital flaw in the system. Perhaps it had been just an oversight, or perhaps a simple and human psychological error which suggested that an inlet demanded more security than an outlet.

It did not really matter either way. The important thing was that the single exhaust vent for the entire complex was protected only by a grille of half-inch metal bars. And it was here that Hailsham and his men would make their entry.

The first faint rays of the early morning sun glinted on the whirling rotor blades of the two helicopters as they lifted from the plateau and rose towards the mountains.

The Hind-As were designed for a crew of four and a passenger capability of eight fully equipped combat troops. Packing Hailsham, Cyclops, Andrew, Tweedledee and the Thinker in on top of Captain Yascovar's complement of eighteen men was a bit of a squeeze, but then they had not been expecting to fly Ambassador Class. Clad as they were in heavy NBC suits and S6 respirators, comfort was hardly a matter for consideration.

Cyclops glanced at Tweedledee. 'Bet you never thought we'd be going in by private air-taxi service,' he said, his voice distorted and blurred by the respirator. 'Makes you feel like a VIP, doesn't it?'

Tweedledee grunted. 'All I feel like is a bloody Star Wars trooper,' he said.

Cyclops nodded. 'Yeah, you look like one,' he confirmed.

It was time for last-minute orders. Hailsham pulled his mask away from his face so that he could speak clearly.

'Right. Now the important thing to remember is that once we do get inside that complex there must be no wild and indiscriminate shooting,' he reminded them all. 'Aim specifically and directly at human targets only – and make sure that there is no scientific equipment of any sort either in or behind your line of fire. I don't need to point out that there could be anything in there, from bacteriological agents to nerve gas. We don't know what's in there, or how deadly it might be. The last thing we can afford is to go spraying bullets around the place. If you're in any doubt at all, hold your fire. Dive for the nearest protection and wait for someone else to cover you from a safe line of fire. Understood?'

The men nodded gravely, all well aware of the potential horrors which might greet them once they reached the laboratory areas.

'And secondly, don't open fire at all unless fired upon,' Hailsham went on. 'We want to make this assault as much of a surprise as possible. Hopefully, Captain Yascovar and his men will be keeping the security forces well occupied on the complex perimeters. We want to keep them from knowing we're sneaking in the back door for as long as we can.'

A slight lurching feeling in the pit of his belly told Hailsham that the Hind-A was starting to go down again. It had been agreed that the two choppers would swoop in low, dropping Hailsham's team off about fifty yards below the complex before climbing again to circle round and make a final approach down from the mountains. If no one had already heard them coming, it might at least suggest that the attack was from one direction only, and focus the defences at a single point. Even if this small advantage was only a temporary one it would help – and they needed all the help they could get.

Hailsham slipped his respirator back in place and checked it. He glanced over at Yascovar, jerking one thumb into the air. Reaching up, Yascovar punched a control button and the bottom section of the horizontally divided door at the front of the passenger cabin began to drop down like a ramp. With another sickening lurch, the Hind-A sank to within four feet of the ground and hovered just long enough for Hailsham and his men to drop over the side and into the thick snow.

Then the helicopter was off again to join its companion in a smooth and almost unbroken movement.

Hailsham watched them both climb and wheel away for a few seconds before returning his eyes to the ground. He unfolded the sketched plan of the complex he had been carrying in his hand and studied it quickly. Tapping Andrew lightly on the shoulder, he pointed up ahead to the right, where the exhaust ventilation shaft could be seen as a black, igloo-shaped hole against a white background. Pausing only to check their weapons, the troopers began to plough through the snow towards it.

The sound of heavy machine-guns opening up from higher up the mountain made Hailsham's head snap up, a curse forming on his lips. The dark mound which had been all he could see of the complex was now twinkling with flashes of light as the roof-mounted machine-guns spat out a hail of fire at the approaching helicopters.

'Damn!' Hailsham grated out, realizing that their chance of a surprise attack was gone. He had hoped to get at least as far as the ventilation shaft entrance before the action started. Obviously the complex boasted an efficient early detection and warning system. They had probably picked up the approach of the helicopters at a range of a mile or more. Hailsham's heart sank. If their surveillance was that good, then they had probably monitored the close approach of the drop-off helicopter as well. In which case, it would not take a genius to figure out the probability of a primary assault force. Or indeed roughly where they were likely to be.

Hailsham certainly did not intend to stick around long enough to test out this observation to its logical conclusion. With a warning yell to the others, he threw himself forward through the thick snow, desperately trying to break into a run. The best he could manage was an ungainly, floundering struggle, but it sufficed. The distance between him and the dark mouth of the ventilation shaft began to dwindle, yard by precious yard.

So, the expected attack had come at last, Tovan Leveski realized as the internal alarms started to pulse out their incessant warning bleeps. It was no surprise. He had been primed for it for two days and nights now, ever since the coded messages had started coming in over the radio. He was prepared; he knew what he had to do. The tension of waiting had focused his attention, channelling the wanderings of his muddled brain into unusual clarity.

He rose from his desk, walked calmly across his office towards the shredding machine and switched it on. The files were already piled beside it, in readiness. Every scrap of paperwork, laboratory note or requisition slip which referred to the Phoenix Project was there. The computer records had already been erased, the hard drives taken out and destroyed so that there would never be the faintest chance of retrieval. Slowly, painstakingly, Leveski started feeding the files into the shredder. Finally he pulled a cigar and lighter from his pocket. Lighting the cigar, he sucked on it for a few seconds. Then, using a twisted bundle of shredded paper as a spill, he lit that and dropped it into the waste bag and watched the flames spread greedily.

Phoenix would keep its dark secrets from the outside world. There remained only the physical evidence, but soon that too would be destroyed. As, indeed, the whole complex would be destroyed.

\* \* \*

Hailsham threw himself into the tunnel of the ventilation shaft, pressing himself against one wall so that the others could crowd in behind him. Exactly as the plans had shown, there was just the single barrier of the metal grille, recessed about three feet inside the mouth of the shaft. Beyond that the tunnel ran straight ahead at a steady incline for about fifty yards, before branching off into several smaller shafts which Hailsham assumed went to the various different levels. The fact that he could see clearly was something of a bonus, he reasoned. He had expected the tunnel to be as black as pitch, since one would not expect an exhaust vent to be illuminated. As it happened, none of the upper levels or outer corridors had been supplied with power for several months, ever since Leveski had sealed and isolated them. It was only now that the complex's alarm system had been activated that emergency lighting had cut in automatically.

'Right, Thinker, this is your department,' Hailsham grunted, but the burly corporal had already set himself to work. Dropping to his knees and opening his bergen, the Thinker took out and unwrapped two bundles of Semtex and began to knead the malleable substance in his hands. Rolling it out into long, thin sausages, he pressed it into place at strategic points where the grille was embedded in the walls of the shaft. Explosives were his speciality, and he was good at his job. He worked quickly and efficiently, knowing instinctively how much to use and where to place it. The entire operation took less than forty seconds. Finally he stuck in the pencil fuses and detonators and nodded his head at Hailsham. 'Fifteen seconds,' he said quietly, deftly setting the timers.

It was more than enough time to retreat and take shelter around the outside of the shaft. They did so – although in truth they could probably have safely stayed exactly where they were. With his typical expertise, the Thinker had used no more explosive than was strictly necessary to do the job. The blast which blew the grille clear out of the tunnel wall did not even disturb the snow outside the mouth of the shaft.

They were back inside and running down the ventilation tunnel before the small amount of smoke from the explosion had cleared. If the original plans still held good, and the air-conditioning system had not been modified in recent years, it was a clear run to the exhaust pumping station. From there they should be able to use the maintenance access directly into the storage bays, and thence get into the internal security area. With luck, most of the guards would still be occupied with the frontal assault, and they could expect only minimal resistance. That was the plan, anyway.

The front access port of the Phoenix Complex had been designed to withstand the most violent of storms and any normal ground-level military attack. Over four decades previously, its makers had not been able to foresee the devastating effects of the steady stream of 'Swatter' anti-tank missiles and 57mm rockets which were being delivered by the two still-circling Hind-A helicopters. Under such a blistering attack, even a door made of eight-inch steel armour plate is still just a door.

As the surrounding concrete walls blew in with a final roar, Captain Yascovar ordered the two helicopters to rake the minefield with a hail of shells from their undernose heavy machine-guns. It was a matter of minutes now before he could safely bring them both in to land and discharge his troops. He wondered how Hailsham and his men were getting on.

The Thinker inspected the heavy steel shutter which sealed off the loading bay from the storage area. 'No problem,' he said confidently to himself, preparing to set another couple of explosive charges.

'Stop wasting time, you plonker,' Cyclops yelled out at him through the intake of his respirator. Pushing past the big man, he bent over and pulled up the bottom of the shutter. It slid up effortlessly, the open padlock dangling impotently.

A burst of gunfire from an AK-47 took him in the legs and abdomen as the shutter slammed into the ceiling above. He screamed horribly and fell back at the Thinker's feet, convulsing and twitching violently for a few seconds before finally lying still.

The Thinker hardly moved, other than to step slightly to one side and bring his SA-80 up into the business position. The single security guard in charge of the loading bay never got a chance to fire a second burst. The Thinker's first four slugs opened his chest up like a split watermelon. The next twelve slid his corpse jerkily across the loading-bay floor, leaving a glistening trail of blood. The Thinker did not even blink.

The very walls of the complex were echoing and vibrating with the sounds of gunfire now, as Yascovar's troops poured into the breached building. Guided by the sound, Hailsham led the rest of his men towards the scene of battle, prepared for further opposition but never encountering it. Perhaps overawed at the ferocity of the assault that had been mounted against them, or dispirited by their months of isolation, Leveski's security guards maintained only a token resistance for a few more minutes, and then put down their weapons and surrendered to the inevitable. Captain Yascovar was already interrogating them by the time Hailsham joined him in the central control room.

\* \* \*

The door to Leveski's office was ajar. Hailsham sent one of the captured guards through it first, just in case. Nothing happened. Cautiously, Hailsham kicked the door fully open with his boot and fired a warning burst from his SA-80 up into the ceiling. Only then did he step forward, flanked by Andrew and Tweedledee.

Leveski sat at his desk, facing the open door. He smiled chillingly as Hailsham entered. 'I've been expecting someone,' he said quietly. 'Although the British SAS is something of a surprise.'

'Your men have already surrendered,' Hailsham told him calmly. 'Now I must ask you to do the same.'

The Russian pushed himself stiffly to his feet, clicking his heels together in a curiously old-fashioned gesture. 'Of course, Major. You must ask – just as I must refuse.' He leaned forward, pressing a small red button set into the surface of his desk.

He smiled again, and Hailsham thought that the man's face was possibly the most evil thing he had ever seen.

'And now we all die together,' Leveski said. 'I have just initiated the auto-destruct sequence which will blow this entire complex apart in just over thirty seconds. There is no way that you and your men can escape in time, Major.'

Hailsham's face was impassive. 'Wrong,' he said quietly. 'We have already disarmed it.'

His hand dropped to his hip, drawing his Browning. Raising it, he put a double tap cleanly through Leveski's forehead.

'That's for Piggy Baker,' Hailsham muttered. 'Never trust a fucking Russian.'